The Star in the East
a winter tale of ancient mystery

The Star in the East
a winter tale of ancient mystery

By John Adcox
Illustrated by Carol Bales

Creators of
Raven Wakes the World: A Winter Tale
Christmas Past: A Ghostly Winter Tale

THE
ST■RY
PLANT

The Story Plant
Studio Digital CT, LLC
P.O. Box 4331
Stamford, CT 06907

Text Copyright © 2022 by John Adcox
Illustrations Copyright © 2022 by Carol Bales

Story Plant hardcover ISBN 978-1-61188-335-0
Fiction Studio Books e-book ISBN 978-1-945839-69-6

Visit our website at www.TheStoryPlant.com

First Story Plant Printing: November 2022

Printed in the United States of America

The Library of Congress Cataloguing-in-Publication Data is available upon request.

For a world in recovery

1

The Graveyard of Secrets

o Beth Bethlen, Rome was a city of scents. The air sang with them. The ancient city wore them like a blanket, the way San Francisco wore fog, or Seattle rain. There was a district where she liked to shop—or had liked to when she'd still been strong enough to walk that far—that always smelled of the sea, even though the wind had left salt and fish long behind by the time it reached those airy, crowded plazas. The streets near her tiny, out-of-the-way hotel always smelled inexplicably of lemons. North, toward Vatican City, the streets smelled of bubbling sauces—tomato, basil, oregano. South, it was cheese—Parmesan, Romano, and something that might have been Gorgonzola, but sweeter, like it was touched with blueberries and honey. A few blocks east, and the aromas of fresh bread—morning to midnight—made her stomach rumble with happy anticipation, even though she never had much appetite. Not anymore, anyway.

Beth crinkled her nose. Here, the only scent on the still, heavy air was the weight of dank, damp decay, moldering stone, and time. This part of the city smelled old. Old, dusty, and forgotten. She glanced down at her phone and wondered why map apps never included smells. In Rome at least, it would surely be a huge help. Wrong smell, wrong district. Right smell, why, you were right on track. She shook her head and glared at the phone. No such luck.

She checked the phone again and nodded to herself, an introvert's old habit, and let out a sigh. Uber rides and phone apps could only get her so far. This deep in the old city, where secrets rested, lost, modern maps were useless. But she was almost there at last. *Thank God.* She took a deep breath, her nose crinkling, and let it out slowly. She was tired, so very tired. She didn't think she could have made it much farther.

Beth paused and adjusted her N95 facemask. With her weakened heart, she had to stop often to rest and catch her breath, even if it was just for a moment or two. She put her small carry-on suitcase down on the cobbled pavement and pulled her Boston Red Sox jacket more tightly across her thin frame. It was too large for her, especially now when she'd lost so much weight, but she wore it anyway because it belonged to her husband—it still smelled faintly of his Old Spice Bearglove aftershave—and she liked to have something with her that made her feel close to him, even if he was half a world away. Beth smiled. He had no idea she was in Rome. He didn't even know she'd left the States. He was going to be just all kinds of surprised.

She thought about sitting down, but she didn't. Her nose crinkled again. She didn't want any more of her person to touch the streets here than was strictly necessary. The soles of her shoes were more than enough, thank you very much, and she might literally just throw them away when she got back to the hotel. She didn't even want to rest against the stone walls of the buildings, which leaned precariously over the narrow street like old men bent over their canes. She rested one knee on her suitcase and then the other. That would have to be enough. God but she was tired. Dammit, she wasn't even thirty. No way she should be this frickin' tired.

She smiled to herself. Frickin'. That was one of her husband's words.

Beth slipped her phone back into the pocket of her Red Sox jacket. Now, she needed the kind of knowledge to which modern technology wasn't privy, so she retrieved a bundle of brittle papers from the side pocket of her suitcase. It had taken her a long time to find those pages, and it had cost a small fortune. She was sure her husband would forgive her when he found out. The surprise was for him, after all. A Christmas mystery. One final puzzle, and the best for last.

9

The first showed a map of a more ancient Rome. Thankfully, Rome wasn't a city that changed much, especially not this part, the one that smelled of dank dampness, one of the very oldest quarters of the city. Senators, philosophers, and centurions had walked these streets. Now that she was close, yes, *yes*, she could follow the map easily. And—she thanked God again—she apparently wouldn't have to follow it far.

She looked up and nodded. There, just ahead. She was in the right place; she was sure of it.

Frickin' finally.

She smiled again. Her husband's word.

The old stone monastery filled several blocks, but it wasn't in any of the guidebooks. Beth knew enough to know that the monks saw to that, just as they had done for centuries. It was a place that hid secrets; it wasn't meant to be found, at least not by those who had no business there. Beth closed her eyes and mouthed a silent prayer, hoping that her errand would qualify. She allowed herself another quick smile. Prayer seemed especially appropriate before entering a monastery.

She shuffled the musty pages and found another map, this one showing a maze of dark catacombs and deep tunnels, ancient and secret. This was the map she would need next, once she was inside. She studied it carefully for a long moment and then took another deep breath, this time for courage. She picked up her suitcase and headed to the monastery's great door, dark wood against dark stone, hidden in shadow, and marveled at how easy it would have been to miss, at least if one wasn't looking for it specifically, and if one didn't know where or how to look. It was old, even in a city where frickin' everything was old. The door was unlocked, but it was even heavier than it looked. She had to use her whole body to push it open. Once, not too long ago, she would have just had to shove it with her arm. She slipped inside, but then she had to pause again to slow her breathing. Her heart pounded. That wasn't good. Her doctors would have a fit. She had to put her suitcase down again and use both hands to push the door closed behind her again. She grunted with the effort.

When her eyes adjusted to the dim light, Beth turned and found herself in a long entrance corridor with walls of unadorned stone. The air was still and stale, and cooler than it had been outside. The dank smell lingered. At the end of the corridor, a monk sat behind an ornate desk that, Beth couldn't help thinking, would have been called an antique when her great-great-grandparents were infants. Frickin' Caesar probably would have called it an antique. A simple wooden cross stood on the desk, along with an open leather-bound book and a fountain pen. Behind the desk stood another tall door, also of wood stained dark by time.

Beth approached the desk and sat her suitcase down again. Her Italian absolutely sucked, so she had to rely on her phone's translation app. "Hello," said Beth. "I'm here for the, uh, Graveyard of Secrets."

The app's synthetic voice repeated: *"Ciao. Sono qui per, uh, il Cimitero dei Segreti."*

She reached into her shirt and pulled out the heavy silver chain she wore around her neck. It held an oddly shaped pendant—an iron key.

The monk regarded the key and for a moment, his eyes widened slightly. He nodded once. *"I Custodi ti stanno aspettando."*

Beth looked down at the translation screen and read: *The Keepers are expecting you.*

The monk made a note in his book. Then, he stood and unlocked the door behind him. He bowed slightly and motioned for Beth to enter. She managed a smile. *"Grazie."* She didn't need the app to say thank you, at least.

The monk nodded and closed the door behind her just as she found the light switch. It clicked loudly when she flipped it, and the lightbulbs buzzed. The walls here, too, were of stone, although there were carpets on the floor. Sconces lined the walls, but they were empty of candles. It took her a minute, but Beth found another door at the far end of the chamber—another one she would have missed easily if she hadn't been looking carefully. It seemed to be made of the same stone as the walls. Beth frowned. She wasn't sure she would have been strong enough to push that door even if her heart

. . . even if she wasn't sick. She closed her eyes, took another deep breath, and pushed all her weight against the stone door, struggling to push it open. As she did, she heard counterweights shifting behind the door and, to her very great surprise, the door swung open easily. She wished her husband could be there with her. The ingenuity of the ancient mechanism would have impressed him. He was fond of old things, as his father the scholar had been, and he admired clever things.

Since she could see a faint glow ahead, she didn't bother with the light switch. Instead, she thumbed on her phone's flashlight and started down a stairway of narrow, damp stone. There were walls of plaster on either side, much of it flaked away to reveal more stone, but she wished for a handrail. The stairs took her down a long, long way.

At the bottom, Beth found that the still air smelled more dusty than dank. Dim and flickering lights—for which she could not see the sources—made strange shadows but provided enough illumination to show her that she had three choices, or four if she counted back up the stairs. The latter was no choice at all. So she could go left, right, or straight ahead. She checked the second map. Straight ahead, then right, and then two lefts.

With the phone's flashlight and the flickering lights to guide her, Beth made her way through the maze of tunnels, a dark and secret way far beneath the streets of Rome. The architecture wasn't quite ornate enough to be

Gothic, Beth supposed, but it was too damn creepy to be anything else. Somewhere to her left, water dripped, echoing in the vast darkness. She took another right, and then a left. After a time, she came to a narrow stone bridge that arced over a dark and deep chasm, the walls of which were lined with rough brick. Far below, she could hear the music of rushing water. She sniffed. It wasn't sewage, thank God. It must be a lost, underground river, or a stream, anyway, too deep in shadow to be seen. She wondered where it let out, if it ever did, or if anyone in the outside world knew of it.

She kept going. Soon she was breathing heavily, so she stopped and set her suitcase down. She checked the map again—so far, so good. Her heart was still pounding, so she found a prescription bottle in her jacket and swallowed a pill, even though she didn't have any water. It wasn't the first time she'd done that, not by a long shot. She was almost used to it; the little bastards hardly ever stuck in her throat anymore. It went down like a pinecone. Once she'd choked it down, she gathered her suitcase and continued on, glancing down at the map one more time as she moved.

Ten or so minutes later, Beth opened a wooden door and emerged blinking into a cavernous, domed room that, she would have bet, had been old in the Renaissance. Bookcases climbed nearly to the ceiling far above. Beth wished she had time to gaze at the titles. The light was brighter here, and Beth found herself blinking. Beyond the bookcases, doorways opened into corridors, and a winding staircase led up. The next thing Beth noticed was that she was not alone.

Three men in monk's robes stepped forward, while nine more held back, making a ring around a stone table. The robes didn't match. Two were white; the others were black or brown. Beth wondered if that meant they were of different orders or something; she didn't think fashion choices were much of a thing with monks. She was glad she hadn't stolen a glance at the book titles. She doubted the men would have approved. She swallowed and approached them. She opened the translation app on her phone and said, "Is this the Graveyard of Secrets?" The app translated.

One of the monks, a plump man with close cropped white hair, fingered the cross he wore around his neck as he answered in English. "Welcome, Mrs. Bethlen." Beth smiled. The man's voice was warm, and his accent was lovely. "We offer you the blessings of our Lord."

Beth's smiled widened. "Thank you, Father. I . . . um, I'm looking for a book. That's why I'm here. *The Roots of the Bethlens.*"

A different monk answered her. This man was younger and thinner, and his accent, she thought, must be from a different region of Italy, one she hadn't visited. "I'm sorry, my child. We can give the book to only the Bethlen heir."

Beth nodded. "That's my husband. Gaspar. Gaspar Bethlen."

"Gaspar," the monk with the close-cropped hair said with a lip twitch that almost, almost hinted at a smile. "That's . . . an unusual name."

Beth nodded. "It's a family name." She tried to smile. "His is . . . an unusual family, I think. He's related to a Hungarian count. Did you know that?" The monk nodded. "I don't think my Gaspar does. I can't wait to tell him! Anyway. I . . . I'm here to, uh, claim it for him. Gaspar. The book, I mean."

The monks shifted and looked at one another. They frowned awkwardly. Beth felt her own smile wilt. *Uh oh.* She forced the smile back into place. "My husband's father spent his life looking for that book. He died looking for it."

The plump monk nodded. "Dr. Bethlen, the Nativity scholar. We know his work. He was a brilliant man."

"And . . . and I have the key," said Beth. "It belonged to Gaspar's great-grandfather. You know it, don't you? Yes?"

Another monk spoke. This man had an accent that wasn't Italian. Beth thought it might have been Scottish. "And his before him, my child, and his before him. That key is ancient."

The second monk, the thinner one, spoke again. "You should know . . . we have only the first volume of three."

16

Beth felt another smile blooming and hoped it didn't look smug. Well, not too smug, anyway. "I already found the other two."

The plump monk's eyes popped open wide. "Did you? Extraordinary." The other monks muttered softly to one another in Italian or maybe even Latin. Did monks still speak Latin? Beth couldn't follow any of it.

The thinner monk ignored the others and frowned. "Be careful. Keep those books hidden. And safe. They are the keys to . . . to a very special legacy."

Beth nodded. "I know. It's this, isn't it?"

Beth knelt and opened her suitcase pocket. She found a parchment in a folder of clear plastic and gazed at it, as she had some many times already, before she handed it to the thinner monk. It showed an antiquated, hand-tinted etching of a jewel set in what appeared to be gold, ornately crafted, nearly the size of her husband's palm. Her husband had very large hands, an athlete's hands. The artist had etched fire onto the stone. Beth had assumed that was meant to be symbolic, although she had no idea what it was supposed to represent. Something mysterious, no doubt. Something numinous, something holy.

The monks glanced at one another with scarcely contained surprise.

"My husband's father had that parchment when he died," Beth said. "I think this is meant to be actual size. It is, isn't it? The gem must . . . why, it must be priceless!"

"More so than it appears," the thinner monk said softly, nodding, "for this gem carries with it a secret. One that has remained untold for more than two thousand years. Did you know that?"

Beth nodded. "I think so. That's why I need the book. It's the last clue. I think so, anyway. It belongs to my husband, yes? I mean, it's rightfully his. Uh, right? The book, I mean. And the gem, too, if I'm right. And if the book is the last clue."

The plump monk smiled and inclined his head, a barely perceptible motion. "My child, we cannot give you the book. Come back to us. With your husband."

Beth closed her eyes and sighed. This was what she had feared. Okay. It was time to play her trump card. It was time to tell these monks the truth.

"No. No, you don't understand." She took a deep breath. "This . . . this is my last trip. Like, ever, I mean. Father—"

"Brother," the monk corrected her.

She nodded. "I'm dying, Brother." She managed a smile, even though she knew it was a sad one. "Heart condition. Degenerative. A few months. Maybe a year. I'm never going to have a baby. I'm never going to be forty. Christ, I'm never even going to be thirty-five." She didn't think the monk was offended. She hadn't meant the Christ as profanity; she'd meant it as a sort of prayer. Nonetheless, she added, "Uh, sorry, Father."

"Brother," the monk corrected her again. Beth saw a smile in his eyes.

Beth had to fight to hold back her tears. "I'm not looking for pity. I'm . . . I'm at peace. I am, truly. But . . . here's the thing, see? My husband will be hurting. He'll be alone. This is my last gift to him. I . . . I want to give him his *family*. He . . . he doesn't know. He doesn't know anything about his own legacy, or the books, or the jewel. Definitely not the secret."

The monks bowed their heads, sadly, all twelve of them, even the ones who hadn't spoken.

"May God bless you, child," the plump monk said.

The thinner monk managed a smile. "We'll show it to you, if you like. Even though we shouldn't even do that much. But you may not take it with you. I'm sorry."

Beth wanted to argue, to plead, to beg, even, but she knew it would do no good. She valued economy of effort as only one who knows she is dying can. She sighed. There was only one thing left to do. "He'll come here. My husband, I mean. After . . ." She swallowed. "After I'm gone. Maybe not right away. But he'll come. Someday. I'll make sure of it. Could I . . . could I leave you something? To give him?"

The thinner monk nodded. "We'll keep it with the book. We will guard it, like all the secrets we are called to protect."

Beth nodded. "Thank you."

"One more thing," said the plump monk. "The Bethlen legacy. Your husband will have to know where to take the books. And he'll need to answer certain questions."

Beth looked up and grinned. This time, she didn't even care if she looked smug. "I already found the answers. Well, all but the last one, anyway. Three of the four. I'm not sure where to go. Yet. I'd need the book for that last one. I think. If not, well, I'm pretty sure I know how to find out."

"And how is that, my child?"

Beth smiled again. "Marco Polo knew."

The monks muttered again, this time with something that might, almost, have been excitement. The thinner monk didn't try to hide his astonishment. "But you answered the third question, yes? Even your husband's father never—"

"I found the answer. Gaspar's father didn't, see, because he was looking in the wrong place. Well, the wrong time, anyway. An astronomer in Rome helped me find the answer." Beth knelt and produced a final engraving, an antique star chart. The colors had long since faded, but the elegant lines were clear. "The sky above Bethlehem," she said. "The first Christmas."

The thinner monk pressed his lips together, an almost-but-not-quite frown, as he bent to examine the legend. "That's not the date scholars usually accept."

Beth grinned again. "No. It's not."

Lengthening shadows made the Roman streets dark, even though it was only late afternoon when Beth left La Banca d'Italia in Palazzo Koch, her final errand completed at last. She pulled her suitcase behind her and bowed her head against the unseasonally cold wind, and wished she'd brought something more substantial than her husband's Red Sox jacket. She wished she was home. Short of that, she wished she could go straight to the airport. She longed to be in her own bed with her own quilt and, most of all, she longed to be with her Gaspar. She couldn't go to the airport yet, of course. She'd have to wait for morning. One more night.

God but she was tired. She thought about getting an Uber or a Lyft back to her hotel, but at this hour, God, it would take forever. She could take a cab, but Roman taxis were terrifying. Besides, if she took the short cuts, it would be faster to walk, despite the fact that she had to stop so often to rest. One last walk through Rome wouldn't be so bad. She loved the Eternal City, and she knew she'd never be back. She wondered what new scents she would discover. Every scent was precious now.

Beth walked. After a block, she turned into an arcade that would shorten the journey by a few blocks. With the shops already closed, it was really just an alley, but it would do. She turned a corner and then stopped abruptly.

21

Three large men in dark suits stood shoulder to shoulder, blocking her way. A fourth man stood back, keeping to the shadows between two closed merchant's stalls. He was thinner than the others, and, Beth thought, older. He wore a long, black overcoat.

Two of the men stepped forward. Beth froze as sudden, icy panic took her. She felt her heart grow numb and her blood go cold.

Her heart . . .

Oh, no, no . . .

The panic swelled to terror. She should take another pill. She should—

Beth closed her eyes and tried to slow her breathing. When she opened them again, she realized that two of the men were speaking Italian rapidly. She couldn't understand either of them, not when they were speaking so fast, and at the same time. She scrambled for her phone.

"Don't!" the third man said in English but with an accent Beth recognized as Hungarian. "Don't move your hands."

Beth froze.

Oh no, oh no . . .

She opened her mouth to scream, but a meaty hand covered the bottom half of her face before she could make a sound. The body that held her still felt like a mountain behind her, and it reeked of sweat and garlic.

Beth didn't bother to struggle; she knew it would do no good. Instead, she tried to calm herself, to slow her breathing, her heart . . .

That didn't seem to be helping too much, either. The cold panic swelled inside her. She wanted to scream, but she couldn't, *oh God*, she couldn't.

The man who spoke English with the Hungarian accent stepped closer to her. He was larger than the other two.

"Be silent," he said. "Your case. You are going to give it to me."

Beth tried to nod, but the man behind her held her too tightly.

"What's happening?" The thin man in the overcoat had spoken, also in Hungarian-accented English. "Does she have it?" The man took a step forward, and the glow from a flickering gas lamp fell on his face.

Beth wanted to laugh—she wanted to cry.

Thank God, oh, thank God!

She knew the man. It was Count Bethlen Tamás, her husband's relative. She'd met him in Budapest.

"Abban," said Tamás, "let her go. At once!"

"Tamás!" said Beth, her voice thick with tears. "Thank God! What's th—?"

"Quiet!" the man who'd spoken before said. "Your case. Give it to me. Put it down on the ground and step back."

"Okay," said Beth. She knelt and put her case on the stone pavement. She rose slowly, her hands raised at her sides. "Okay. There. See? I—"

"Quiet!" the man snapped again. "Back away."

Beth took a step back, trembling, and then another. Icy pain knifed through her chest, and the numbing panic surged with it. It was her heart. She had to calm her breathing; she had to make herself relax, she had to . . .

Oh God, oh God—

Beth took another step back and then, after a final, fleeting look at Tamás, she turned. She'd thought to run, but there was nowhere to go.

The man who'd held her, the man called Abban was there, and he aimed a gun. He held it at his waist, half hidden by his coat, but it was leveled at Beth.

The panic swelled to terror. The sharp pain was worse.

Oh God, oh—

Beth tried to raise a trembling hand to her chest, but she couldn't manage it. Her arms were numb.

From behind her, she heard Tamás's voice. "What is it? What's happening?"

Beth was dizzy and she was cold. *Pills . . .* She needed her medicine. She tried to speak, but her tongue was ice. "H . . . heart . . . need—"

Beth gasped and then she fell. It seemed to take a long time for her to reach the ground, almost like she was floating. She landed on her back, and there was no pain. Above her, the clouds had parted, letting through a single shaft of pale and fading light from the setting sun.

"What is it?" someone demanded. No, not someone. It was Tamás. *Oh, Tamás, why?* "What's happening? Tell me!"

"I don't know!" someone replied. She thought it must be the man who had held her, the man with the gun, the man called Abban. His voice sounded very far away.

Someone knelt next to her. She couldn't see which man it was. Maybe it was Tamás. Maybe he'd realized his mistake. Maybe . . .

"Should I call an ambulance?" The voice spoke English with an Italian accent. It wasn't Tamás.

"Never mind that," said Tamás. "Get my books! Hurry!"

Dimly, Beth was aware of one of the men opening her suitcase—he must have broken the lock—and searching through it. Her chest didn't hurt anymore, but her whole body was cold, so very cold . . .

Beth tried to lift herself from the pavement, but she couldn't move. Her head slumped to the side. The man was emptying her suitcase, throwing her clothes and toiletries carelessly aside. Her pill bottle rolled along the pavement. It was just an inch or two from her outstretched hand. It was a million miles away.

The man looked up. "She doesn't have them!"

The world was growing darker, but Beth recognized Tamás's voice. "That's not possible!"

"I tell you, the man insisted, "There is no book here! Not even one."

Tamás kicked the suitcase furiously. "God *Dammit!*"

"Hear that?" the other man said. "We need to get the hell out of here."

Beth's eyelids fluttered. The darkness deepened, and the cold. The pain was gone, though, and only the numbness remained. She felt suddenly very light.

The men were still speaking, but she couldn't hear them. They were too far away now, too far, and it was cold.

Beth breathed one last word, the dearest word, the dearest word of them all, of all the words she knew.

"Gaspar—"

The world grew darker, and darker still, and then it was filled with golden light.

2

A Win and a Loss

he crowd at Fenway Park rose to its feet, every last man, woman, and child as one, screaming for all they were worth, and Gaspar Bethlen imagined they could probably hear the noise all the way down in, like, Atlanta or somewhere. Baseball was like that in Boston, especially in autumn, when there was a pretty darn good chance that this year, the Sox might still be playing in October.

In the on-deck circle, Gaspar shifted the bat in his hands. There were two outs in the bottom of the ninth, and the Sox were down to the Astros 2 to 1. But if O'Doul could somehow manage to break his oh-fer and get on base, Gaspar would get a chance. He grinned. He lived for moments like this. It was a perfect Sunday afternoon in September. The sky was as blue as it ever gets, and the air was already crisp. If Beth were home, she'd have worn a sweater to the game. She always looked great in sweaters. Autumn baseball was the best.

Gaspar watched as the right-handed reliever dealt. Low and outside. Ball one. The crowd roared.

Then news showed up on the scoreboard—the Yankees had lost. If the Sox could somehow pull out a win, they'd be only one game back. The crowd roared again and started the familiar chant: *YANK-EES SUCK! YANK-EES SUCK!* That always made Gaspar shake his head and grin. Red Sox Nation screamed that chant every game, usually more than once, no matter who the opponent was. At least the Boston and Houston faithful had something to agree on.

Two more pitches, both balls. Gaspar used the opportunity to lock in his timing. It always took a little longer when he batted from the left side, and the first pitch might be the best one he saw. He had to be ready. The crowd was even louder, and now Gaspar wondered if they could hear the thunder all the way down in Cuba, or maybe even the South Pole. *Probably,* he decided. There would be some pretty startled penguins down there.

The next pitch was a called strike, and the cheers turned to boos—even though the pitch had been right down Newbury Street. The Boston faithful never took kindly to calls that went against the Red Sox nine. The next pitch, though, was a ball in the dirt—and O'Doul managed to check his swing. He was on. The roar swelled to thunder, and Gaspar was almost certain he could feel Fenway's antiquated steel girders shaking. He wondered if this was what an earthquake felt like.

Gaspar's heart raced as he stepped into the left-handed batter's box. A base hit would keep the inning alive.

That's all. Just a simple base knock. . . .

He grinned and shook his head. He didn't want a simple base knock any more than the Fenway faithful did. He didn't want to extend the game; he wanted to win it, and with just one swing. He wanted the walk-off. He shifted his bat and waited for the pitch.

It didn't come.

The Astros manager popped out of the dugout, walking slowly to the mound. Just before he got there, he signaled to the pen with his left hand. He was bringing in a relief pitcher, a lefty.

Gaspar stepped out and waited while the reliever trotted in. It was the new guy; they'd just called him up. *Jeez, what's his name again?* Steele, yeah, that was it. He was supposed to have a big curve and a fastball they said touched triple digits. Gaspar hadn't seen him in the minors—he'd been promoted to the Show before the kid reached Triple A—so he wasn't sure what to expect. He watched the kid warm up and whistled. *Impressive.* The kid had a bright future ahead. Gaspar planned to make sure the bright part started tomorrow.

When the kid had finished his tosses, Gaspar stepped into the batter's box—the righted-handed one this time. The noise swelled and now he was sure he could feel the very foundations vibrating.

The first pitch was the hook, and it was a good one, even if it looked low and outside to Gaspar's eye. The umpire disagreed, and Gaspar turned to see him raising his right fist. "Strike one!" Gaspar sighed and forced himself not to say anything. He didn't even let himself make eye contact. A pissed-off umpire was the last thing he needed with the game on the line.

The next pitch was the fastball, and Gaspar was ready. He unloaded. When you hit the ball too close to the hands, it hurts. When you hit too close to the end of the bat, it just feels weak. Gaspar hit the ball right with the sweet spot of the bat, and he almost didn't feel it at all. It was like he'd swung through the ball. The impact sounded like a rifle shot, though, even over the noise of the crowd. He didn't pause to admire the ball as it arced over the Green Monster, as much as he wanted to. He didn't want to show up the kid, not in his first game. His home run had won the game, pushing the Sox one step closer to October. That was enough.

He couldn't hide his grin, though. He didn't even try.

He only wished Beth could be there to see. He couldn't wait to tell her about it, every last detail.

The clubhouse wasn't much quieter than the field had been. In fact, Gaspar couldn't help thinking, it was pretty much pandemonium. A part of him wanted to tell the guys to save it for when they actually clenched, or at least until the TV interviews were over, but he didn't bother. They knew their business, and damned if they hadn't earned the celebration.

A cameraman had his video camera trained on Gaspar and an attractive reporter held a mike to his face. Dammit, he should know her name. Or he should at least remember which of the local stations she was on. He'd want to be sure to record the segment for Beth. Beth always liked to see his interviews.

Gaspar smiled as he answered her question. She'd wanted to know about the home run, of course. "Well, you never know. I thought I'd made pretty good contact, I had my arms extended, so I was hoping . . ."

The reporter quirked her head to the side and raised an eyebrow, an incredulous look if he'd ever seen one. He laughed. "Okay, okay. Yeah, I knew it was gone. Moment I hit it."

Before the reporter asked what Gaspar hoped would be a less obvious follow-up, O'Doul approached, still in his muddy game uniform. "Hey, Bethlen. Skip needs to see you."

Gaspar nodded at the still running camera. "Uh, kinda busy here at the moment, Lou."

O'Doul didn't smile, and he didn't back away. "He said right away."

Gaspar looked back toward the manager's office. Through the large glass window, he could see Dave O'Brien, the manager, a grizzled vet, watching. His face was grim. Something was wrong. Gaspar felt his blood go cold and his gut felt hollow. He muttered something to the reporter that he hoped might qualify as an apology and walked quickly without looking back.

O'Brien closed the door as Gaspar entered. Then O'Brien sat on his desk, not behind it like he usually did. "Sit down, okay?"

"I don't want to sit down." Sitting down was for bad news. There was no bad news. There couldn't be. Gaspar had just won the game for God's sake.

"Bethlen, please. Sit down, son, okay?"

Gaspar, concerned and confused, obeyed.

O'Brien stood up and then sat down behind his desk. Gaspar could see him trying to find words and failing. O'Brien stood, walked closer, and then knelt beside him. Gaspar waited for him to speak, but still no words came.

Gaspar shood his head. "Dave, what is it?"

O'Brien took a breath, and then another. Finally, he said, "It's Beth."

Gaspar opened his mouth but didn't answer. The chill in his blood was colder.

"There was, uh, a call for you," O'Brien said. "From Italy."

Gaspar shook his head. "Italy?"

"Italy," O'Brien confirmed.

"No. No, she's not in Italy. She's in Florida."

"It was her heart."

Gaspar shook his head again. "No, no. The doctors say she's got months. Maybe years. They—" He didn't finish.

O'Brien closed his eyes. "Dammit. I'm sorry, son."

"No. No. No, that can't be right. You heard wrong."

O'Brien didn't answer. He didn't look away; he kept his eyes locked on Gaspar's.

"She . . . she's not in Italy, Dave. She's in Florida. I just talked to her last night."

"They left a number for you to call. You can use my phone if you want."

Gaspar shook his head one more time. When he spoke again, his voice was barely a whisper. "But it's not time yet."

In the clubhouse, the other players gathered to watch, silently, solemnly, through the glass window of O'Brien's office. They saw Gaspar collapse, broken, as his world fell apart. O'Brien held him as he sobbed. Not one man moved to leave, even if all they could do was watch awkwardly and wait. They were his team, after all. They were there for him.

It rained at Beth's funeral, which later was about the only damn thing Gaspar could remember about it. A small crowd followed to the burial after the service, where it rained again. A man and a woman sang "How Great Thou Art," and O'Brien put his arm around Gaspar's shoulder and covered him with his umbrella. Gaspar sobbed.

A few weeks later, Gaspar left a small Beacon Hill market, clutching a small bag of groceries, stuff he'd been out of for nearly a week. The leaves on the scraggly trees were starting to fall. Autumn had come early to Boston, and it was already cold. Gaspar wished he'd brought a coat. Thankfully, the walk back home was a short one.

As he passed a pub a block or two from his townhome, he happened to glance in. A few regulars had gathered around a TV and were watching the Red Sox game. Despite the cold, the pub's door was open. Gaspar stopped. He hadn't seen a game since Beth had died.

He didn't even know how the season was going. If the remnants of Covid had a silver lining, it was that with the N95 mask and his fedora, he could stop for a minute without being recognized. It was hard to be a ghost without anonymity.

He watched through the open door for a moment, holding his bags close to his chest, and wished he hadn't. He sighed. The Boston batter—Gaspar wasn't close enough to see who it was—had popped out weakly. The announcer called the end of the game. "And that's your ballgame, folks. The Red Sox lose, three to one. With rising star Gaspar Bethlen's unexpected retirement, Boston's hopes are fading fast. They're four games back now . . . ."

Inside the bar, the Boston faithful muttered. Gaspar didn't listen. He turned and walked away. No expression, not even a shrug. A dead man's walk.

At home, Gaspar passed a week's worth of newspapers he hadn't bothered to collect and let himself in. He put his grocery bags down on the kitchen counter and glanced at his answering machine. Like the townhouse itself, the answering machine was a legacy from Gaspar's father. He'd kept the thing partly out of inertia, but mostly because he clung to anything that had belonged to his parents with an orphan's desperate grasp. Beth had wanted to keep the machine because she thought it was kitschy and fun, like the antique Victrola they kept next to the CD player, a legacy of her own family. He wondered, not for the first time, if he and Beth had the last one in all of Boston.

No, if *he* had the last one. Beth was gone. He still hadn't learned to think of her in the past tense. He wondered if he ever would.

The light was blinking. Without thinking, he pushed the button and heard the machine's mechanical voice: "You have ninety-three messages."

A young woman's recorded voice came from the machine. "Hi, Mr. Bethlen. This is Kelly from the children's hospital. I just wanted you to know that the kids here really miss your visits. If—"

Gaspar stopped the message. He pressed another button.

The mechanical voice spoke again: "All messages erased."

He fell into a kitchen chair and buried his face in his hands. He didn't bother to put his groceries away, not even the milk and eggs. Maybe he'd do it later, maybe not. Just . . . not now. Now the weight of exhaustion and sorrow were just too damn much.

3

The Last Mystery

aspar looked out his bathroom window and, to his surprise, saw snow on the ground. Somehow, winter had arrived when he wasn't looking. *Baseball season must be over,* he realized with a start. He wondered how the Sox had finished. He didn't know what surprised him more, that he didn't know or that he couldn't make himself care. He thought about checking the news on his phone. He didn't bother. The thing was on the fritz anyway. He thought about calling Dave O'Brien, or maybe texting some of the guys.

He should absolutely do that.

Probably.

He didn't. Instead, he sat alone, huddled in a chair, wrapped in a blanket. He stared at the TV, but he didn't turn it on. He saw his bleary-eyed reflection staring back at him. He hadn't shaved in days, and he looked like hell.

He thought about making breakfast, or maybe lunch. He had no idea what time it was. He didn't get up.

His phone buzzed. Gaspar didn't move. After a minute, the landline rang. Again. Again. The machine, which may or may not have been the very last one in Boston, picked up. He heard Beth's recorded voice, and his heart shattered into a million pieces.

"This is Beth and Gaspar. Leave us a message, okay?"
Beep!

After a second, Gaspar heard a second voice take a deep breath before speaking. He knew it was O'Brien even before he spoke. "Uh, Gaspar? Yeah, hey, it's Davey. None of us have heard from you, and I . . . Jeez. I don't know what to say. I just wanted you to know that, uh, the team's all thinking about you, huh? And, uh, you know. Merry Christmas and all." Gaspar heard O'Brien take another breath. "Yeah, Listen, I'm so sorry about Beth. Let us know you're okay, okay? Uh, yeah. Anyway." Another breath, and another. He was trying to think of something to say. That's one thing Gaspar had learned as a widower. No one ever knew what to say. "Hey, did you ever figure out what she was doing in Rome?"

O'Brien hung up. Gaspar frowned.

What the hell *had* she been doing in Rome?

He stood and walked down the corridor past their—past *his*—bedroom. The door to Beth's workroom was closed. It just about always had been back when Beth was . . . back when Beth was still using it. Her workroom

38

was her private domain, the place where she did her research and her writing, where she made her art, and where she tinkered with her many projects and hobbies. It was her special place where she did things that didn't involve him, and Gaspar had never felt comfortable venturing within, even though she'd laughed and said he was being silly. After all, he'd had a place to do his own thing that didn't involve her. He'd called it Fenway.

Gaspar let himself in and sat at Beth's desk, still exactly as she left it. He started the computer. While it was booting, he opened her top drawer. She always kept notes and such for her current project there. If there was a clue, that's where he'd find it. Sure enough, he found a folder inside. It was labeled in her neat, tiny handwriting:

Gaspar's Christmas Mystery

He smiled, even though he had to wipe away a tear. One of Beth's traditions would endure, for one last Christmas, anyway. It had been a long time since he'd smiled, and it felt a little weird.

Gaspar opened the folder. Inside, he found two receipts, both signed by someone named Will Klaus. He frowned. Beth had paid the guy a couple hundred dollars, but the receipts didn't say for what. He turned the two receipts over, looking for contact information, or for any clue at all, but he found nothing. There was nothing else in the folder.

As Gaspar put the folder back in the drawer and opened the larger one beneath it. There he found a package, neatly wrapped in gold paper with silver ribbons. He smiled again. Beth had always been a master gift wrapper. There was a tag, also written in Beth's tidy script:

For Gaspar, your first clue!
Love forever, Beth

She'd probably meant to give it to him on Christmas morning. She'd have moved it under the tree while he was sleeping. Or maybe . . . maybe she'd known, somehow, and she'd left it there for him to discover without her. That would have been so like her. Beth, yeah, Beth was a planner.

Gaspar opened the package and found an iPhone, one of the brand-new ones, along with a sheet of paper with columns of numbers, also written in Beth's hand. He shook his head. He already had a phone. It was a few years old, sure, but it got the job done. Well, usually. He could ignore calls and texts on that one just fine, thank you.

He turned his attention back to the rows of numbers, but he couldn't make heads or tails of them. Maybe it was a math puzzle? One of Beth's custom super sudokus or something? Gaspar ran his fingers along the paper, knowing it was one of the very last things Beth had touched, and looked more closely. Yup, that's what it was alright—a puzzle.

"Aw, Beth," he said aloud, turning his eyes skyward. "You know I always need a hint with the math clues!"

He sighed, but then an idea occurred to him. Beth had given him a phone. Maybe the numbers she'd written out were phone numbers? Maybe for this Will Klaus fellow? They certainly didn't look like phone numbers, but maybe they were international? Like, Italy, maybe? Was Klaus her contact in Italy?

Gaspar booted the phone. Of course Beth had already set it up for him; of course she had. When it came to life, an app launched automatically. He shook his head. It was a GPS map application. *So where the hell am I supposed to go?*

Gaspar turned his attention back to the numbers Beth had written out so carefully. Could the solution to the puzzle be an address? That didn't seem likely, since the solution would just involve numbers, no letters. So no help there, at least not yet. He'd have to solve the puzzle and then figure out what to do with them.

He'd have to do it without Beth's help. He didn't want to; he didn't even want to think about it. But it's what she would have wanted. So, wishing again that he had a cup of coffee, he sat down at the kitchen table and started to work.

A few hours later, he had it. He'd been overthinking the problem. All he had to do was add the columns up, both horizontally and vertically. *Yes!* Most of the totals made dates that had been important to Gaspar and Beth. *There, that's the date of our wedding. This is my birthday, and this is hers. This is the date we left on our honeymoon.* Gaspar smiled. The latter had been a few years after the wedding, but when they'd finally managed to make it happen, it was the trip they'd dreamed of.

Gaspar's smile wilted to a frown. The dates had brought back memories, but they hadn't contained a clue. He was missing something.

Aw, Beth!

Of course it wouldn't have been that easy. He chewed on the eraser of his pencil.

He thought again about making a cup of coffee, but remembered, again, that he was out. He wondered if his newfangled phone had a delivery app. He was about to check when an idea occurred to him. Maybe there was a puzzle within the puzzle? On a hunch, he added the columns again, this time selecting only the even numbers—Beth always had liked even numbers better; she thought they were more elegant. He rubbed his chin thoughtfully. The numbers clearly weren't dates—there weren't enough digits—but they were naggingly familiar all the same.

He thought. He stood and paced. He sat down and checked his math again. He stood and paced again.

And then he remembered. Of course the numbers were familiar. The solution was the number and combination to their old safe-deposit box, the one he'd almost forgotten they even had. Gaspar knew the answer wouldn't be there. No, Beth wouldn't have made it that easy. But the next clue surely would be.

He pulled on his long, black woolen overcoat, a warm scarf, his mask, and his black fedora—the one that had been his father's. Less than thirty minutes later he arrived, only to remember that, close to midnight, the bank was, of course, closed. The next morning, he tried again. There with all the important documents and such was a bright green envelope adorned with a red bow. He smiled.

It took Gaspar another day to solve the puzzle he found in the green envelope. When he did at last, he grinned. He was pretty close to sure he finally had an idea of what to do with the fancy new iPhone and its Maps app. He put on his coat, scarf, mask, and hat again.

4

The Bookshop

light dusting of snow covered a narrow street. The sidewalks were busy. Quaint storefronts were dressed in holiday finery—garlands on streetlamps, green wreaths with red ribbons on the doors, and glittering lights in the windows. Street vendors were selling hot chocolate and roasted chestnuts. Gaspar ignored them all. His attention was on the phone's Maps app. He checked the coordinates against the sheet of paper with four rows of carefully scribed numbers he'd found by solving Beth's puzzles. He was getting closer.

Gaspar passed a group of carolers without noticing them. A few more yards, and then he stopped. The numbers on the GPS app matched the first two rows of numbers on the paper. Gaspar looked up at a wooden sign that hung from an iron post out over the sidewalk. He found himself standing in front of:

KLAUS AND SON
Antiquarian Book Shop

Klaus!

He looked at the paper again. The third row of numbers matched the address painted neatly in the window above the shop's front door: 826. *Bingo.*

Bells jingled as Gaspar entered the shop. Inside, a floor of dark-stained hardwood had been warped by time and humidity into a subtle geography of uneven slopes and gently worn valleys. Rows of crooked shelves, over-filled with dusty, cloth- and leather-bound volumes, climbed toward a high ceiling lost in dim shadow. Pale fingers of wintry light reached through windowpanes of beveled and stained glass, casting round shadows from the four green Christmas wreaths that hung there like stockings. Ropes of evergreen and holly garland surrounded the room, twinkling with white lights, making Gaspar feel as though he'd stepped into a package gift-wrapped on the inside. He took a deep breath, filling his lungs with the shop's heady scent: musty and stale, like sweet smoke from a cherrywood pipe. He liked the place. Beth and his dad would have loved it. This was the sort of place where he would have shopped for both of them.

For a long moment, Gaspar hesitated, considering for a moment the seductive call of stories and secrets hidden in the maze-like rows of shelves, which crossed like the twisting, haphazard streets of some ancient city, shouting like an old friend found unexpectedly at the bar of a favorite tavern. He hadn't been much of a reader, unlike his father, but his Beth had changed that. For that fleeting moment, he thought he could wander the narrow rows for hours, a lost tourist, finding eccentric, threadbare treasures while drinking the odors of old paper, stiffened cloth, and cracking glue. But no, no. Not now. He had an errand. This was not the time for distractions.

"Hi there," a friendly voice called from a tall stool behind a vintage cash register. "Can I help you find something?"

A young man had spoken. His red-blond hair was longish: longer, if only by a bit, than the collar of his tweed jacket. He wore black jeans, a blue wool sweater, and gold, wire-framed glasses. He'd been working studiously on a laptop behind the counter, with books and papers spread around him. A hint of a welcoming smile curved the corners of his mouth before he pulled his mask back into place, and his eyebrows were raised expectantly. He was wearing a Red Sox ball cap.

"Uh, yeah," said Gaspar. "Maybe."

As he stepped closer, Gaspar saw the young man's eyes widen with a double take. "Whoa, wicked."

Gaspar held back a sigh. He was used to this. The hat and the N95 mask helped, but the reaction was still all too common. Ignoring the gape, he handed the young man the paper with the numbers.

The young man recovered quickly and tried to be cool. He grinned. "Not exactly a box score, huh?"

Gaspar raised an eyebrow. The young man smiled sheepishly and pointed his thumb back to a Boston Red Sox pennant on the wall behind him, along with a few autographed balls and framed ticket stubs. It was a shrine.

The young man grinned again. "I almost didn't recognize you with the mask. Gaspar Bethlen. Switch hitter. Career three-oh-five batting average. Three-oh-one from the left side, three-sixteen from the right." The grin widened. "But power from the left."

Gaspar felt surprisingly defensive in spite of himself. "I've totally got power from the right."

The young man shrugged. "Not to argue, but . . . last year, you had twenty-two homers batting left-handed, nine as a righty."

Gaspar raised an eyebrow. "That's 'cause left-handed pitchers know better than to challenge me."

"Well, statistically, lefties threw fastballs thirty percent—" The young man noticed Gaspar's glare. "But now that I think about it, not in what you'd call a challenging sort of way."

Gaspar didn't respond. Chagrined, the young man looked back to the paper. "So what's this?"

Gaspar showed the young man the phone with the GPS app. "I think these first two numbers are GPS coordinates. See?"

The young man was impressed. "Wicked. Where to?"

Gaspar pointed patiently to the GPS map. "Here," he said. *Duh.*

"Oh! Uh, yeah. Of course."

Gaspar pointed to the third row of numbers. "And this looks like—"

"Our street address. Sure."

"Which brings me to the last numbers," said Gaspar. "Those . . . well, not so much with the cracking yet."

The young man grinned. "Ah! There I can help. Now that we've narrowed your search down to these coordinates, and indeed to this very address, why, I can surely recognize one of our own stock control numbers. See, since we specialize in rare and antiquarian volumes, we can't always use the ISBNs like the big chains. And I happen to know exactly which volume that number refers to, without even referring to one of my index cards. C'mon, follow me."

"Is your name Will Klaus, by chance?"

"It is. I'm the son of Klaus and Son. How'd you know?

"Lucky guess," said Gaspar.

Will led Gaspar to the shop's back room and opened a vintage safe. Inside, he found a package wrapped in plain brown paper. "I was told a gentleman would come by to fetch this book, probably around Christmas." He smiled sheepishly. "When the gent is Gaspar Bethlen of the Red Sox, you kinda remember."

"Formerly of the Sox," said Gaspar. "I retired."

"I know," Will said softly. "Man, everybody knows. I'm sorry for your loss."

Gaspar ignored the sympathy and opened the package to find a leather-bound volume. A slip of paper was with the book. There was no title on the cover or spine. "What is it?"

"A book of Eastern European genealogy. *The Roots of the Bethlens, Volume 3*. I had a hell of a time tracking it down, lemme tell ya. It's the only copy that exists."

"Is it like, uh, valuable, this book?"

"I wouldn't have thought so," Will said hesitantly. "If a book's popular, they generally make more than one copy. But a man's been by asking about it. Twice, in fact. He was rather insistent and downright furious when I wouldn't let him have it. I have no idea at all how he knew it was here."

"Jeez! What that was all about?"

"To be frank, I was hoping you could tell *me*. Uh, not that it's any of my business, of course." Will looked around nervously and then leaned closer and lowered his voice. "And I'd swear I've seen figures lurking about at night, like they were just waiting for a chance. I don't mind admitting, I've been more than a little nervous walking to my car after closing time."

"Wow. I'm sorry to hear that."

"But to answer your question, if someone wants a thing, it is, by definition, valuable."

"But I'm guessing not to just anyone," said Gaspar.

Will shook his head. "No. I mean, how many Beth-lens can there be, anyway?"

"Yeah, we're not exactly Smiths or Joneses."

"Anyway. I take it that doesn't solve your mystery?"

Gaspar shook his head. "I'm afraid it's just the next clue in an unwinding puzzle. Say, you didn't happen to find it in Rome, did you?"

"Rome?" Will shook his head. "No. Why?"

"Beth . . . Beth was in Rome. That's my wife."

Gaspar saw Will shift uncomfortably. Whatever this dude was about to say, well, Gaspar just plain didn't want to hear it. He'd heard it all enough, thank you, and besides, he didn't want to risk crying in front of a stranger. He turned his attention back to the book and spoke quickly. "I can't read this."

"No Hungarian, eh?"

Gaspar shook his head, perplexed. "Not so much."

"Any idea what it's about?"

"Again with the I can't read this."

"Your wife said your great-great-grandfather's in here."

Gaspar looked back at the book. He felt his brow furrow. "You knew my wife. I, uh, saw receipts. You, uh, did something for her?"

Will nodded. "Yeah. Beth. She hired me. She was great. Look, I was really, really sorry to . . . uh, you know."

Gaspar managed a ghost of a smile, just for a second, and nodded before he changed the subject abruptly. He seriously didn't want to cry in front of this guy. "Why'd she hire you?"

"She thought you might need help. With a mystery. Hey, listen. I'm about to close. Let's get a beer. I'll tell you all about it. What'd'ya say?"

Gaspar shook his head. The tears were too close. "No. Thanks and all, but I . . . I really need to get home."

Will smiled. "You saw the receipts. I'm already bought and paid for."

"It's okay. You're fired." Gaspar turned to leave.

"But . . . but she already paid me."

Gaspar didn't look back. "Keep it. Look, dude, I'm just not up to this. Okay?"

Gaspar reached the door. Will called after him. "She said you'd be like that."

Gaspar turned back, surprised, a little hurt, a little angry. He opened his mouth to give this Will a piece of his mind, but the guy spoke faster.

"It's what she wanted."

Gaspar closed his eyes and sighed. Will had just said the one thing that might change his mind.

"Beer, huh?"

—❊—

The bookshop stood just a few blocks from Faneuil Hall in one of the oldest parts of Boston, where narrow, cobblestoned streets ran from Government Center, past quaint taverns and pubs that had endured since the days when patriots gathered in darkened corners to speak of freedom in hushed, furtive tones over frothy pints of handcrafted ale, and finally to the winding Italian neighborhoods of the North End. The streets were still dusted with a light frosting of snow, and in the light of the full moon, the city glowed with incandescent light, as though the whole land were the halo of some giant angel, bigger than the world. All the buildings were dressed in holiday regalia—red, green, and the glittering silver and gold of stars, turning every block into a constellation. Beneath every lamppost at every corner, vendors sold roasted chestnuts, cinnamon almonds, and steaming mugs of hot chocolate and spiced cider.

With his paper-wrapped parcel held tightly against his chest, Gaspar followed Will to the Bell in Hand Tavern on Union Street. It was a touristy kind of place, but it was close, and it would do. As they walked, Gaspar found himself falling in love with his home city all over again, despite his best efforts at humbuggery. He had always fallen in love with Boston at Christmas, with its swirling veil of snowflakes and its tinsel and blinking lights; he had done so each year anew since Beth had taught him to understand the subtle but fierce love with which beauty can bind the heart. But it had been a long and lonely time since anything had struck him as beautiful, and the reborn feeling was as unfamiliar as it was unexpected, like a first kiss, and it took him a long moment to recognize the sensation as pleasure. It had been a long time since he'd remembered pleasure. He felt a little guilty about it.

Inside, the brick walls were adorned with wreaths, and a crackling fire blazed on a stone hearth. They found a table in the back corner, away from the bar where most of the merry crowd had gathered. The Christmas beers were in, and they both ordered a pint. When the first few sips were warming them, Gaspar asked, "So how'd you meet my wife?"

"In person? Your wife came into the shop—gosh, it must be fifteen months ago now. But that wasn't the first time we'd met. At least, it wasn't if you count *virtual meetings* on the Internet." The younger man made air quotes with his fingers when he said the words *virtual meetings*. "We actually met through the message boards of a European genealogical website. Turns out we were both researching Hungarian ancestors. It seems Dad and I have inherited a business in Budapest, if you can believe it. And we happened to be more or less neighbors, which is somewhat unusual, even in a city like Boston."

"Klaus is a Hungarian name?"

Will shook his head. "That's where my family was before they came to America. I don't think they originated there. Same as yours, I think. I think both of our families just kind of stopped there along the way."

"I see."

"Anyway, when your wife found out I was both a researcher and an antiquarian book dealer, she hired me, and I helped her with some research. Well, a contact of mine and I did. A friend in Hungary. Her name's Hapsburg Anasztázia. Ana. In Hungary, they put the last name first, you know. Traditionally." He grinned. "She's . . . gosh. She's an amazing woman. Ana, she—"

Gaspar cut him off. "What kind of research?"

"Oh. Uh, well, genealogy, partly, and tracking that book down, mostly." Will grinned. "There aren't as many people interested in Hungarian genealogy and who happen to know the rare book market as you might think."

"To be honest, I wouldn't have thought there was one."

Will shrugged. "My point is made."

"And this Ana is a genealogist?"

"No, no. She's a banker by day. I met her because of some . . . uh, some stuff having to do with that other business. The one Dad and I inherited. But genealogy is a hobby of Ana's. She sure knows a lot about your family, let me tell you. Well, the Hungarian branch, anyway."

"Beth was looking for my family," said Gaspar, his voice thick with emotion. "Wasn't she? She was looking for my roots."

"How'd you know?"

"It was something we talked about. Something my dad was interested in."

Will nodded. "She'd been researching for months already, I think, when we made contact. And she'd learned that the entire history of your family is recorded in a set of three volumes, of which only a single copy survives—if, indeed, any others were ever produced. She wanted my help with that."

"In Hungary? She sent you all the way over there?"

"Not exactly. I've never really traveled much. Not yet. I'd seriously like to. Jeez. Someday, though. . . . Uh, sorry. I'm rambling. Anyway. Not in Hungary. On the Internet. See, I'm more of a reader."

Gaspar nodded. "Gotcha."

"That can be an adventure, too, let me tell you."

"If you say so."

"Uh, anyway, that's what I do. I track down old books and odd facts. Missing branches in the family tree, historical tidbits. Stuff like that." He offered a lopsided grin. "It's like being a detective. Just without all the danger and guns and, you know, anything that might make it even remotely cool."

Gaspar tilted his head to the side. "That's a job?"

55

"Well, that and the store. Hey, I'm working for you, aren't I?"

"Only 'cause firing you didn't take."

"And you gotta admit, detective sounds way cooler than research assistant," Will said.

"Again with the if you say so."

"I do say so! I mean, like, what's cooler than detective?"

"Baseball player," said Gaspar.

"Touché. But hey, I found your book, didn't I? So c'mon. Let me help. Detective. Already bought and paid for. Tell me about it?"

It had been a long time since he'd been around other people, so Gaspar had to rummage around for a smile in the cluttered, long-neglected attics of his memory. He found that, despite long weeks of disuse, it still fit, if awkwardly. "It's kind of a tradition. Y'see, every year, Beth makes . . ." Gaspar swallowed. ". . . *made* a mystery for me."

"Right," said Will. "The annual Christmas mystery. She told me a little about that. You have to solve it to find out what your present is."

"Yeah. That's the gist, more or less. What else did she say?"

"That's pretty much all she told me, really. I take it there's a story?"

Gaspar nodded. "There is." Maybe it was the beer—the Christmas brews were always pretty strong—but to his surprise, he found he wanted to tell it. He took another sip and began. "When my wife and I were first married, we were just starting off in life. You know? The world was, like, totally our oyster, as the old saying goes, but if it held a pearl, you couldn't have proven it by us. Minor league ballplayers don't make much, you know, and grad students make even less."

Will nodded. "Money was tight, I take it?"

"Tighter than Bigfoot in baby shoes," Gaspar agreed with a nod. "Of course, Beth thought it was even tighter than it really was, because whatever extra I could squirrel away remained safely hidden so that, come December, I could afford to buy her a little something nice, yeah?"

Smiling, Will nodded his head. "Of course you did."

"Damn right," said Gaspar. "I always had a knack for finding, well, that one little special something that she'd never buy for herself. But sweet Beth, she didn't let a little thing like our beggar's bankbook keep her from giving me a Christmas present, no way!"

"What did she do?"

"Well, my Beth, she knew there was very little in the world I loved more than a good mystery. She used to pick up mystery books from the library, and at night, we'd build a little fire and read to each other, matching wits with the likes of Sam Spade, I. M. Fletcher, Miss Jane Marple, and yeah, even the great Sherlock Holmes himself. So what did my darling give me?"

"Why, a mystery, of course."

"A mystery," Gaspar confirmed. "Handcrafted by my Beth, and just for me. That first time . . . on Christmas morning, I found an envelope in my stocking. That's it! Just an envelope. Inside was a note—of which I could read not a single word."

"A code?" Will guessed.

Gaspar nodded. "Took me all morning to even guess how to begin! While Beth cleared away the breakfast things, I chewed the end of a pencil until I was afraid I'd get eraser poisoning."

"Uh, is there such a thing?"

"I am thankful to report that, apparently, there is not. It was nearly lunchtime when I finally cracked that code—and revealed a riddle. Would you believe I can't remember a single word of that riddle? Not one word. I still have it, though. Maybe I'll get it out tonight. Anyway, the answer led me to the attic, where I found another code, and another riddle, which, sooner than you can say 'Merry frickin' Christmas,' had me digging up an old mason jar in the little barren patch we called a backyard. While my dear heart fussed and cooed over the pretty new jacket I'd picked out for her, I deciphered the next clue. That led me out to the loose step on our front porch, which steered me in turn to the corner cupboard in our kitchen, and then back to the attic again, if you can believe it. The other end, this time. The sun was setting when I finally solved the final clue, which prompted me to peek right under my own bed. I found a box there, all tied up with a bright red ribbon. Inside was a sweater that my Beth had spent the better part of our married life knitting for me. One sleeve was longer than the other, and it itched like crazy, but dude, let me tell you. I never treasured a Christmas gift more."

Will smiled. "'The Gift of the Magi,' eh?"

"The Gift of the frickin' Magi," Gaspar acknowledged with a nod. He drank some more of his beer.

"And thus was a tradition born?"

"That's how it happened. Neither Beth nor I had much of a family to speak of. Mom died when I was a toddler, and Dad, well, he passed not long after we were married. Pretty much the same with her. But if there was ever a closer, happier, richer family, I never saw or heard of them."

"A regular mini Waltons clan, eh?"

"The Waltons? Dude, like, how old *are* you?"

Will chuckled. "I used to watch the repeats with my dad. He ate it up."

"Right," Gaspar said with a nod. "Me, too, believe it or not. Okay then, so yeah, Beacon Hill was our Walton's Mountain. At least it was after I made the Show. And not even a TV family could make Christmas as magical as we could, even if it was just the two of us. And the annual Christmas mystery—that was the very best part of it. The presents were always treasures, for how could a gift from Beth be anything else? But the mysteries! The stories! Handcrafted with love and care, and just for me. I never loved a Christmas present more; *no one* ever loved a Christmas present more. No one, ah, no one ever could. They got harder and more complex every year, the mysteries, but even the simplest of them would have made prim Agatha Christie and old Arthur Conan Doyle turn greener than a holly wreath with envy. Sometimes it would take me 'til New Year's Day to solve them—a time or two it took me all the way to Valentine's, and once to frickin' Saint Patrick's Day!"

"And she made you one more before she died," Will guessed. "The last mystery."

"One last Christmas mystery." Gaspar managed a nod. "Beth—see, she knew the end was coming. I think . . . I think she knew she wouldn't be there to see me solve it." He swallowed. He was *not* going to cry in front of this guy. "Anyway, they found some of the clues. The Italian police, I mean. She had them with her when. . . ."

Gaspar couldn't make himself finish the sentence.

Will forced a smile. "It must be hard."

Gaspar shrugged. "Like you said. It's what she wanted."

"And you just found the clues? Today?"

"Few days ago. She had some in her desk. Then I found something else that had come in the mail. The cops in Italy sent it along with all the rest of her stuff. A sheet of parchment. I was probably supposed to find it later, somewhere else along the trail, but she never got to put it . . . uh, wherever she was going to put it." Gaspar shrugged and tried to smile. "So I guess I'm a little bit ahead of the game."

"What took you so long to get started?"

Gaspar sighed. He had to dab at his eye with the napkin. He hoped the dude hadn't noticed. "That's a hard question to answer. I guess . . . a part of me just couldn't face the idea of solving a Christmas mystery without her—without seeing how her eyes would shine when she'd catch me hot on the trail of a red herring, or how she'd beam like a full moon in a winter night when I'd finally crack a clue! The Christmas mysteries—they were the joy of the season to me, man. But I don't know what joy *means* anymore, because joy was something I shared with Beth. Without Beth, the Christmas mystery would be just one more hole. That's what's left when you lose someone, you know. Holes. All the holes where that person should be—the dent in the bed where she slept all those years, her chair at the table, her spot by the window. Can you imagine that? Can you? The empty place torn in the very fabric of your life? The jagged, aching hole in your heart where . . . where even the memory of joy bleeds away."

"What an astonishing love you must have shared."

Gaspar took a sip of his ale. "That it was, man. Yeah. That it was."

"What else?"

"I hadn't gotten around to opening the mail, so I hadn't seen what the cops had sent from Italy. Beside that? Well, the puzzle was hard! There was math. And Beth . . . well, this time she wasn't there to help with the math."

"I guess not."

"Another part of me . . . well, I guess I knew that this was the last mystery she'd ever make for me. When this one was solved, well, it would mean she really was *gone*. That she was really and truly gone forever, and I really was alone."

"So what made you finally change your mind?"

Gaspar smiled. "Just like you said. It's what Beth wanted. She worked so hard, even as she knew she was dying. It's her last gift for me. And . . . and when I solve it at last, I'll have something to hold onto, right? Some little, like, memento to grasp, tightly, through all the long and lonely years left to me, like a life preserver to remind me of what I've lost. It'll be like a little piece of her, even if it's all I've got. I want that, man. I really, really do. I want . . . I want something to hold onto."

Will had the grace to change the subject. "What were the, uh, clues?"

"The first was the new phone. When I found it, I also found a puzzle." Gaspar pulled a square of paper out of his breast pocket and unfolded it carefully.

Will bent closer to examine it. "Oh, it's one of those—what do you call them? Number crosswords. The Japanese logic puzzles."

"You're thinking of sudoku," said Gaspar with a nod. "My Beth loved them. We used to have contests over breakfast to see who could solve them faster. I never could beat her. I'm telling you, dude, she always had hers finished before she was ready for her second cup of coffee. Of course, she couldn't catch a baseball to save her life, so I guess it evened out. But no. This is similar, of course, but my Beth thought sudoku puzzles were too easy, if you can believe it. This little cipher is her own variation. As you can see, it's a little more complex than what you see in the papers. Look, she made this one herself. She was a wizard with the things."

"Wow." Will whistled. "She *must* have been a wizard."

Gaspar nodded. "And I'm not even, like, an apprentice. Of course, I had another clue, too."

"The one that came in the mail? You mentioned that."

Gaspar nodded. "Here." He pulled a sheet of parchment from his pocket and slid it to Will. "Funny, I guess. The cops mailed it to me with the rest of her stuff, all the way from Italy. Did I tell you that already? Anyway. I never even bothered to open it till I found the phone and the coordinates."

Will unrolled the parchment and found an illuminated engraving of a jewel. His eyes sprung open. "Wicked!"

"No kidding," Gaspar agreed.

"What . . . I mean, jeez! What is this?"

"Yeah, see, that's pretty much the question. Detective. Anyway, I found some notes on Beth's computer. Thankfully, she made it pretty easy for me to find them. She said this picture used to belong to my dad. Which, for the record, was news to me. She says to find that gem, we'll have to solve a mystery that's puzzled scholars for more than two thousand years."

Will's eyes popped open like a pair of window shades. "Two thousand—! Well. How hard can that be?"

"Yeah," said Gaspar. "Good thing she hired me a detective."

Will's eyes narrowed. "Maybe the next clue's in the book."

"That might explain why somebody was after it. I mean, if there's, like, really an actual jewel, and not just a picture. I guess that's not likely, is it?"

Will shrugged. "One way to find out. Solve the last mystery."

"If only I could read Hungarian."

"My friend can help," Will said eagerly. "Ana. In Hungary." He caught himself and grinned. "She's amazing. Uh, I mentioned that, didn't I?"

Gaspar rolled his eyes, but he smiled. "Amazing. Yeah. Seems like."

Will smiled back sheepishly. "I've been practicing myself. I'm not bad with languages."

Gaspar opened the book. As he did, a folded, yellowed receipt fell out. He picked it up.

"Clue?" Will asked.

Gaspar shook his head. "It's an ATM receipt. Maybe from the previous owner?"

"I doubt it," said Will. "Look, that's from a Florida bank. See? The book came from Europe."

"Beth must have put it in here," said Gaspar. "Maybe it is a clue after all."

"What does it mean?"

Gaspar felt his brow furrow as he considered. He shook his head. Finally, he said, "It means I have a mystery to solve."

"So you can get your gift?"

"So I can find out what the hell my wife was doing in Rome."

Outside the pub, a man in dark clothing kept to the shadows as he watched Gaspar Bethlen and the kid from the bookshop shake hands. After a moment, the kid walked away, probably back to his bookshop, and Bethlen climbed into his Tesla. As soon as he drove away, the man in dark clothing tapped his phone and spoke.

"Bethlen has the book."

After a moment, he spoke again. "Huh? No. Just one book."

Another moment, then, "No. You heard me. One book. Not three. One."

———※✦———

Just before Will opened the shop's door with his key, he stopped, frozen.

The door was already open.

It had been forced.

Will took a deep breath. He entered, slowly, cautiously, moving as quietly as he could. He crept through the stacks. The store was dark. No one was there. He kept moving.

The door to the back room was open. Will tiptoed closer.

Inside, he spotted a rough-looking man kneeling at his safe. He'd apparently just gotten it open and had shoved the cash and rare volumes aside. He was looking for something else.

"Hey!" Will shouted.

The man turned and pulled a gun out of his coat. Will gasped and dove for cover. The man fired. The bullet splintered the wood of a bookcase. Before Will could stagger to his feet, to hide or bolt, the man fled into the night.

5

Find Them

aspar woke slowly, smiling, from a dream he was already forgetting. The dream had been brewed in a cauldron of memory—the time he'd tried unsuccessfully to teach Beth to play catch before she'd utterly humiliated him with a soccer ball, the time they'd grilled shrimp on the beach before they'd danced, just the two of them, to the harmonies of wind and ocean. The time he'd surprised her with a blouse she'd loved but thought was too expensive. He'd been pretty sure she'd known he was lying when he said he'd found it on sale, but she'd cherished it anyway. He'd dreamed of her laughter, and her whispers, and how her eyes always sparkled just before her smile widened into a mischievous grin.

Pale and silver fingers of moonlight spilled though the frosted window and fanned over the empty sheets next to him, and for a single moment, through his half-closed eyes, it made the rumbled sheets look like a woman's body, soft, curved, and luminous. But when he reached out for it, his fingers touched only cold cotton. He wanted to reach out again and touch that empty place that had been Beth's with gentle strokes, soft and aching with love, but he was wise enough not to break the illusion's cruel and fleeting gift, so he lay still, listening for the lost echo of her breathing. In the end, he reached for her absence because he couldn't stop himself, and the spell shattered like crystal, like ice, and then even the dim memory of the wind-stirred ocean's music was lost. He went and found the blouse in her closet and he held it close, because it still held the ghost of her scent.

The hours after midnight were the longest and the loneliest, with sleep an ever-more-infrequent visitor, a friend from his youth with whom he was gradually losing touch. He knew it wouldn't come again, not that night, anyway. He wept softly again before he finally pulled himself out of bed.

In the kitchen, Gaspar opened his refrigerator. It held only a pizza box and the last four cans of a six-pack. He opened the pizza box and sighed. It was empty. He threw it away. The groceries he'd bought the night before were still on the counter, but the cold stuff, at least, was shot. He threw the whole bag away. He thought about making coffee, but that bin, too, was empty. He went back to the fridge and took a beer. *Breakfast of Champions.*

Gaspar sat at his table where he pushed aside a stack of unopened mail. He sipped the beer and flipped through the book, *The Roots of the Bethlens, Volume 3*. He pursed his lips. Beth would have known he couldn't read it. So how could it be a clue? The engraving of the gem was on the table. Gaspar shook his head. No clue there. Well, there probably was, but he wasn't ready for it yet. So he was missing something.

On the other side of the table, Beth's chair was empty. He looked at it with sad, longing eyes.

I need your help, baby. I don't . . . I don't know if I can do this without you.

For a moment, he fingered the pages with Beth's handwriting, a tender and lonely gesture. The yellowed ATM receipt was there, too.

Now what the hell is that about?

Then he sat upright, suddenly, as an idea occurred to him. He snatched up the receipt and looked at it more closely. There was an address at the bottom. Will had been right; it wasn't from an overseas ATM at all. It was from a Florida bank. More specifically, it was from a bank in Sarasota, Florida. He knew that bank. It had been a minute, sure, but he'd been there, back when he played A-ball for the Sarasota Red Sox. He'd been there with Beth, back when they were newlyweds and he was a young, struggling minor leaguer and the Show in Boston was a million years away. Memory fell over him like rain.

The ATM had been brand, spanking new in those days—he remembered that because the bank had finally gotten around to replacing the old one that never seemed to work. He had Beth had been making a withdrawal on the way to the airport. It wasn't much of a withdrawal; they hadn't had much to withdraw in those days. Gaspar had offered Beth a smile and hoped it didn't look sad. "I guess it's not much of a honeymoon."

Beth smiled back and touched his cheek. "It's always a honeymoon when I'm with you."

"I wish I could give you more."

"You gave me everything." Beth's smile widened to a grin. "Hey! Someday we'll go to Europe. How about that? Huh? We can start planning it soon as we're back from this one. C'mon. We'll make a scrapbook."

"I'd like that."

"We'll go to Hungary," Beth had said. Gaspar remembered it like it was yesterday. "How about that?"

"I'd like that. My dad always wanted to do that. Did you know?"

Beth nodded. "Silly. Of course I knew."

"He wanted to trace his ancestry."

"We'll finish what your dad started," Beth said. "That'll be my gift to you, my sweet orphan boy. Someday. I'll give you your family."

Gaspar leaned in to kiss her. "You already have."

Beth tucked the cash and receipt carefully into her purse.

Gaspar looked down at the creased and yellowed receipt and smiled. Beth had saved it, that memory of the beginning of their modest honeymoon, the first memento of their marriage. For all the years, so many and too few, she'd saved it.

They *had* made that scrapbook. They'd worked on it for years until they'd finally had enough money to travel. Gaspar wondered if Beth had kept it. He shook his head and grinned. Sure she'd kept it. Beth kept everything.

Gaspar looked back at the book. *The Roots of the Bethlens.* They'd talked about tracing his ancestry, about finding his roots.

Beth would have known he'd remember the scrapbook. She'd always known what he was thinking and usually before he'd thought to think it. That's what she wanted him to find; he was sure of it. He felt his brow furrow. Now where the hell was it?

Moments later, Gaspar stood on a chair, feeling around on the top shelf of Beth's closet. He found a dusty box hidden behind a pile of sweaters (hers) and t-shirts (his—the old, ratty ones she'd hidden from him) and pulled it down.

Well. At least I have my good ol' shirts back.

At the table, Gaspar opened the box and pulled out the old scrapbook, so familiar even after all the years. This was where they had dreamed and planned a life, he and Beth together, a life they'd barely begun to live. He opened it and found the carefully selected collection

71

of worn travel brochures and articles, old friends. Then
he smiled. *Bingo*. He discovered among the memories a
crisp new envelope addressed in Beth's dear hand:

My Beloved

He opened it . . . and was not surprised to find a
hand-drawn grid filled with neat numbers. It was another puzzle of Beth's own clever design. With a sigh,
Gaspar reached for a pencil, and chewed the eraser
thoughtfully.

*Aw, Beth, honey, you know I need your help with the
math.*

He wished again for a pot of coffee, but he was too
eager to wait. So, in the deep of the night, he put pencil
to paper, and he began to solve. It took him a good long
while.

It was close to lunchtime the next day when Gaspar
made his way back to the bookstore, carrying a metal
briefcase. Despite the cold, he'd decided to walk—by the
time he got his car out of the garage, fought traffic, and

found a place to park, he'd just about make better time on foot, and he was eager to get started.

Gaspar found Will behind the counter with a thin, graying man that looked so much like him that Gaspar knew me must be the elder Klaus of Klaus and Son. Two uniformed police officers were just leaving after shaking hands with Mr. Klaus. A handyman knelt by the door, making repairs.

Gaspar felt his eyebrows rise. "Holy crap! What the hell happened here?"

Will looked up. "Wild party. The guest of honor was a burglar."

The older man scowled. "Bastard shot at my son. Can you believe it? What's this city coming to?"

"Holy shit!" said Gaspar. "You okay?"

Will nodded. "I'm fine. He fired a shot and booked, pun intended."

"Did he get anything?" Gaspar asked.

Will shook his head. "Nothing. He had the safe open, but he totally ignored everything in there."

"Cash, rare books, everything," the older man confirmed.

"Oh," Will said. "This is my father, by the way. Jim Klaus. Dad, this is Gaspar Bethlen."

Gaspar offered the man his hand to shake. "Pleased to meet you, Mr. Klaus."

"Call me Jim, please, and the pleasure is all mine. My son and I are big fans, big fans!"

Gaspar nodded. "Thanks. Did the cops find any-thing?"

Will shrugged. "They said they'd get back to us."

"Which means no," said Jim.

"Damn," said Gaspar. "Man, that really sucks."

"Eh," said Jim. "Nobody died; nothing valuable was taken. I can see how it might not be top priority for them."

"What do you think he was he after?" Gaspar asked. "Your, uh, guest of honor, I mean."

"If I didn't know better," said Jim, "I'd swear it was that book of yours."

Will nodded. "I told you about the guy who came here looking for it."

Gaspar gaped. "My book? You're kidding!"

"You didn't leave it behind, did you?" said Will.

Gaspar hefted the briefcase. "No, as a matter of fact, it's right here."

"I don't think carrying it around is necessarily safer," Jim pointed out.

"Good point," said Gaspar. "I guess it really is valu-able after all."

"To someone," Will agreed. "And if it's a clue, it makes me wonder if someone else knows about that jewel in your engraving."

"So you think there's a . . . literal jewel. It's not like a, uh, family symbol or something?"

"Search me. But someone really seems to want that book, and that's the only thing I can think of. Speaking of, did you find more clues?"

"As a matter of fact, that's why I'm here," said Gaspar. "I think I might need your help again."

"You've got it," said Will. "Uh, Dad?"

Jim grinned and waved. "Help Mr. Bethlen. I can finish up."

"Thanks, Dad." Will led Gaspar back toward the front desk. "So, what can I do for you?"

"Here, take a look." Gaspar handed Will the paper he used to solve Beth's puzzle.

"You solved it?" Will asked.

Gaspar nodded. "More coordinates. Or rather, the same ones again. Man, Beth went to, like, a whole lot of trouble to make up new puzzles that had the same answer."

"Here again?" Will guessed. "The coordinates, I mean."

Gaspar nodded. "And three more of your stock number things. Just like the last one."

Will glanced at the numbers. "That's funny. I don't recognize these."

"You actually know your stock numbers?" He left the word *nerd* unspoken, but he was pretty sure Will heard it all the same.

"You'd be surprised. But here. Let me check." Will punched the keys on a slightly antiquated terminal. He shook his head. "Just as I thought. Nothing."

"I don't understand. These are your numbers, right?"

"Sure looks like our system, yeah," said Will. He turned the monitor around to show Gaspar. "But look, see? Nothing."

Jim called back from where the repairman was working on the door. "Why not check the shelves? If computers could tell you everything, we wouldn't need all these books, would we?"

"Are these in numerical order?" Gaspar demanded. "Where do they start?"

"Sort of," said Will. "The first two are the category. See? This first one is Travel. Then—hey!"

Gaspar was already moving.

"Wait," Will called after him. The Travel section's back here, the other way."

Gaspar checked his paper again and followed the numbers. *Closer . . . closer. . . .*

Then, between two volumes clearly labeled with inventory stickers on their spines, he found an unstickered book—right where the missing stock number should be. He pulled the book from the shelf. It was a travel guide to Budapest, Hungary.

Will had to stretch to look over Gaspar's shoulder. "Huh. I'd swear that's not one of our books."

"Maybe it was ordered special," Jim called to them.

Gaspar opened the book. Inside, he found another envelope with Beth's familiar handwriting:

Merry Christmas, My Love!

Gaspar smiled.

"C'mon," said Will. "That next one should be in Foreign Language and then, uh, yeah, Business and Finance. . . ."

In the Foreign Language section, they found a Hungarian phrase book. "Bingo," Gaspar said when he found another note from Beth.

"C'mon," Will said again. "This way!"

Will led them to the store's Business and Finance section where, at the top of a ladder, Gaspar found a third book: this one was a tiny bankbook.

"Okay," said Will, *"that's* not a special order. Now how the hell did that get on the shelf?"

Jim called out again from behind the front desk. "What, you think you were the only one who helped Mrs. Bethlen?"

Will chuckled. "Apparently not. C'mon. Let's go to the back and take a look."

The stock room was small and cluttered. Books were stacked precariously on every flat surface, and a few that weren't. Faded art prints, old calendars, and a few vintage Red Sox posters covered the walls—Lefty Grove,

Yaz, Carlton Fisk, Cy Young, even a pre-Yankees Babe Ruth. The place smelled of dust, mold, candle wax, and old leather.

Will cleared a spot, and then he and Gaspar spread the books on the desk, along with three envelopes, all addressed in Beth's handwriting. Gaspar looked at the travel book, his lips pursed thoughtfully, while Will opened the bankbook.

"What's this?" Will asked.

"The bankbook? You know what I know. I can't read it. Is it from your friend's bank, by chance? Ana?"

"No. It's a different logo. We can try the phrase book, I guess. My Hungarian is still not perfect, I'm afraid. How 'bout the envelopes?"

Gaspar reached for the one that had been in the travel guide. "Here we go." He made himself smile, hoping it would hide his nervousness. "Beth's last mystery."

Will smiled, too, solemnly. "Thank you for letting me share the moment. I'm honored."

Gaspar nodded and opened the first envelope. Inside he found two more page of Beth's hand-written numbers—another code—and an old, black and white photograph.

Will glanced at the pages with the numbers. "Well. That clears things up."

Gaspar frowned. "Those aren't like the others. Let's save them for now."

"What about the picture?"

"Careful," said Gaspar. "That's more than a century old."

Will nodded and reached for the photograph, touching it just with his fingertips. The corners were sticky; he suspected that, until recently, it had been forgotten in an old family album somewhere. It showed a family, wearing or carrying everything they owned, standing on the cold and windswept docks of Ellis Island, with the fog-shrouded promised land of New York City and all of its harsh and jagged beauty waiting in the cold distance, just a harbor away. The past, with all that was known and comfortable, was forever behind them, in that moment when the camera blinked, and the future, with all its cruel and dangerous mystery, rich with desperate hope, lay before them, newborn. Will turned the photograph over and found two words written backwards in a careful hand:

Find Them

"Interesting," said Will. "Mirror writing. And it looks recent."

"My wife's hand," Gaspar said with a nod. "It's one of her clues."

"Find them," Will mused aloud. He grinned. "That may be a trick. How old did you say this picture is?"

Gaspar rolled his eyes. "But look, it's written backwards. See? *Find them* means looking back. Uh, I think so, anyway. And since the other gift is a book of genealogy—well, my man, it's clear I'm meant to *find them* by tracing back. I'm supposed to find their beginning. That's my current guess, anyhow."

"How do you think she found this photo?"

"Oh, I've got boxes and boxes of old family photos up in the attic. I actually spent quite a bit of time with them when I was a kid, dumb as it sounds, since I have no idea who they are. The people in this photo are my ancestors, but they're strangers to me. My parents never had the chance to pass on their stories."

"Isn't that sad?" said Will. "What's more tragic than a lost story? It is one thing to be gone, quite another to be forgotten utterly."

"I guess so. All the same, the idea of having a family . . . you know, like, roots and all . . . it was always a comfort to me, even if they're strangers."

"Find them. Your family."

Gaspar nodded again. "My family. So anyway, I guess I'm supposed to trace my roots back."

"I think so," Will agreed. "She'd been researching for close to a year, I think, when we made contact on the genealogy sites. At least that long. And she'd learned that the entire history of your family is recorded in a set

of three volumes, of which only a single copy survives. I mean, think of it, right? The entire history, going all the way back to the beginning!"

Gaspar chuckled. "All the way back? To, like, some half-monkey creature in the prehistoric African jungle? Do your books go back that far, huh?"

Will laughed with Gaspar.

"Likely not," he admitted, "although I haven't actually seen volumes one and two, so who knows? But seriously, the important families of Europe typically traced their lines back to one significant ancestor, a king, a noble, a knight from the crusades, a holy man, an explorer. You get the idea. Someone of note, and usually someone whose undisputed bloodline helps them maintain a grip on something."

"What kind of something?" asked Gaspar.

"Oh, it varies, I suppose," said Will. "Land, wealth, a title, power. Or even some minor claim to trivial fame. For example, my own humble family claims to originate with some Turkish Christian bishop, Nicholas of Myra, I think. Something like that. Anyway, it kind of seems to lend us some very minor notoriety, as it were, even if it's not the sort one can cash in at a bank. In any case, families tend to trace ancestry back to that one individual who first claimed or attained that something, whatever it happens to be. In England, there are families who can trace their lines all the way back to William the Conqueror, and even back to Normandy. But very few of them seem interested in tracing back to the French tanners and peasant farmers that existed before the line rose to prominence. What interests them is the some-thing—title, land, or bragging rights—that it allows them to claim."

"Any idea what that might mean for my family?"

"Well," said Will, "as with most of the old European families, yours once had many, many branches. But today, only two survive. You are the last heir to one branch. Now here's the interesting part. Each of the two branches is heir to a part of the family legacy, a legacy that stretches all the way back to the family's origin. One branch has inherited property and wealth."

"Figures that's not *my* branch. What about the other?"

"The other—well, something *else*."

"Yeah?" asked Gaspar. "What is it?"

"As to that. . . ." Will began hesitantly, "well, to be honest—I don't know. When we met, your wife was just beginning her research. At that point, she'd only found hints and rumors. The references were vague but fascinating, or so she said. Some hints suggested a treasure, some priceless heirloom."

"The gem?" said Gaspar.

"Maybe," said Will. "An object of some sort, anyway, something of great antiquity and value. Others seemed to suggest it wasn't a physical thing at all, but rather a *secret*."

"So, uh, which is it? Gem or secret?"

Will shook his head. "I don't know, Gaspar. I'm sorry. It could be either, I suppose, or both of them at once."

"Or nothing at all, I suppose."

Will shook his head and frowned. "I find that unlikely."

"Why's that?"

"I only met your wife a few times, and I certainly don't pretend to have known her well. But she didn't strike me as the type to go to all this trouble just to set up a wild goose chase. I think she found something. Something special. And besides, it's pretty obvious that someone wants that book you've got there. Badly enough to shoot at me."

"Good point." Gaspar realized he was holding his case a little more tightly. "You must be right. I mean, Christ! I wonder what she found? And who

. . . who was the first? The father of the family? Where does the line begin?"

"Beats me. But whatever Beth learned, it seems she's left you a trail to follow. Don't you think? To your family."

"Like Dad always wanted. Wait a minute. The book . . . *The Roots of the Bethlens.* There are supposed to be three volumes, right?"

"Yeah. But I haven't actually seen volumes one and two. Hey, I wonder if the thief thought we had the other volumes?"

"Where are they?" Gaspar demanded.

"No idea," said Will. "But I bet Beth knew."

"And she left them for me to find. Somewhere. If I can crack the clues."

Will smiled. "Your Christmas mystery." He slid the unopened envelopes to Gaspar. "Here. Try the others."

Gaspar opened the second envelope and pulled out some papers. "My birth certificate? Huh. I wonder what that's about?"

Will looked at the other papers. "Yes. I helped her with these—certified copies of your ancestry going all the way back to Ellis Island."

"What for?"

"To prove you're who you say you are, if I had to guess. In case there's something for you to claim."

"From who? Or where?"

"I guess we'll find out. Anyway, I think there should be more stuff there. One last envelope, right?"

Gaspar opened the last envelope and he frowned. "Travel vouchers?"

Will nodded. "Like gift certificates. Flight and hotel."

"In Budapest."

"Budapest," Will acknowledged. "I think there might be more in there. Right?"

Gaspar looked again and found another gift certificate, this one made on a home computer. It was for:

Will Klaus,
Consulting Research Detective

Gaspar looked at Will and raised an eyebrow. "So. It looks like Beth hired me a helper. One who grins like a monkey caught with his paw in the banana jar."

Will shrugged. "I told you. One detective. Uncool, but bought and paid for. I'm, uh, part of your present." He grinned sheepishly. "Merry Christmas."

"This wasn't something you could have, you know, mentioned? Like, at any point before now?"

Will laughed and held up his hands in surrender. "Okay, okay. You got me. Yes. I know more—although likely not so much as you're hoping, I'm afraid—than what I've told you. But in my defense, if you'll recall, I *did* say something about a promise to a lady, didn't I? Forgive me?"

Gaspar returned the grin. "I wouldn't have forgiven you if you *had* told. As you say. A promise to a lady is sacred. Especially to Beth. So. The next clue's in Hungary."

Will nodded. "So it seems. Budapest. That might be just a step, though. Like I said. Neither of our families originated there."

"Right. And yours was . . . what did you say? Turkey? That pope dude?"

"Bishop. Nicholas of Myra, or something like that, anyway. I haven't quite made it all the way back that far. Not that I'm not absolutely loving all the family legends.

But it seems, in fact, that I may well be the last of my line. Er, so far, that is. But anyway, they were in Hungary more recently."

"And you said . . . you said you inherited a business there?"

"I'm afraid so," Will confessed with a lopsided smile. "I have just recently discovered that I am, in fact, the heir to a nearly bankrupt business. Yay me. I'll have to sort it all out, it seems. But let's stay focused on your stuff, huh? Look, over here. This is my personal travel shelf. I'm mean, you've got Beth's books and all, but you never know what you might need. I mean, it's all about preparation, right? Just like baseball."

"It's really not anything like baseball."

"Uh . . . right. I guess not. Anyway. Here. Take a look."

Gaspar glanced at the titles. All were guides to exotic global locations. "Wow. You must really like to travel."

"Uh, yeah. It's really, like, more of an aspirational thing."

"You don't travel. But you have all these books."

"I read," said Will. "A lot. Okay?" Will scooped up a couple of the books. He sighed. "But someday."

"Huh. I have a funny feeling that someday is coming soon. I mean, it would be better to deal with your business in person, right?"

"In person—! Wait, what?"

Gaspar didn't answer. "Dammit, what's the name of our travel agent again? Oh, wait." Gaspar pulled the new phone out of his pocket. On impulse, he thumbed the contacts icon. On the Favorites screen he spotted the number of a travel agency he and Beth had used frequently. He grinned. "Oh, of course. Beth programmed the number in." He looked skyward as he tapped the number. "Thanks, hon."

"Who's that?" Will asked.

Gaspar didn't answer him. Instead, he spoke into the phone. "Yes, I need to know when the next flight to Budapest is. From Boston. This is Gaspar Bethlen. I have some vouchers. . . ."

"Here's a couple of books on Budapest," said Will. "I kept them special. Just in case I, uh, ever got to meet Ana."

Gaspar ignored him. He was listening to his phone. "Yeah, soon as possible. Two passengers. Wait, say that again?"

Gaspar's eyes widened. "That early, huh? Uh . . . yeah. I can make that." Then, more quietly, he added, "Maybe."

"Make what?" said Will. Gaspar still ignored him.

"Gaspar Bethlen and Will Klaus. You already have our information? Ha! Now why doesn't that surprise me? Never mind. Yeah, we'll be there."

He ended the call.

"Huh?" said Will. "Wait. What's happening?"

"You better go pack," said Gaspar. "Tomorrow's someday. And grab your coat. We've gotta go get rush Covid tests."

They heard Jim call to them from the main store. "You'd better hurry!" There was laughter in his voice.

Will shook his head. "Wait. Whoa. Where are we going?"

"Today? We gotta get a Covid test," said Gaspar. "Not just a drugstore—it has to be good for travel. And, uh, really quickly. Tomorrow morning? Airport. And way, way early. Flight's at 6:35. Which sucks, but we can sleep on the plane."

As Gaspar buttoned his coat, Jim brought Will a Red Sox jacket and cap.

Will shook his head again. "Airport? What's there?"

"Planes," said Gaspar. "Long lines. Bad food. . . ."

"You're seriously going to Leslie Nielsen me in my own shop?" said Will.

"You had that one coming," said Jim.

"Pulling frickin' teeth. . . ." Will muttered.

"Hey," Gaspar said, "You got a passport, right? Uh, since you don't travel?"

"I *meant* to travel. So yeah, I have one. It's an . . . aspirational passport."

"And proof of vaccination?"

"Well, sure," said Will. "Uh, jeez, somewhere. . . ."

"They're in the drawer under the register," said Jim.

Will shook his head yet again, and Gaspar began to wonder if it was going to fall off. "They are?"

"Here, I'll get it." Jim grinned. "I had them ready for you. Again, do you think you're the only one who talked to Miss Bethlen?" He nodded to Gaspar. "Rest her soul."

Gaspar held up his gift certificate. "Bought and paid for, right? Detective?"

"You fired me," Will reminded him.

Gaspar was already moving to the door. "Didn't take. Remember?" He stopped and sighed. After a moment, he turned back to Will. "Dude, look, I wasn't there when Beth died. I . . . I wasn't with her. This . . . this is the best I can do. For her. You understand that, right?"

Will closed his eyes and nodded. "Of course I do."

"This is something I have to do. And as much as I hate to admit it, I think I need your help. Beth thought so, anyway, and that's enough. You see that, right?"

Will still hesitated. "I do. Really! But . . . I can't just . . . Dad. . . ."

Jim handed Will his passport from behind the counter. "Here. Also, here's an address where you can get a Covid test for travel. Now then. Go on. Have an adventure."

"But—" Will protested.

"I can watch the store, and I've already called some college kids in to help. Now get away from this counter for a little bit and see some of that beautiful world out there. It's high time, son."

"Dad—!"

"See the things you've been reading about, huh? Meet this amazing Ana you've been pining over."

Will's sudden blush made Gaspar want to grin, but he suppressed the urge. Will nodded his head back toward Gaspar in a very clear *not in front of the company!* sort of way. Hissing through clenched teeth, he said, "Ana's just a friend, Dad."

Jim was clearly no more convinced than Gaspar was. "If you say so. Now go! See some of the world. See . . . see your friend."

Gaspar started moving again. He was already through the front door when he glanced back over his shoulder. "C'mon, dude. We got a get a test before they close. You'll come, right?"

"I—" Will began.

"Go!" Jim commanded.

Will took a breath and nodded. "Okay. Sure. Even if your wife hadn't already put me on the payroll, so to speak, I'd help. Not that I wouldn't have minded a little notice. Without Beth's help and generosity, I never would have been able to accomplish as much as I have— and this legacy I've inherited would have just been dissolved by the courts and lost forever. Whatever you need, I'm your man."

Gaspar nodded. "Thanks dude." He winked. "Let's book. See what I did there?"

Will sighed and rolled his eyes. "That was my pun first. Oh, that reminds me! I gotta grab something."

"Hurry," said Gaspar. He saw Will grab a dusty old book before hurrying to follow, cradling it like a treasure.

"Give me that test address, okay?" At the sidewalk, Gaspar held up his hand. "Taxi!" A cab passed. It didn't slow.

"Uh, Beth didn't put, like, Lyft or Uber on that new phone?"

"I have no idea," said Gaspar. "But everybody uses Lyft and Uber. And at this time of day? That'll totally take forever. Nobody takes cabs anymore, so there should be plenty."

"Strangely, that almost makes sense to me. Not quite, but almost."

"Taxi!" Another cab passed. It didn't have its light on.

"I didn't pick up my laundry!" Will protested. "I don't even have time to pack!"

"Me either. Trust me, dude. Checking luggage is a bitch. Best to travel light—just a carry-on. We can grab stuff more when we get there. But I'm pretty sure they have stores in Hungary. Uh, they do, don't they? Taxi!"

"How the hell would I know?"

"You've been reading all those travel books, right?"

"In an aspirational sort of way! And I was, like, planning, you know? This . . . this isn't anything like planning!"

"So be spontaneous. Taxi!" The second cab didn't slow, either.

"There's a right time and a right place for spontaneity."

"Besides, if someone comes back for *The Roots of the Bethlens,* I don't think it oughta be here. Do you?"

"Okay," said Will, "that's a good point."

"Taxi!"

A taxi pulled over. "Well," said Gaspar, "that was fast. See? We're off to a great start."

Gaspar climbed into the cab and Will scrambled after.

"Driver," said Gaspar, "we need to get a Covid test like really, really fast. If you make that happen, I'm going to tip you like you won the lottery."

The driver looked in his rearview mirror and his eyes popped open. "Holy shit! Are you Gaspar Bethlen?"

Gaspar sighed and pulled his face mask back into place.

6

Budapest

aspar adjusted his mask and rubbed his eyes before opening them. It took him a moment to get his bearings; he'd been sleeping on his back, not his side as was his wont, on a reclining seat rather than the long-familiar queen-sized bed. More than anything, it was the sense of gentle motion that reminded him where he was: on a jet liner in business class headed for Europe.

"You okay?"

Gaspar turned and found Will in the seat next to him, his eyes wide with concern. Gaspar fumbled with the control that raised his seat back to its upright position.

"Yeah," he mumbled. "Fine."

"It's just that you cried out in your sleep," Will said, probing. "Were you having a nightmare?"

"No, no," said Gaspar. "Nothing like that. It was a good dream. Happy times."

"About your wife?"

"Yeah." Gaspar knew that his smile was sad as he nodded, and he was glad the mask hid his expression. "About Beth."

"One usually doesn't cry out like that after a good dream," Will pointed out. "Not in my experience, anyway."

Gaspar fiddled with his safety belt. The buckle was making him uncomfortable. "It wasn't the dream that made me cry out. It was the realization that it *was* a dream, and that the time had come to leave it. That pretty much sucked."

"What was it?"

"I was with Beth, surrounded by music and the light of a hundred thousand candles, twinkling like a whole galaxy of stars. We were dancing, and then we were sitting together in our place by the fire, snuggled under a wool blanket, and everything was warm and the color of gold. . . . That was the dream. But waking, yeah, turns out the world is harsh and cold again, and the great mass of sorrow and loneliness weighs heavy on my tired shoulders like a glacier. Glaciers move slowly, let me tell you, carving the rock of my soul into a new landscape of sadness. It is a heartrending and dreary world to return to, when Beth isn't here. I miss my wife, man. I miss my wife."

Will managed another smile, and Gaspar appreciated the effort. "Then let's solve her mystery together. What do you say? Maybe that will bring you some comfort and peace."

"I sure as hell hope so." Gaspar knew he didn't sound especially optimistic. He yawned and stretched, and then looked over to see that Will had arranged the sheets of codes, *The Roots of the Bethlens* book, the Hungarian phrase book, and a notebook across his meal tray. "So what've you got there? Any luck?"

"As a matter of fact, I just had a eureka moment. I cracked the code. Well, one of 'em, anyway. It's a book code."

"Come again?"

"See, it's a kind of a code that uses a book," Will explained. "A word replaces a series of numbers. To crack the code, you need a copy of the exact same edition. Any slight variation, and it won't work. See these numbers along the top here?"

Gaspar nodded.

"That's the page number, the line number, and the number of characters away from the left margin. That gives you the first letter. These numbers give you the second. And so on. Without the right book, even a computer couldn't crack it."

"Huh," said Gaspar. "Not bad. What about the other?"

Will let out a sigh. "Yeah. Those. They've pretty much got me stumped."

Gaspar grinned smugly. "Not me."

Will's head spun around. "Huh?"

"You need the other two volumes. Detective. Or one of them, anyway."

Will gave him a blank stare. "I so can't believe I hadn't thought of that." He chuckled. "You're not so bad with the problem-solving yourself."

Gaspar shrugged. "I'm an athlete, not an idiot. My dad was a scholar, you know."

"Right. I read one of his books. On the Nativity."

Gaspar chuckled. "Of course you did."

"Right. Like you didn't read any of them."

"I read 'em all."

"Was he disappointed you didn't follow him? Your dad, I mean."

"Are you kidding? He was thrilled. Hell, he was a bigger Sox fan than you are." Gaspar smiled. "Beth was the scholar. Dad was crazy about her."

"I'm glad I got to meet her. She was—"

"Amazing?" said Gaspar.

Will laughed. "Good word. I was going to say terrific; Ana is amazing. And the funny thing is, I wouldn't have even met her if it wasn't for your Beth. I mean, it's not like I'd have had a reason to investigate Hungarian genealogy books, like, just on a lark or something. I don't think any of my folks are in a set of rare family history books, if you know what I'm sayin'. So in a way, she made my life better, too."

Gaspar's felt his sadness return, falling over him like a blanket. His hint of a smile faded, and he was glad his Covid mask didn't let it show. It is a private place, the land of grief. He turned to the window.

"So what did you find out?"

"Not much," Will admitted. "The coded message says, *Find the beginning; seek what he sought.* The rest is just numbers. More coordinates for your GPS, maybe. If so, then the next could be street number again. The rest . . . well, I've got nothing. Oh, I also translated a bit of *The Roots of the Bethlens*. Enough to figure out how your granddad was related to the rest of the family, I think."

"I guess we'll see."

"My friend Ana can help. I'm sure of it."

A sudden thought struck Gaspar. He turned back to Will. "Say, did you happen talk to Beth about this Ana?"

Will shrugged. "A little. Maybe. A time or two. The word amazing might have come up."

"I thought so." Beth had always been a natural born matchmaker. "So why haven't you met her?"

"Ana? Oh. We're just friends. Really. Okay? She helped me with Beth's research, and I helped her find some references here in America. She did her thesis on Chekhov. Can you believe it? Chekhov!"

Gaspar shook his head. *"Star Trek?"*

"Russian playwright."

"Oh, him. Right. *Cherry Orchard* dude."

"I've talked to her. I talked to her when I was look-ing for the book for Beth. But then . . . we just talked for—God! Hours. She's—"

Gaspar grinned in spite of himself. "Amazing?"

"Okay, so my vocabulary can use a boost. But yeah."

"And you've seriously never even met this chick?"

"Not even once. Well, except by phone, but it's like we were already best friends. It's like I've known her all my life. Can you believe it? When we talk, it's just . . . it's just, like, magic. You know? I know that sounds just all kinds of stupid."

"Yeah, dude. It does sound stupid. But I understand. Believe me. I've been there."

"Yeah. I guess you have."

"Anyway. So, you've been working on the code all this time?"

"Well, it beats the rest of this crap."

"What is it?"

"More paperwork from that business in Hungary I've inherited."

"Any luck?"

"Lots," said Will. "But none of it good. Seems like I'll just claim my inheritance, declare bankruptcy, and close it down. Which is just too damn bad."

"Why's that?" Gaspar asked, feeling his eyebrows climbing his forehead.

"Because it seems like such a dear, sweet business," said Will. "And it's endured for two centuries. Can you believe it? They had to go underground when the Communists came, but in the past decades, they'd made a go of the old family business again. Things like this, things with grace and heart, should endure, Gaspar. I hate—I hate like hell—to have to be the one to have to shut it down."

"So no hope at all?"

Will waved his hand futilely at the piles of spreadsheets and documents arranged chaotically on his tray table. "None that I can see. And I've kept a bookstore afloat!"

"Why don't you let me take a look? I've got a decent enough head for business. No, really. I manage my own investments, after all. That's my dad's influence. Oh, don't look so impressed. I only barely made it to arbitration, you know, so the really big baseball money never really hit." Gaspar shrugged. "I suppose that's not much of a qualification, but a fresh set of eyes can't hurt, I mean, right? Maybe I can spot something you missed."

"Gosh, I hate to ask that—"

"Nonsense," said Gaspar. "It'll give me something to think about. And you a chance to sleep. I think that'll be good for both of us."

"That's terribly kind, man."

"It's my pleasure. What sort of business is it anyway?"

"Toy makers, if you can believe it. They've been making handcrafted wood toys for two centuries—metal and clockwork ones later. Marionettes, trains, castles, sailing ships, fire trucks, dollhouses. You name it. I've got some pictures here. See?"

"I see," said Gaspar. "Wow. You'd think that there would be a place for wonders like those, especially when all the megamart shelves are filled with cheap, plastic nonsense. Surely there's a market out there. Even if it's only for, like, collectors."

"You'd think," said Will. "And odds are, you'd be right, at least with some careful management. But the place has been bleeding money for far too long, I'm afraid. Twenty years or more. When my family petitioned to regain the business after the Communists fell, well, they weren't really businesspeople. They're all gone, anyway, and it's just me. It's likely too late, now."

"Why's that?" asked Gaspar. "Why the money-bleed, I mean?"

Will laughed. "It would have helped, I think, if they hadn't given so much of their profit away. Too many gifts to orphanages, churches, charities, poor families. . . . That's my legacy. The giving of too many gifts. I guess the long line will be broken at last." He shook his head and laughed again, sadly. "With me."

"Generosity seems a sucky damn reason to go out of business," Gaspar said. "God knows this crappy old world needs more of it. Here. Let me look at those spreadsheets. You never know. Maybe I can find something. Probably not, but I need something else to think about."

—⊰⊱—

The airport in Budapest seemed small to Gaspar—in a strange sort of way, it reminded him of the small-town bus stations he used to visit as a minor leaguer. They deplaned on the tarmac and climbed stairs to the gate. Otherwise, it seemed like a miniature of all the other airports he'd visited. Hurried passengers rushed past newsstands and crowded bars to gates. The language was new to him, but the messages were familiar—flights were arriving or boarding, individuals should meet their parties or seek a gate agent. The line at customs was long. The uniformed officials took their jobs seriously; they did not speak as they carefully examined Covid test results and passports and made their stamps with brusque efficiency.

Will found a cab and, with a little help from Google Translate, spoke to the driver in Hungarian. The driver nodded and sped them away. They passed through countryside that turned quickly into what Gaspar assumed were the Hungarian equivalents of weathered suburbs. His first impression was of impoverishment—the newest buildings looked to be more than half a century old, including some monstrosities of Soviet brutalism, and none seemed well maintained. He saw few signs of new construction.

With traffic, it took them nearly an hour to enter the city. The afternoon was fading to evening, and the city was already adorning itself in sparkling evening jewels, and Gaspar tried to see it as Beth would have. As twilight dimmed, the last signs of poverty were swallowed in a night-dark cloak of shadow, and reflections of city lights twinkled in the Danube, turning the river into a mirror of heaven. Budapest wore history like a uniform, there for none to miss. Everything spoke of centuries that were ancient memories when infant America was still a dream. The office buildings were not the majestic, steel and glass structures of a city in the States; rather, they were distinctly, almost defiantly, old European— blocky but elegant, ornate but not fussy, made of sensible stone meant to endure. Many of the buildings were already dressed in their festive winter holiday finery.

After a quick shopping excursion to grab the items they'd forgotten to pack, another taxi carried Will and Gaspar across the famous Chain Bridge to the Four Seasons Hotel Gresham Palace. Will whistled appreciatively. "Beth had good taste."

"That she did."

The cab came to a stop, and the two men grabbed the shopping bags, Gaspar's briefcase, and their carry-ons—their only luggage. They had to circle around a crew setting up cameras and lighting rigs to get to the entrance. "Huh," said Will. "Think we're going to be on the news?"

"I think that's probably a movie crew," said Gaspar. "Believe me, I've seen enough TV news cameras to know one when I see one."

"Ha! I guess you have."

Gaspar handed his bags to Will. "Go check in, okay? Oh, and throw my stuff in my room? No, not the briefcase. I'll take that."

"You're not coming?" said Will.

Gaspar shook his head. "You go ahead. I'm going to take a walk."

"Give me a minute and I'll come with you. Shall we do a little sightseeing? I thought we might cross back over the Danube and figure out whether we're on the Buda or the Pest side. I hear the bridges are lovely. And the museums! I bet the museums here are fabulous."

"Maybe later. To tell you the truth, I've had my fill of sightseeing."

Will quirked his head to the side. "That surprises me, especially from a worldly guy like yourself. There's such joy in seeing beautiful things, experiencing a culture—"

Gaspar smiled again, a slight smile that didn't light his eyes. "Joy doesn't come so much from what you experience but in what you share. I'll just see things that will make me ache because I can't share them with Beth."

Will nodded. "I understand. But I wish you'd change your mind."

"Besides, I really want to check the clue out. I think I've got just enough time before everything closes. If I hurry, that is."

"You need me to—?"

Gaspar shook his head. "I *need* you to check in. I'll be fine for one stop. If I need a detective, I'll be sure to let you know. I think I've got those coordinates right, and it shouldn't be far from here. If this shiny new iPhone is right, it's the bank district. Which I'm thinking would explain the bankbook."

"Yeah, a bank would sure make sense. These digits would be a street number, as with my shop. This might be an account number—or a safe deposit box, maybe."

"I guess that could be. I'll know soon enough." Gaspar managed a grin. "Call amazing Ana. Tell her I said hello."

The mention of Ana stopped Will's last protest. "See you when you get back."

The man who followed them from the airport was not the same man who had followed them in America, but he was of the same sort. He was not tall nor unusually heavy, though his round belly protruded slightly over his belt. His suit was worn and shabby but not so much that one might mistake him for a vagrant. He had a scar on his chin and his knuckles were dark with bruises that never seemed to heal, but he kept his hands to himself, he wore his face mask, and he pulled his hat low. In short, he was the type of man one wasn't likely to notice at all. But if passersby never gave him a second look, it didn't bother him. His cloak of ordinariness was, in fact, the very quality that made him good at his job.

He paused, leaning against the corner of a building, in a spot that afforded him a good view of the hotel entrance. Keeping to the shadows, he tapped a mobile phone. When a man answered, he spoke softly in Hungarian.

"Mister Bethlen? They have arrived on schedule and checked into their hotel. Yes. The Four Seasons.

"Of course. I'll follow them, and if they locate the volumes, I will let you know at once.

"Ah. Yes. As to that, there *is* a back entrance, and one on the north side as well, near the car park, although I think it unlikely that they'll use either of those. Tourists tend to use the door they know, even if it happens to face away from their destination. All the same, I can call in men to watch all sides if you don't mind the extra cost.

"Of course, sir. I will do so. As you say.

"Don't worry, Mister Bethlen. I'll stick to them like glaze on a pastry.

"I will, sir. When they have the books, I will contact you and await your order."

⟶⦾⟵

The streets of Budapest were both timeless and modern—main thoroughfares congested with traffic divided by a network of narrow streets that had last been called modern at the dawn of the 1800s. Many of the streets were crowded with tourists in the bustling city center, the heart of a thriving metropolis struggling to revitalize itself. The air smelled of car exhaust, coffee, garbage, exotic spices, and people.

The walk was longer than Gaspar had expected. He thought about hailing a cab, but without Will, he wasn't sure he'd be able to manage the obstacles that language would present. He scowled. Recognizing a foreigner, a cabby would likely take him the few blocks he needed to go by way of Prague or Vienna.

Checking the directions on his GPS app one more time, he continued on his way, moving slowly but steadily up the slope. He passed rows of buildings—old, he knew, even when his ancestors abandoned them for the uncertain hope of America. The buildings had been constructed close together, touching, as though their long-dead architects had known that someday they would need to huddle together like old men for support.

Here and there, one of the buildings has been restored to something suggesting its former majesty. Most were shabby, their glories barely memories, faded after decades of neglect. A few looked almost new, and strangely out of place. More than a few were gone utterly, leaving only bits of rubble and dust in the gap, like missing teeth in an unsightly smile. Gaspar was both charmed and saddened—proud that the culture of his grandfathers still hung on defiantly, if only by the tips of its bloody fingernails, but dismayed at the signs of time and paucity's inevitable victory.

Thirty minutes later, after a delay caused mainly by his getting turned around in the old and unfamiliar streets, Gaspar found himself standing in front of a bank. The building was large, an imposing structure of old stone, square and formidable, with steps leading to a porch guarded by a row of tall and stately marble columns. According to the phone, he'd come to the coordinates indicated, and the street number matched the third row of digits in his notes. He had come to the right place; he was sure of it. He checked his watch; he probably had twenty minutes before they closed. He smiled, and for a moment he could almost, almost feel Beth with him, peering over his shoulder and beaming with pride as he solved the next clue. The moment was fleeting; loneliness fell on him again, and the ache inside him was as cold and profound as ever.

Pulling his mask back into place, Gaspar entered. The doors opened into a wide lobby. Gaspar approached a teller who spoke quickly and in Hungarian.

"Uh, wait . . . just a second, okay?" Gaspar managed as he scrambled for the Google Translate app on his new phone.

The teller smiled and motioned to a manager. The manager took her place at the window. "May I help you, sir? I speak English." He spoke with a crisp accent that sounded, to Gaspar's inexperienced ear, like a cross between Hungarian and British. It reminded him a little of Boris Karloff's Dracula from the old movie he'd watched with his dad, and he had to force himself not to smirk.

"Uh, yeah. I think I'm here about an account." He showed the man the digits Will had decoded. "Is this one of your numbers?"

"Is this your account, sir?" the manager countered.

Gaspar shook his head. "No. It's . . . I think my late wife might have opened it." He handed the manager the bankbook. "Here's the book. I think."

"I'm sorry for your loss," the manager said.

Gaspar nodded his thanks. The manager entered the digits into his computer and made a few mouse clicks.

"It's a safe-deposit box," the manager said after a moment. "I'll need to see some identification."

Gaspar produced his passport and the manager examined it. "Thank you, Mr. Bethlen. "It seems that someone intended the contents for you, and you alone. You have the combination, of course?"

Gaspar glanced at the last row of numbers from the clue. "Maybe. What happens if I don't?"

The manager sniffed. "Then I should imagine the box will not open."

"Great," Gaspar muttered.

"There are two sequences of numbers that must be entered—one by us, and one by you, sir. I don't have access to your set of numbers, of course."

"Then let's hope I have the right combination."

The manager nodded. "As you say, sir. If you'll follow me?"

Gaspar nodded and stood. The manager made small talk as he led Gaspar across the vast lobby toward the open vault on the far side of the room.

"Are you of Hungarian descent, Mister Bethlen?"

Gaspar nodded. "Turns out I am."

"I thought so. Bethlen is a very old and prestigious name in this country. Although I'm sure you must know that. They are nobility, or they were when we had such, going all the way back to the time of the Hapsburgs. They were once among the wealthiest families of Eastern Europe. They didn't fare well under the Communists, alas. But then, who did? Still, much of their ancestral property has come back to them, if not their wealth. Why, you might be related to Count Bethlen Tamás himself! Ah!

I see you are confused. In Hungary, it is common to use the family name before the given name."

"Actually, I *did* know that," said Gaspar, mildly irritated by the man's condescending tone. And from the volume Beth had given him, and that Will had helped him read a bit of on the flight, he knew that he was, in fact, closely related to Bethlen Tamás. "But—Count? I thought you had no royalty. Not since the time of the Communists, anyway."

"We do not, as you say," said the manager. "But Bethlen Tamás is the heir, and would be the count, if the title still existed. Everyone calls him the Count. Including himself. And he is one of the few who regained his ancestral . . . how would you say? Manor. Yes. His ancestral manor and estate. Most of the others have been destroyed . . . or are in the hands of international corporations. So Tamás is something of a relic, if you will. A living reminder of old ways that are vanishing."

"That's a shame," said Gaspar.

"Yes," said the manager. "Our ancient culture is changing, lost to a bad economy and Western homogenization. Ah! But come, here we are."

They entered the yawning mouth of the vault, and the manager led them to a row of safe-deposit boxes. The manager checked the card he carried, and then entered a series of numbers into a keypad. He stepped aside and nodded to Gaspar, who checked the last row of digits Will had deciphered and entered them carefully. To his relief, Gaspar heard the satisfying clicks of the locks releasing their grips. He let out the breath he'd been holding.

The manager opened the box. Gaspar peered inside and found a package wrapped in brown paper. Judging by the size and shape, it likely held another volume of *The Roots of the Bethlens*. There was another package inside as well, this one wrapped in bright Christmas paper, and an envelope. Gaspar put the items in his briefcase and snapped it shut.

The manager cleared his throat. "I can offer you an office if you'd like to examine the contents in private."

"Huh? Oh. No, no. That won't be necessary. I'll just take this with me. Thank you."

The manager nodded. "And will you be maintaining the account?"

Gaspar shook his head. "No. I don't think that will be necessary. Thank you."

"Of course, sir. Please don't hesitate to contact us if we can be of any further assistance in the future. And sir, I'm very sorry for your loss."

7

Trouble Along the Danube

aspar walked back toward the hotel with his head bowed and his coat buttoned tightly against the wind and winter chill. He walked two blocks or so and found himself again among the rows of crumbling buildings. He was close to the Danube, so close that he could hear the river's music and the buzz of distant laughter and conversation.

Lost in his own thoughts, he almost didn't see the stocky man in the worn coat and hat until he had nearly passed him. Gaspar might not have noticed the man at all, had he not spoken. Another larger man in a black turtleneck and a leather jacket stood behind the first man with his arms crossed over a massive chest. Both men stepped together to block Gaspar's path.

The first man said something in rapid Hungarian. Gaspar turned and raised his eyebrows, shaking his head to indicate that he had not understood.

The man spoke again, in heavily accented English this time. "Mister Bethlen."

"Yeah?" Gaspar tilted his head to the side.

"Your case. Give it to me."

The case? No way. No way in hell. Beth had given him the case, and the books it contained. Gaspar felt his eyes narrow. "Uh, no. I don't think so."

The stocky man stepped forward. The man clearly didn't expect any resistance.

The man took another step, and another.

He reached out with his right hand to grab for the briefcase.

Gaspar turned, planning to flee back the way he'd come, but two more thugs—that was the only word he could think of to describe them—were waiting there in the shadows, ready to block his retreat. Gaspar turned back to the first two men.

"Perhaps you'd like to think again," the first man said.

Gaspar sighed. He nodded and held the heavy metal briefcase out. The man stepped closer.

Gaspar looked to the sky and muttered under his breath. "Beth, babe, I hope whatever's in here isn't breakable."

As the thug stepped forward to grab the briefcase, Gaspar swung it abruptly, as hard as he could, catching the thug under the chin. The man dropped, moaning.

The other thug, the man in the black turtleneck, charged forward. He was big, but Gaspar was a professional athlete in the prime of his career. He blocked the man's punch with the case and then swung it, knocking the man down as it connected with his jaw. The man staggered back, and Gaspar swung the case again, bringing it down hard on the top of the man's head. He crumpled, too, holding his forearms over his head and moaning.

Behind him, Gaspar could hear the other men running, close and coming closer. Gaspar didn't wait. He bolted blindly.

Gaspar reached the end of the lane and turned right—but saw two more men approaching and coming fast. He turned back to his left—the way seemed clear— and he ran.

In high school and college, Gaspar had run track to improve his stamina, just as he had practiced kickboxing to help improve his hand-eye coordination. He hadn't really enjoyed either; baseball was his love. He'd thought about giving them up; he seldom had to run more than ninety feet anyway, and when he had to go farther, well, it was usually at a trot. Now, he thanked holy God above for the discipline and conditioning that kept him ahead of the men behind him. Nonetheless, he was breathing hard when he reached a T intersection at the end of the street. He looked left and saw a row of dumpsters in front of an obvious dead end. He ran the other way.

Gaspar looked back over his shoulder. The four men were gaining. The leader thug, the one Gaspar had slugged with the case, was right behind them.

Gaspar turned his head forward and ran harder. The alley ended, and there was only one way to go, left again, which he thought might lead him back toward the river. *Good*, he thought. *There should be people there.*

Unfortunately, the alley ended in a dead end. Gaspar skidded to a stop and turned. The men behind him were closer. He could hear their pounding footsteps. He turned again. Since back wasn't an option, there was only one way he could go—up. Gaspar scrambled onto a dumpster and tossed the briefcase to a ledge above. He was able to leap and reach the ledge with the tips of his fingers. Fueled by adrenaline and desperation, he shifted his grip and pulled himself up after the case, grabbed it, and leapt to grasp at another ledge, just above. From there, he was able to scamper to the roof of the three-story building.

Gaspar ran across the rooftop. He reached the far edge and stopped for one heartbeat. *Aw, crap. I hate heights.*

He took a breath and thought back again to his track and field days. *It's just the long jump again. That's all it is. It's just the long jump.*

He'd never been great at the long jump.

Gaspar took a few steps back and ran again. This time, he didn't slow. He jumped across the narrow alley to the next rooftop, sprinted, and then, without giving himself time for rational thought, jumped to the next.

Gaspar paused to catch his breath. He looked back over his shoulder to see four of the thugs making the leap across the first alley.

They were still coming, relentless and determined.

"You gotta be frickin' kidding me," Gaspar muttered aloud.

Gaspar ran again, leaping to the next rooftop, and then to the next.

Renovation was underway on the next rooftop. Scaffolding and framing, along with piles of lumber and building materials, blocked the view to the next building. Gaspar didn't slow. He sprinted through the labyrinth of obstacles.

At the edge, he skidded to an abrupt stop, flailing his arms to slow himself. The next building was missing utterly—only a pile of rubble remained in the foundations far below.

Gaspar looked around frantically. He could hear the sound of closing pursuit. He couldn't go back.

He looked down. There was a dumpster filled with what looked like old insulation. Full trash bags had spilled out and covered most of the alley. Maybe they'd be enough to break his fall.

Maybe.

Maybe hell, he sure wasn't going to find out. There was no way in the world he was jumping from this height.

He looked around again. He had one chance. He rushed back to the pile of lumber and grabbed a long timber beam and dropped it across the gap, making a precarious, makeshift bridge.

Gaspar closed his eyes and took a deep breath. "I frickin' *hate* heights. . . !"

—◆—

The man in the worn hat and coat led the other men across the rooftops after the fleeing American. *"Rohadt köcsög!"* he swore softly under his breath. They'd underestimated the man. They'd known he was a professional athlete, but they hadn't expected him to fight, and they certainly hadn't expected him to be so *kibaszott* fast!

The next roof was littered with construction materials, and there was no sign of the American. No worries. The American could only have gone forward. The man didn't slow until he reached the far side. The next building was gone, utterly demolished.

"Where the hell is he?" one of the other men shouted.

The man in the worn coat and hat pointed. "There!"

The American had dropped a beam across the gap, forming a sort of crude bridge. They truly had underestimated the man. "Go!"

Carefully, gingerly, the four men started across the plank. They were about halfway across when the man in the worn coat and hat heard a sound—behind them. The man stopped. He couldn't turn his body; the beam was too narrow, too precarious. He craned his neck, trying to look back.

The American appeared from behind a pile of bricks—he hadn't crossed; he'd been hiding. The *mocskos, büdös faszszopó* had tricked them.

Before the man in the worn coat and hat could react or even shout a warning, the American raced forward and kicked the plank bridge. The man in the worn coat and hat bent his knees and extended his arms.

"A kúrva anyád!"

Somehow, he kept his balance. The man in front of him wasn't so lucky. He fell, screaming, until he hit the dumpster three stories below. The man in the worn coat heard the fallen man moaning and cursing.

The others realized what was happening and began running across the bridge as fast as they dared, desperate to reach the safety of the far side. The man in the worn coat and hat knew they weren't going to make it.

Grunting with effort, the American kicked the plank again, and again, harder.

The man in the worn coat and hat was the last to tumble off, and he, too, screamed as he fell. He, too, moaned and cursed when he landed in the dumpster.

—�️⟨—

Gaspar looked down and winced. Down below, the men who'd been chasing him looked like they were hurt, but probably not too badly, and they looked like they were seriously, seriously pissed off.

Then, from behind, he heard the sounds of men running—more pursuit. Two more thugs were coming, and fast.

Gaspar gaped. "Oh come on!"

Without thinking—he knew that if he stopped to think, fear would paralyze him—he turned and sprinted across the bridge.

The two men reached the plank before he made it to the other side. Gaspar turned his head. Together, they grunted as they tried to lift the plank, attempting to dislodge the beam and send it falling.

Gaspar flailed his arms to keep his balance. "Hey! That's *my* trick!"

The men grunted. The plank shifted.

Gaspar ran. He tried not to look down. He looked down.

He was past the dumpster where the first two men had landed; there was only broken rubble beneath him.

Panic took him. His heart pounded and his palms were slick with sweat. He could feel the beam moving beneath his feet. If the fall to the debris didn't kill him, the pissed-off men would surely be happy to finish the job.

I'm not gonna make it. I'm not—

There was only one thing he could do, one last, desperate chance. He threw the briefcase to the next roof and leapt.

The plank fell and crashed in the rubble far below.

Gaspar grasped the edge of the next building, his chest hitting the rough stone, barely holding on. Grunting with the effort, he pulled himself up to the rooftop, swooped down to grab his briefcase, and ran without looking back.

Behind him, he could hear the last two men shouting in Hungarian, but he ignored them.

He ran.

At the far side of this building, he found the upper parts of a fire escape, but most of the structure was missing. His whipped his head back and forth, looking for a way down. At last, he spotted a heavy, iron drainpipe. He closed his eyes and took a deep breath.

I hate, hate, hate *frickin' heights!*

Then he wiped his palms on his pants and knelt. He dropped the case down on another pile of construction lumber and wrapped his hands and legs around the drainpipe. Without opening his eyes, he slid down until it ended, and then he dropped the last few feet to the alley below.

He retrieved the briefcase and sprinted to the end of the alley. There, he skidded to an abrupt stop as he nearly collided with the man in the black turtleneck, the one he'd slammed with the briefcase, and one other man.

"Oh come *on!*" Gaspar said.

The men came closer, approaching slowly.

"Great. You're down here, too. Seriously, like, how many of you guys *are* there, anyway?"

Gaspar backed up. He dropped the briefcase and stood in front of it, protectively. Reaching back to the construction lumber, he found a better weapon. One of the planks of wood was just about the same length and weight as a baseball bat. It was even sort of rounded. He smiled.

The two men came, slowly, carefully, professionals ready to attack. Just as they reached him, Gaspar raised the plank—just like a bat. Before the men could react, he swung for the fences, taking them down with two fast swings, both right-handed.

Gaspar allowed himself a grin. Then he ran, sprinting for all he was worth.

He ran all the way back to the hotel. He'd already reached the lobby when he finally thought to call the police.

8

Amazing Anasztázia

ill took the elevator down to the hotel lobby, carrying his notes and Gaspar's book. When the doors opened, he spotted Gaspar near the entrance, where he was talking to uniformed two police officers. He hurried over, but Gaspar was already shaking hands with the men. As they departed, Will asked, "What was that all about?"

"I was attacked," Gaspar said. He described the events quickly, ending with the two men he'd taken down with the bat-sized plank. He grinned again. "Anyway, I mention that last bit just to remind you—I totally have power from the right side."

"For God's sake, you're making *jokes?*"

"No jokes. Dude, those were really good two swings. And, I remind you again, righty."

Will shook his head. "Holy crap! Gaspar, seriously, are you okay?"

"I'm fine. Really. And the cops are watching the hotel now."

"But—"

"I'm *fine,*" Gaspar repeated. "So what's been happening with you? Did you call this amazing Ana?"

"Huh? Oh. Yeah. Yeah, she's meeting us." Will checked his watch. "Uh, pretty soon now, as a matter of fact."

"What, *now?*"

Will nodded. "In the bar right in front of the restaurant. Uh, is now bad?"

Gaspar rolled his eyes and shook his head. "Apparently not. I mean, who needs to change clothes or, like, catch their breath anyway? Well, c'mon then."

Gaspar walked quickly. Will followed. The hotel bar, located just outside the restaurant, was fairly crowded. Will looked around, craning his neck to see the far corners.

"Is this Ana of yours here?"

"We're a little early, I think. I—"

Gaspar interrupted. "What does she look like?"

"Uh . . . to be honest, I don't know."

Gaspar gave him a wry look. "Don't tell me. You just read about her."

"Well, that. And like I told you. We talked on the phone! God, for . . . for *hours!*"

"Don't you nerds know about Zoom?"

Will shrugged, embarrassed.

Gaspar rolled his eyes again. "Probably some stuffy old librarian type. Bankers and librarians. They're pretty much the same, right?"

"No."

"Bug eyes, thick glasses, hair in a bun—"

Before Gaspar could finish, Will spotted a woman approaching them from the far side of the bar, smiling and waving. Will nudged Gaspar and nodded his head in the woman's direction. Even as he did, he felt his jaw drop, and then he flushed with embarrassment. She was tall and wore a very professional blue, woolen skirt with a matching jacket over a cream-colored blouse. Her skin was pale beneath hair of dark red that fell past her shoulders, and she was without question the most beautiful woman he had ever seen in his entire life. In that first moment, Will knew, without a single quantum of doubt, that this woman was Ana. This was the woman that, he finally admitted to himself, he'd already fallen in love with. With effort, he forced himself to close his mouth, knowing that he'd just blown his chance to make a smooth first impression.

"Not bad for a librarian," Gaspar said.

Will could only nod. "You know, I think I'm gonna have a lot of overdue books."

The woman reached them, still smiling, and extended her hand. "You *must* be Will. I knew it the moment I saw you."

A second too late to be cool, Will accepted her handshake. She took his hand in two of hers. "Wow," was all he could manage to say.

Ana gazed at him with big, dark eyes, quirking her head to the side and raising her eyebrows, her full lips pursed expectantly. Will felt his heart stop. "Excuse me?" said Ana.

Gaspar grinned, obviously amused, and Will wanted to slug him. "Hi there. I'm Gaspar Bethlen. This is my hired assistant, Will Klaus."

"Detective," Will corrected him.

"And you must be Ms. Hapsburg Anasztázia," said Gaspar.

"Ana. It's a pleasure to meet you." She turned her smile to Will, and he felt his knees go weak. "Although after all the late-night talks, I feel I know you already."

Ana glanced down and then looked up at Will through her lashes. Her smile widened.

"Oh," Will said. "Wait." He reached into his coat pocket and pulled out the old book he'd almost forgotten in the shop when he and Gaspar were rushing to get their pre-travel Covid tests. "Here, I brought you a present. Sorry I didn't have time to wrap it."

Ana accepted the book and beamed. "Chekhov! In the original Russian!"

Will nodded. "The first printing."

"Better than flowers," said Ana. "The way to my heart. You know me so well already. However did you find this?"

Gaspar shook his head. "Oh dear God. There's two of 'em."

"Never mind," said Ana, "tell me later."

Will knew he was grinning like an idiot, but he couldn't make himself stop.

Ana tucked the book under one arm and took Will's elbow with the other. "Come, I have a table already." She turned to Gaspar. "Would you believe this is the first man I've ever met that's as well-read as I am?"

"I can see this is gonna be a fun conversation," Gaspar muttered as he followed. He smiled nonetheless. He'd always bought books for Beth when he traveled without her. She wasn't much for souvenirs or flowers, so he'd developed a talent for discovering titles that she would like, but that she wouldn't have thought to buy for herself. It was a sort of puzzle to solve anew in every city with a Major League Baseball franchise—Susan Petrone in Cleveland, Ray Bradbury in Los Angeles, Benji Carr in Atlanta. Will, bless his nerdish heart, seemed to have the same knack.

Once the drinks had arrived, Gaspar decided it was time to talk business. The sooner he did, well, the sooner he could leave Will alone with his dream girl. Who, for some reason, seemed equally smitten with him.

"So, Ana, Will here tells me you're an expert on my family."

"Genealogy is a hobby of mine," Ana said, and Gaspar couldn't help thinking she was hedging a little. "Yours is a very . . . notable family in my country, Mr. Bethlen."

"Gaspar. Please."

Ana nodded. "Gaspar. If I may?" She reached for *The Roots of the Bethlens,* the volume that Will had brought down from the room.

Gaspar nodded. "Please."

Ana opened the book and showed Gaspar a chart. "Today, only two branches of the Bethlen family survive. You are the last heir to one branch." She pointed. "See? The other . . . you have a distant cousin here. Did you know that?" Gaspar couldn't help noticing that Ana seemed mildly uncomfortable.

"I don't know much about my family," he admitted.

"Count Bethlen Tamás," Will said, and Gaspar suppressed a grin. The dude was showing off like a Low-A level rookie who'd gotten an over-slot signing bonus. Gaspar raised his eyebrows and Will shrugged. "Research, you know. Detective."

Ana lifted her wine glass, but she only took a small sip. "Each of the two branches, yours and Tamás's, is heir to a part of a legacy that stretches all the way back to the family's origin. One branch has inherited property, wealth, and title."

Gaspar chuckled. "Figures that's not my branch."

"What about the other?" Will asked.

Ana shrugged. "Just . . . legends and rumors, really. Something about a legacy that's more than land or title. Something special. Something secret."

"The gem," said Gaspar. He reached into his coat pocket and retrieved the etching that Beth had been carrying.

Ana's eyes widened as she unrolled the parchment. "Where did you get this?"

"My late wife found it in some notes my father left," said Gaspar. "I think. Could this be connected to the, uh, legacy thing?"

Ana took another sip of her wine, a deeper one this time. "I think your wife may have discovered something wonderful, sir."

"And she left us a trail to follow," said Will. He looked at Ana and didn't even try to hide the hope in his eyes. "Uh, maybe we can talk more tonight. Over dinner, maybe?"

"I'd like that," Ana said. "I'd love to show you my city. Both of you! Oh, Will, and your toy shop!"

Gaspar shook his head. "You two go ahead."

"C'mon, man," said Will. "It's time to live a little."

Gaspar shook his head again. "No. I . . . uh . . . just no."

"Gaspar—" Will began.

Gaspar cut him off. "I'm not gonna argue. Look, I'm here because it's what Beth wanted. Don't push. Okay?"

Ana smiled again, and Gaspar couldn't help thinking how much Beth would have liked the girl. Beth always liked smart people. "But there's such joy in experiencing a new culture. Don't you think?"

Gaspar shook his head. "Joy doesn't come so much from what you experience, but from what you share, I think. I'll just see things that will make me ache, because I can't share 'em with Beth."

Ana nodded, and Gaspar was grateful to see understanding in her eyes. "You must have loved her very much."

Gaspar smiled sadly.

On their way out, Will and Ana passed the movie set. The crew seemed to have finished setting up, but nothing else seemed to be happening. "What do you think this is?" Will asked.

"It's some kind of futuristic spy drama," Ana said. *Challengers* is the title. It's been on the news, and my bank is providing some of the financing."

"I wonder what they're waiting on?"

Ana spoke to one of the cameramen in Hungarian. He shrugged and answered her.

As they walked, Ana said, "They're waiting on some custom props. They were supposed to have arrived by special delivery. High-tech weapons and such. But with Covid, supply chain logistics are a nightmare."

"Ouch," said Will. "There's no local source, I take it?"

"I don't think those are the sorts of things one can pick up at a corner market, are they?"

"I guess not."

9

The Last First Kiss

rom the first moment he entered the toy shop, *his* toy shop, Will was utterly enchanted. Shelves of toys, remarkable, wonderful toys, climbed toward the timbered ceiling and the sky beyond. And the toys, oh, the toys were utterly fantastic, more so by far than he could possibly have dreamed. He stood in the doorway for a long moment, staring, gaping, unable to move.

Though it broke his heart, he was never able to find the words to describe the miracles in Klaus's Shop of Wonders to his friends back in the States. He found dolls that could walk and talk and cry and laugh. He watched trains with colorful engines, boxcars stamped in exotic languages with the names of faraway, exotic places, and elegant passenger carriages that chugged mightily along tiny steel tracks, through tiny villages where old men and children waved and shouted and counted cars. He laughed when the tiny whistle blew. He peered through the windows of toy houses with running water and electricity. He gazed, with mouth gaping and eyes wide, at steadfast tin soldiers, velveteen rabbits, many-towered castles capped with tiny banners, bright picture books, dancing puppets, and model airplanes that zoomed and looped, performing dazzling feats of aerial acrobatics.

"You like?" Ana asked, smiling.

Will couldn't find the words to answer.

A small but cheerful fire crackled merrily in a charming fireplace of old brick behind the wooden cashier's desk, making the cluttered room deliciously warm after a brisk walk through the wintry city, and the air was sweet with the rich, distinctive pungency of dust and old things. An old woman sitting at the cashier's desk asked him something in Hungarian.

"She wants to know if she can help you," Ana translated.

"Hello," Will replied in English, wishing his Hungarian wasn't so clumsy. "I'm Will Klaus. From America."

Before Ana could translate again, the old woman nodded sadly and answered in English. "Come to close us down at last, have you? I see you brought the lady from the bank."

Will smiled and tried to think of something cheerful to say. Words failed him. The contents of his stomach seemed cold and heavy.

"He's come to see if he can help," said Ana. "And I'm going to help him do it."

—⋙⋘—

Ana took him to the Jazzgarden Café in the oldest part of the city, a favorite of hers, where they dined and drank wine. Will had been worried that he wouldn't know what to say to her; he had an extensive history of short, awkward dates filled with long, uncomfortable silences. But even before the first appetizer arrived, it was just like all those four-hour phone calls all over again. Talking to Ana was as natural as breathing and, Will couldn't help thinking, as necessary. They talked about books, theatre, and cinema (their tastes were remarkably similar), and they talked music and art (their tastes diverged).

"I am definitely going to have to introduce you to some music from this century," Ana chided him gently. "Some of it might involve more than just a singer-songwriter with a guitar."

Will smiled. "Just go slow. And be gentle with me."

"I make no promises," Ana said, grinning back and looking up at him through her lashes.

Mostly, they talked about themselves and each other, whispering intimate dreams and secrets they'd never dared share with anyone else before.

Over dessert, the conversation turned more serious, and Ana steered the subject to the toy shop. "Businesses like the shop are important," she said, "because they are a vanishing part of our traditional Hungarian culture. After all the years of Communist oppression and the current economic situation, there's not much left. The traditional past is vanishing, and that's sad. I've worked like hell to keep the shop in business this long, and that was before I even knew you. My superiors at the bank have given me another month to let you come up with some sort of last-ditch plan."

"That's something," Will acknowledged. "Speaking of, I don't suppose you've come up with any brilliant ideas from looking at the records, have you?"

"I'm afraid not," Ana admitted. "Not yet, anyway. To be honest, the late former owners dug themselves quite a deep hole. If I could have gotten my hands on the books ten years ago, or even five. . . . But now? I'm afraid it doesn't look good, Will. Not without a serious infusion of capital."

"I'm a little short of infusions," said Will. "My dad and I can keep the bookshop afloat, and even make a decent enough living, but that's about it."

"Well, I'll keep looking. Maybe I'll turn something up."

"I'd be grateful."

"Me, too, Will. Me, too."

—❦—

Everywhere they went, Will heard Christmas music. A scarce few of the songs were new to him, but most of the tunes were familiar and dear. The words, however, were strange; his Hungarian was too limited, even with Ana's help, and she didn't know the English lyrics. Nonetheless, they sang together, finding that *blah blah blah* is a universal language—it fits every melody and is more than sufficient for expressing sentiments like joy to the world and peace on earth. They sang, and they laughed until they ached.

They strolled through an open-air Christmas market, a tradition dating back to the Middle Ages, where craft booths lined crowded, narrow pathways and the air was drenched with the intoxicating scents of wine, cinnamon, and chocolate.

"The toy shop should totally have a booth here, Ana," Will said.

"They used to," Ana said. "Before Covid. Maybe next year, if the tourists come back . . ."

"Mmm. Maybe I could open a bookshop, too!"

"Budapest has wonderful bookshops," said Ana. "But perhaps you could specialize in international language books. For the tourists, yes? English, Spanish, Italian, Russian . . . oh, and German, certainly. We get a lot of Germans. Oh, and—"

"I imagine it would be a long list."

"It is indeed! Why, we can also open a second toy shop next to your bookshop in Boston! How about that? We can spend our lives flying back and forth."

Will beamed. "I think I'd like that life." Especially, he couldn't help thinking, if it involved living it with the amazing Ana.

They walked to a museum; Will wasn't sure which, since it had been closed when they arrived, but they took their shoes off and, laughing, looked the danger of frostbite right in the eye and splashed in the old stone fountain.

They found an open café and warmed their wet toes in the light of a fire and talked until the darkest hour of the night, the last before night would have to be called morning. When the place closed at last, they walked back toward the hotel slowly, pausing on a stone bridge that arced over the river like a taut bow to watch the light of gas lamps and stars twinkling and dancing in the dark water far below. Will took her in his arms then, and they danced to the distant music of church bells.

Ana took her mask off. Will took his off. Then he kissed her, knowing even then that it was his last first kiss, the one, best kiss he would remember until the end of his days.

―✦―

137

When they neared the hotel at last, Will noticed uniformed police officers still keeping careful watch. He smiled and nodded to a pair of them as they passed. The movie crew was packing up to leave. "I guess they finished?"

Ana spoke to one of the crew members in Hungarian for a few moments.

"They've given up," Ana said. "The custom props never arrived. They were supposed to have been delivered hours ago. They don't know when they'll be able to start again. What a shame!"

"Huh," said Will. "You know, I think that might just give me an idea."

10

Calling on the Count

he toy store was amazing, Gaspar!" Will gushed. "Amazing! Just . . . Jeez, I wish I could think of another word, because I don't think you can stand to hear the word amazing one more time, can you? But . . . oh, my God. It's just . . . just . . . ."

"Amazing?" Gaspar suggested, raising his eyebrows.

They sat at a corner table in the hotel restaurant, eating bowls of thick, steaming oatmeal with fresh bread and nursing cups of hot coffee. The menu described the coffee as American style. It wasn't, and the dainty little demitasses were way too small, but Gaspar liked it all the same. His briefcase rested on the floor next to his chair. Gaspar had found that he didn't want to let the thing out of his sight.

"Exactly," Will confirmed with a nod. "My God. The craftsmanship, the art . . . I truly had no idea they made things like this, not anymore. I didn't think toys like this even existed, not outside of a museum. Or ... or, like, a TV Christmas special or something."

"Do the kids still like them, I wonder?" asked Gaspar. "Near as I can tell, they usually go in for the flashing, noisemaking, computerized, battery-powered robo gizmos that shoot foam darts or plug into the TV."

"Did you?"

"It was always bats and gloves for me, dude. So is a work of art fun to play with?"

Will chuckled and pointed at Gaspar with his spoon for emphasis. "Ah, but *fun* is exactly what makes them a work of art in the first place, isn't it? And Gaspar, you should have seen the photographs they showed me—oh, the light on those kids' faces, the gaping mouths, the wide eyes. Even cynical kids born in the information age know magic when they see it, my friend. Why, Ana told me all sorts of stories about when they took loads of toys to the orphanages or to kids who lost everything. . . . It would break your heart, man. I'm telling you. It would break your very heart."

"Ana, huh?"

Will rolled his eyes. "Great. Is it that obvious? Yes, Gaspar, she is amazing."

"Amazing again."

"So my vocabulary still needs a boost. Work with me here."

The waitress returned and poured more coffee for Will.

"I have to," said Gaspar. "The firing didn't take, remember?"

Will smiled, and for a moment, his flush deepened. "You know, until I met you and heard you talk about Beth, I never believed in love at first sight."

"Was it really love at first sight? Because it seems to me, you were pretty infatuated long before first sight. Seriously, you guys didn't know about Zoom?"

"I concede the point. But still, listening to you, I *believed*. I wonder . . . would things have been different if I'd met Ana before I'd learned that lesson? To believe?"

"Love without faith?" Gaspar shrugged. "It would take a smarter guy than me to answer that. Who knows? Maybe the one brings the other, or at least opens the door. But does it matter which comes first? I don't know. That's a little out of my league. There's probably a baseball joke there, but this isn't the time, huh?"

"Do you believe it? Do you . . . do you really think love can happen, you know, like, so fast?"

"Beth thought so. Now Beth, she would have had, like, all kinds of advice."

"I wish I could have heard it."

"Me, too, my dude. Me, too."

"Because Gaspar, I already think I love her."

"Wow. How 'bout her? She feel the same way?"

"You know what? I honestly think so."

"Good for you," said Gaspar. "Did you tell her?"

"What, you, like . . . just come right out and say it?"

Gaspar nodded. "That's what I mean."

"You mean just . . . blurt out I love you? On the first date? Dude!"

"If you know it, you say it. Period. Otherwise, it doesn't count."

"Doesn't seem like the way to play it cool, doesn't?" said Will.

Gaspar rolled his eyes. "There's nothing cool about being a chicken. You should have told her. So now it doesn't count."

Will seemed eager to change the subject. "Jeez, listen to me. I didn't even ask about your evening. You still haven't told me what you found at the bank. Did you find the next clue?"

Gaspar nodded as he put the case on the table and opened it. "Another book. I used it to decode the other message."

"Another book code, eh?"

"Yeah. But only *after* I solved the math puzzles." He sighed. "Beth knew I always needed help with the math clues."

"Apparently, you don't."

"Apparently. So once that was done, on to the book code."

"Wow," said Will. "How does that even work?"

"I had to figure out the math puzzles, solve another to turn the numbers into letters—well, some turned into different numbers—and then use the book from the bank to decode the real answers."

"Huh," said Will. "Beth really wanted you to stay busy, huh?"

"So it seems."

"And what did you come up with?"

Gaspar looked down at his notes and read aloud. "Remus's and Peter's graves, Adam's birth above. Text your answer to four-seven-six-one-three."

Will pursed his lips thoughtfully. "Did you try the number?"

Gaspar nodded. "I sent a few random answers. The only reply is a question mark."

"Beth must have set up an auto reply. Wow again; that's just wicked clever."

"That's my girl. I was going to Google, but I figured I'd wait for you. Any idea what it means?"

"Easy. You know Remus's brother, right?"

"Uh, Br'er Rabbit?"

Will chuckled and shook his head. "That's Uncle Remus."

"I was making a joke. Which I thought was better than no, nerd, I don't know."

"She means just plain Remus, no uncle, twin brother of Romulus." He grinned and tapped his forehead. "Detective. Steel trap, man." Will mimed a trap snapping

143

shut with his hands and made the sound: "tw-*WAP!* A fact would have to chew off its own leg to get out of this brain."

Gaspar blinked twice. "My instinctive response is . . . gimme your lunch money, nerd."

"No way," said Will. "I'm gonna need it if we're going to Italy. Hope those voucher things are still good."

Gaspar felt his eyes narrow. "Italy?"

Will rolled his eyes. "C'mon. You gotta know this. Oh, okay. Romulus founded the city of Rome when he killed his twin brother, Remus. Saint Peter is supposed to be buried there, too."

"What about Adam's birth? That'd be, like, Africa, right?"

"The Creation of Adam. Dude, it's the painting on the Sistine Chapel ceiling! I'm tellin' ya. Steel trap."

"Lunch money."

Will chuckled. "So you were a school bully, then?"

"What? Oh, hell no. This impulse is utterly new. But it's way strong." Gaspar grinned and winked. "So. Rome, huh? I guess I should have known."

"That's where Beth was," Will said softly.

Gaspar studied the sludge in the bottom of the porcelain thimble they called a coffee cup here. He didn't answer.

"We know our next stop. Want me to check out?" Gaspar nodded. "With everything that's happened, the break-ins at the shop, the dudes that chased you. . . .

Whatever Beth found, well, it must be very valuable. Someone must want it. Badly."

Gaspar nodded again. "I was thinking the same thing. But dammit, they can't have it! Will, whatever it is, this . . . this *thing* that's waiting at the end of the mystery, maybe it's worth something. Maybe it's worth a lot. Dude, I don't know. But that doesn't matter, no, not a bit. Not to me. To me, it's priceless. I say that without even knowing what it is, because it's a gift from my Beth, from my *Beth*. It's her last gift to me. It's the last thing I have to hold on to, to cling to for the rest of my stupid life. You know? Do you? Huh? It's the last damn thing I have to remember her by, Will. I'm sure as hell not letting it go."

"Don't worry. We'll find it. We'll keep it safe. But I think you have to agree . . . this is getting big. Big as in dangerous. Whatever it is, we need to get there before the bastards that attacked you come back."

Gaspar frowned thoughtfully. "Yeah. And I think . . . I think maybe we need some help. Someone with influence."

"Right!" said Will. "And you just happen to have a relative in town."

"Beth wanted me to find my family. Well, dammit, let's do that. I think it's time we paid a visit to this Count Bethlen Tamás."

"Got a number?"

Gaspar shook his head. "Unlisted. But I got an address. Ready to go be a brash American?"

"Sure. Just lemme call Ana. Aw, never mind. I'll call
her on the way."

———◆———

By the time Will joined him outside, Gaspar had
already called a cab with the concierge's help. "Any luck?"

Will shook his head. "I got her voicemail. I left a
message though."

The drive took them out of the city, past the point
where ramshackle suburban neighborhoods gave way to
scenic, Eastern European countryside—green, sloping
hills rising above farms and pastures. Will watched it all,
mile after mile, with, Gaspar couldn't help noticing with
a grin, his face close enough to fog the window.

Gaspar occupied his time by flipping through the
latest volume of *The Roots of the Bethlens*, with its lists
of names along with marriages, births, and deaths. He
couldn't make out much, only the strange names, but
the chronicle fascinated him all the same. This was a
touchstone to his past, to his roots; here was his family.
But they were only names in a book, forgotten men and
women survived only by their names. Like Beth, they
were lost to him. Gaspar was an orphan and a widower.
He was utterly alone.

Gaspar sighed and closed the book before locking it and its twin back in the briefcase.

At last they passed a small village square, with buildings that Gaspar assumed must be a grocery or drug store of some sort and a small pub. Soon after, they came to a drive that ran between two farm buildings of white stucco with gently sloping roofs of rust-colored tile. The drive climbed up a low hill to an imposing stone building flanked by twin towers.

"That must be the house," said Gaspar, feeling himself gaping like a fool.

"I think," said Will, "that something that large can no longer be called a house. It stretches the definition. The word's just not big enough to contain . . . to contain *that*. That, my friend, is a castle."

The driver spoke hurriedly in Hungarian. Will translated the gist of it for Gaspar.

"He says the people are very proud of this place, the manor house of Count Bethlen Tamás. It's one of the few remaining great houses returned to the possession of one of the old, great families. Most of the others in the country are standing empty. The ones in the city were destroyed—or sold to foreigners who turned them into offices, hotels, or shopping malls. Here, old Hungary still clings to life. He's very proud of that. Hungary still has a soul here, he says, despite all she has suffered."

"My God," Gaspar muttered as the cab drew nearer. "We totally should have called."

147

"The man's number is unlisted," Will reminded him.

"We should have sent word. I mean, dude, we're just, like, dropping in unannounced! It's so . . . it's so. . . ."

"American?"

"Well, yeah," Gaspar said with a nod. "Exactly."

"Relax," said Will. "The servants will probably send us away. But maybe we can leave word or something. A message. After all, you're family. Then we can hike back down to that pub and have a pint while we wait for another cab."

The cab pulled into a circle driveway and stopped in front of what Gaspar assumed must be the main entrance. The front door was meant to impress, or even to intimidate, not to welcome. Gaspar paid the driver, and the two grabbed their bags and climbed out. Gaspar was acutely aware of the effort required to keep from gaping; he saw Will's jaw firmly clenched and knew the dude was having the same problem.

Their gazes met. Gaspar rolled his eyes and led the way to the entrance. The great oaken door was adorned with ornately carved panels.

"I don't even know where to knock," Gaspar muttered. "I'll break my knuckles if I rap hard enough to be heard in the depths of that monstrosity."

"Too bad you didn't bring a bat. Oh. Wait. Look, there's a cord there. I guess that's the doorbell."

Gaspar chuckled. "Thank God."

He gave the cord two sharp tugs. After a long moment, he gave two more. Gaspar sighed. He was about to suggest a walk down to the pub to discuss their next move when a sudden noise made him jump. With a groan and a squeal, the door began to slide open on great hinges that plainly didn't see regular use.

A man stood blinking as he looked out into the bright afternoon sun, regarding them from the shadows of the entrance foyer. He was thin but wiry, although Gaspar recognized an athlete's taut frame, and his neatly trimmed hair was more salt than pepper. He wore a crisp white shirt with a tie over black trousers along with a smoking jacket that (Gaspar couldn't help noticing) looked faded and slightly threadbare. Gaspar suspected the man had not outfitted himself for company or for going out; he had the look of a man who dressed out of habit more than anything else. He did not smile, and there was no hint of welcome in his small, dark eyes.

He snapped rapidly in Hungarian, and Will answered quickly. Gaspar could not understand what Will had said, but he recognized his own name. Gaspar saw the man's eyes open wide with shock, but he seemed to recover quickly. A smile stretched across the man's face, but it didn't reach his eyes.

"Please," the man said, switching to excellent English, "forgive my manners. I am not accustomed to visitors, least of all distant relations coming to call, and so . . . suddenly. Won't you please come inside?"

He stepped back, pulling the heavy door open wider. Gaspar and Will exchanged a glance and shrugged. They followed the man into an entrance foyer. Ahead of them, a magnificent stairway wound its way up to a second-floor balcony. Much of the furniture was covered with heavy sheets, and a few lighter spots on the bare floors hinted at pieces that were missing.

"Pardon my dust," the man said. "As I indicated, I wasn't expecting visitors, and most of the servants are off tonight. So . . . I am here alone, and hardly prepared to be much of a host. But family forgives, isn't it so?"

"Of course," said Gaspar, "and, uh, you must forgive me for simply showing up like this, like, out of the blue and all. I believe my assistant here has introduced me."

"Detective," Will interjected.

Gaspar cleared his throat and continued. "But to be polite, I am Gaspar Bethlen of Boston, Massachusetts. And unless I am mistaken, you, sir, must be Mister Bethlen Tamás."

"*Count* Bethlen Tamás," the man said, offering Gaspar a limp handshake. "I am he. But come, come, do take a seat, won't you? Come, there's a sitting room just here."

Without waiting for an answer, Bethlen led them through an arch and into a small room decorated with antique furniture, worn but still elegant, which seemed frail enough to make Gaspar almost afraid to sit. A rolltop secretary in the corner nearest the entrance was littered with the paraphernalia of correspondence:

disordered stacks of unopened envelopes, pens and paper, heavy stamps and sealing wax. A number of fencing foils and masks were mounted on one wall, along with a pair of rapiers. Gaspar also noticed a number of trophies and plaques. He was not, in fact, the only athlete in the family.

An unexpected wave of poignant emotion washed over Gaspar, the stirrings of his long-suppressed orphan side, when he realized that the paintings and framed photographs on the wall might be of his own distant ancestors. Despite a faint but lingering cloud of perfumed potpourri, the room smelled stale and dusty, and of something vaguely medicinal, like a hospital.

"Please, sit," said the Count.

Will and Gaspar exchanged a quick glance and obeyed, slowly and awkwardly, lest their weight snap the groaning, brittle wood. Gaspar smiled a little as he noticed a globe-shaped marble paperweight on the coffee table in front of him. It was just about the size of a baseball. Something, at least, was familiar, and for the first time in ages, his fingers itched for the familiar shape.

"Here," the Count continued, turning his back on his visitors to rummage around in a cabinet. "Let me get you something to drink, eh? I believe I have a nice Tokaji here somewhere. . . ."

"Truly, that's too kind," said Gaspar. "Really."

"Nonsense," the Count said, still fumbling, not turning around. "One must remember the rules of hospitality, mustn't one, eh? Else, what becomes of civilization? And isn't conversation always ever so much more pleasant with a nice spot of something? Am I not right? Besides, it's already opened. You know it doesn't keep. Here, I have some glasses here somewhere. . . ."

Ana entered her tidy flat and dropped an armload of groceries on the counter. Then she sighed with relief. There was her phone, still on its charger. So—*thank heaven!*—she hadn't lost it in the market after all. *Huh.* She'd missed a call and had a message. She tapped play and put it on speaker.

She shrugged out of her coat as the message started, and she smiled. It was Will's voice. "Hey, Ana, it's Will. Sorry I missed you. I'll give you a call later, okay? Gaspar and I are riding out to the country to visit that relative of his, Count Bethlen—"

Ana spun, startled, spilling her bag on the counter. *"Óh ne!"*

She grabbed her coat and keys and ran, leaving the groceries on the counter.

"Truly," said Gaspar, "I don't mean to intrude on your hospitality *or* your privacy, sir. If I can just tell you why—"

"Oh," said the Count, "I know exactly why you're here. In fact, I've been going to quite some trouble to locate you! Of course, had I known that you'd come straight to my doorstep like a gift from God's angels, why, I could have saved myself a great deal of time, trouble, and expense."

Will and Gaspar exchanged another glance; this time their eyes were wide with surprise.

"You've been looking for *us?*" Will exclaimed.

"Indeed I have," said the Count. "As I said, I know *exactly* why you're here. Yes, I know precisely, don't I? You've come to rob me! You've come to take what is mine, haven't you? Ah yes, here we go."

The Count turned, but he wasn't holding a decanter. His pale hand grasped a revolver, and it was pointed directly at Gaspar's heart.

Gaspar leapt to his feet and heard Will doing the same. "What—what the actual *f—?*"

"There," the Count said calmly. "I'll thank you to stay where you are. I assure you, this weapon is loaded and serviceable, and I shall not hesitate to use it. *Bah.* Only Americans would be so bold, coming cap-in-hand to rob a man in his own home!"

Will held his hands up, struggling to keep his voice calm. "I'm sure we don't know what you're talking about. But we can all stay calm, I'm sure we can resolve this—"

"That's close enough, young man!" the Count cried, turning his pistol at Will. "I believe I was clear when I asked you politely to remain where you are. Now, then. I believe you have something that belongs to me."

"I don't know what you're talking about," said Gaspar.

"Pray, don't insult me in my own sitting room," said the Count. "You have a set of books detailing the history of my family."

"*Our* family," Gaspar pointed out.

"Keep your arrogant pretensions to yourself, *American*," the Count snapped. "Those books are rare and valuable, and are the property of this estate, however you came by them. I want them returned. Now."

Gaspar picked up the heavy globe paperweight. It was indeed the size of a baseball. It fit right in his hand. *Yeah, perfect.*

"Catch," said Gaspar. He threw the paperweight toward Bethlen. Without thinking, the man scrambled instinctively to catch. As he fumbled with the paperweight, he dropped the revolver.

Gaspar moved quickly and kicked the revolver. It slid across the room and under a tall antique cabinet.

The Count dropped the paperweight and Gaspar gave him a hard shove. Bethlen fell. Rather than attempting to climb back to his feet, Bethlen scrambled after the weapon.

"Run!" Will shouted.

Gaspar darted back to the foyer and toward the main door, hearing Will close behind. In the foyer, they saw two men coming down the stairs from the second-floor balcony. Both of them were bruised and bandaged, but Gaspar's blood went cold as he recognized them. They were some of the same men that had chased him from the bank.

Gaspar turned for a second. Back in the sitting room, the Count had retrieved his revolver. The Count fired, but the bullet went over their heads.

"Abban!" the Count called to the two men. "Jael!" The men raced to the Count. Gaspar and Will could hear the Count shouting, but they didn't slow. They fled back toward the foyer. As they ran, Gaspar said, "See? Guns. Guess you're a cool detective after all."

"I was okay with the uncool," said Will.

From behind them, they heard the Count shouting, "Abban, Jael! Stop them!"

Driven by blind panic, Gaspar bolted for the main entrance. Will followed right behind him. Once outside, they didn't stop at the driveway; they sprinted toward the main road.

"What the hell were we *thinking?*" said Will. "We totally should have asked the cabbie to wait!"

Gaspar didn't bother to answer. He ran. Without slowing, he looked back over his shoulder. The two men, Abban and Jael, came spilling out of the castle's main entrance—from a distance, both looked large and strong. For a moment, Gaspar thought about dropping his case.

"He said the servants were off," Gaspar muttered.

"Guess hired muscle doesn't count as servants," Will said, panting.

At that moment, a small car turned off the main road and started up the driveway. The driver sped toward Gaspar and Will and then stopped abruptly, raising a cloud of dust. The passenger door swung open.

"Get in!" a woman's voice called. "Hurry!"

"Ana?" asked Will, astonished.

"Hurry!" she repeated.

Will didn't hesitate. He climbed into the tiny vehicle, and Gaspar scrambled after. There was no back seat, so the two men crowded into the passenger seat. Behind them, Gaspar heard the men shouting in Hungarian. The driver was already speeding away before Gaspar could get the door closed.

"Ana!" said Will. "My God! What on earth are you *doing* here?"

What on earth are *you* doing here?" she countered.

Gaspar frowned. "You're not going to believe what happened to us! That crazy old man tried to kill us!"

Ana sighed. "Oh, I believe it. Bethlen Tamás, the self-anointed count, is *not* a good man."

"You know him?" exclaimed Will.

"Of course I know him," said Ana. Her knuckles were white where her fingers gripped the steering wheel. She did not look away from the road. "He's my grand-father."

—※—

From the front of his manor, Count Bethlen Tamás watched the car disappear into the distance. Cold fury danced in his eyes.

"Anasztázia," he said aloud.

His granddaughter. His own bloody granddaughter had betrayed him.

11

from Budapest to Rome

nger and fear wrestled with humiliation for control of Ana's emotions. For Will's sake, and for his friend's, she made an effort to keep those emotions from showing. For their sake, she wore two masks. She took only one of them off, the N95, when their drinks arrived.

"Do you really think he would have murdered us?" Will asked.

"Uh, the bullets pretty much convinced me," Gaspar said.

"He is a small and desperate man who believes he is entitled," Ana told Will. She gnawed her lower lip and shook her head. "Just because of his name and his wealth, even though most of the latter is gone. That makes him ruthless."

Will reached out to touch her shoulder, and she took his hand gratefully. She shaped her mask into a smile and was surprised to find it was genuine. Something about Will's presence comforted her.

Ana had taken them to Fortuna, a comfortable inner-city restaurant in Budapest's castle district, a place of light wood, gilded mirrors, and white lace tablecloths, where she'd promised them the best meal in the city. It was a favorite of hers; it had been since she was a girl. Large windows let in late-afternoon sunlight and afforded them a view of the narrow street outside. They would see anyone coming long before they arrived.

They'd ordered a bottle of Tokaji. Two small glasses later—one gulped quickly, one more slowly—they'd managed to relax enough to exchange stories. Ana was thinking seriously about ordering a second bottle.

"I would have warned you sooner," Ana said. "But . . . well, I guess I didn't think you'd just . . . go to him. It didn't even occur to me, frankly. I should have warned you."

"You saved our lives," Gaspar said.

"I should have warned you." Ana forced a smile. "My grandfather is something of a relic. A living reminder of old ways. He fought like a demon to regain the estate. He was one of the very few old nobles to do so, you know. All of Hungary rejoiced. But times were hard after the fall of Communism; in many ways they were as hard as the days of our oppression. My grandfather regained his ancestral home; he reclaimed his inheritance. But the effort broke him, both literally and figuratively. He exhausted himself physically and mentally; he was never the same man again. He drained the last of his fortune, too. Now the creditors are calling, and I don't think the castle will be his much longer. He probably told you the servants have the night off, didn't he? No. He hasn't been able to afford servants in years. He has already begun to sell some of the furniture, the silver, all the priceless treasures of our family's past. Soon it will all be gone at last, and the Bethlens will be a memory, one more fossilized relic of Hungary's vanished past, its dying culture."

"Yeah," said Gaspar. "The gun kinda killed my sympathy."

"I don't blame you. I loved my grandfather for the man I thought he was. I've never quite forgiven him for being the man he is."

Ana's memory darted back to a time some seventeen years before, the last time she'd been in the castle with her mother. She remembered her grandfather shouting, spittle flying from his mouth, his eyes hot with fury. She hadn't understood the words, but they'd frightened her. Her mother had stood defiantly and refused to back down.

"My mother tried to stop him," Ana told Gaspar and Will. "They argued—something about swindling some landowner or cheating some banker."

In Ana's memory, her mother had stood tall, speaking calmly but firmly. Tamás had swept a stack of papers off a table as his anger swelled to rage.

"She tried to remind him what it means to be no-ble."

Ana remembered what had happened next. She'd knelt in the corner, sobbing, while her grandfather slapped her mother, his own daughter, hard enough to make her fall. Then he'd pointed at the doorway.

"He responded by disowning her," Ana told him. Remembering her mother's strength, she didn't look away from Will and his friend as she spoke. "He hasn't spoken to any of us since."

"Oh my God," said Will. "Ana, I'm so sorry."

"I'm sorry, too." She gave his hand a squeeze.

Will was right, Gaspar decided. Ana was an excep-tionally pretty woman, stunning, even. In her way, she was as lovely as Beth had been, although Ana's beauty was fiery: long, lush red hair, flashing dark eyes, and pale skin that seemed to glow with incandescent light. Beth's beauty was of the forest, of still water, of the night, with her olive skin, her lush black hair, and her deep, dark, soulful eyes. Still, something in Ana's casual openness, in her smile, in the way she tossed her hair reminded Gaspar of his lost Beth, and it made his heart lighter, unexpectedly so, to see Will so obviously besotted. With effort, he forced his mind back to the matter at hand.

"At least," said Gaspar, "we know what he wants from us. Or I should say, from me. He must think I'm trying to use my family line as a claim to his house and wealth. That must be the secret Beth discovered when she researched my roots."

"No," said Ana. "No, that's not it at all."

"What is it, then?" asked Will.

Ana smiled and touched his hand again as she answered. "The secret. Your branch of the family's legacy. Whatever it is."

"The gem," Will guessed.

"I don't know," Ana admitted. She took another sip of her drink. "Maybe. In any case, whatever your branch's inheritance is, my grandfather wants it. I don't remember much about what my grandfather believes the legacy to be. Just bits and pieces of story, really. It's been a long time since . . . since my grandfather asked my mother and me to leave, and my mother never spoke of it, or him, again. This is what I remember. The other branch of the family, yours, was the heir to a legacy. I told you that much already. To claim the legacy, the true heir had to return to the place of Bethlen's father. But only the true heir."

"Where's that?" Gaspar demanded.

Ana shrugged. "I don't know."

"I bet Beth did," said Will. "That's got to be what we're chasing."

"You may be right," said Gaspar. "But how does one prove they're the rightful heir?"

"With the books," said Ana. "The heir must bring the books—all three volumes."

"Likely with ID," Will added. "That must be why Beth had you bring all those documents."

"Yes," said Ana. "And the answer to certain questions. At least . . . from what I remember. I don't know why. Like I said. It was just stories."

Will smiled. "You of all people should know . . . there's no such thing as just stories." Ana smiled back at him.

"I'm going to go out on a limb," said Gaspar. "You don't know the questions, do you? Much less the answers?"

"That would be a safe assumption," said Ana. "If my grandfather knew, I don't remember him mentioning it. I think your Beth might have been ahead of him there."

Gaspar smiled. "That's my girl."

"At least we know why the Count wants you so badly, Gaspar," said Will. "He wants the books. And whatever they lead to."

"I'm afraid so," Ana agreed. "In the desperation of his madness, he thinks it's his by right, or at least that his need overcomes any moral responsibility. Beware of him, Gaspar. He's used the last of his fortune to hire those men. I don't know what he'll do next. I don't know what he's capable of."

"What do *you* want?" asked Gaspar.

"Me?" Ana shrugged. "I don't want to see the culture of my homeland die any more than any other Hungarian. I don't want to see the home of my ancestors become a hotel. Any more than I want to see Will's toy shop replaced by a Pizza Hut or something."

"I see," said Gaspar.

"But be that as it may," Ana continued, "I don't want to see the house in my grandfather's grasping, miserly hands, either. I don't want to see a proud legacy tainted. Maybe it *is* time to let the past rest, so that we can move forward, and see what the future holds for our nation. But enough of this. The Count won't stop. You men have a secret to uncover, don't you? Do you know your next step?"

Will looked at Gaspar, uncertain how to answer. "We don't know a lot," Will admitted.

"I'm going to put my cards on the table," said Gaspar. "For better or for worse, I would rather trust in the help of others than be a lonely, desperate asshole like that Count Tamás. We're going to Rome. I think the next clue is there. Will and I will go to the airport and get on the very first flight."

Ana shook her head again. "No. My grandfather will have men there. He's truly desperate now; this is his last chance."

"What do you suggest?" asked Gaspar.

Ana thought for a moment. "Take the train."

"The train?" said Gaspar. "Like . . . how long will that even take?"

"The better part of a day," said Ana. "I'd think fifteen or sixteen hours, most likely. But I think it's the safest option."

"Alright," said Gaspar. "Will, get your vaccination card ready. You're gonna need it again."

——✦——

At Gaspar's insistence, they took a cab to the train station.

"Not that I don't appreciate the timely rescue, Ana," he explained, "but your tiny car is too small for me. I'm a big dude. I prefer my own seat, rather than sharing one with Mister Klaus here."

It was dark when they arrived. Gaspar went to purchase tickets while Will said goodbye to Ana. When Gaspar returned to the platform, he found them talking softly.

"You know," Ana said, "when you get back to Budapest, we're going to have to talk about the financial situation at the toy shop."

"I know," Will said. He closed his eyes for a moment. "I guess we both know what's going to happen, don't we?"

"I'm afraid so," she said, touching his arm. "But I'll stall as long as I can. Who knows? Maybe your idea will work. It's a good one. There are always possibilities, no?"

"Thanks again," Will said. "I—"

Will didn't finish, because Ana stood on tiptoes to give him a kiss. He took off his Red Sox cap, took her in his arms, and kissed her again, long and deep. Gaspar held back for a moment and pretended, tactfully, not to notice.

"Come back to me," Ana said.

"I will. I can't wait."

Gaspar had to suppress a smile, because Will was floating as they boarded the train. "Did you tell her?" Gaspar asked.

"I didn't have to," Will said. "That kiss told me she already knows."

"Still doesn't count," said Gaspar.

The porter showed them to their compartment, a roomette with facing seats and a tiny bathroom and shower. The seats could fold out for sleeping, a handy thing, since they'd be traveling through the night.

As the train started to move, Gaspar glanced out his window and sat bolt upright.

"What is it?" Will asked.

Gaspar pointed. "Look. There." Two men were running toward the train. "See those two?"

"What about them?" Will asked grimly.

167

"One of them was with the men who attacked me after the bank. The guy in the turtleneck."

"I guess the airport wasn't the only place where the count had men stationed," Will said. "Dammit! Gaspar, they might have bribed the ticket agent. They could know which compartment we're in!"

The train gained speed. The men sprinted. They were closer, closer.

Gaspar's heart pounded. His palms were slick with fear.

And then the train pulled away from the platform and the station.

"Did they make it?" asked Will.

"I don't know," said Gaspar. "But . . . yeah, I think so."

"We can't stay here."

"I know," said Gaspar. He handed Will a stack of bills. "Here. Use what you have to. Bribe someone. Get us moved to another compartment. Preferably at the front end of the train, away from where those men boarded. Pay the porters enough to keep them quiet."

Will nodded and pulled his Red Sox cap back on, and Gaspar followed him into the narrow corridor. They found a porter. Will spoke to him in Hungarian. The man shrugged and shook his head, but Will pressed some bills into his hand, and then more. Finally, the man whispered something. Will nodded. The man turned, motioning for them to come with him.

"What did he say?" Gaspar whispered as they hurried after the man.

"There are no more empty compartments, but we're going to stay in his roomette," Will explained. "There's a crew car near the front. We'll have to be quiet and make sure we're not seen."

"That was pretty much my plan, anyway," Gaspar agreed. "The whole not being seen thing."

They passed through two more sleeper cars, and then a club car and dining car. Finally, they came to a door between cars with a sign that said, in several languages, *Crew Only. No Passengers Beyond This Point*. The porter used a key card to open the door, looked cautiously, and then motioned for Gaspar and Will to follow. He led them to a roomette that was rather like the one they had just vacated, although it clearly had not been serviced as recently. It smelled vaguely of cologne and tobacco.

"This will do," said Gaspar. He nodded to the porter.

"For a while," said Will. "But those men will find us sooner or later. At the station in Rome, if not before. They'll see us get off the train."

"Wait," said Gaspar. "Will, ask the man to wait a moment."

Will spoke to the porter in Hungarian.

"Ask him if he can find two men about our size. Men that are getting off at the next stop, or the one after. Anywhere before Rome."

Will relayed the question and translated the reply for Gaspar. "He doesn't think that will be a problem. Why?"

"Give the man some more money," said Gaspar. He was removing his topcoat and fedora. "Here, I'm going to need your coat and cap." Gaspar began emptying his bag.

"Hey!" Will protested. "I just got that coat!"

"Don't worry. I'll replace them. Ask the porter to find some men about our size and offer these things in trade. Tell him we'll pay them some money, but make sure they're wearing our things when they get off the train."

Will grinned. "You know, that's not actually a bad idea. Uh, unless we're, like, putting innocent people in danger."

"I doubt it," said Gaspar. "Those men will realize their mistake pretty quickly, and I don't think hired thugs hurt people for free. They're professionals. They won't want the attention. They'll be fine."

Every time Gaspar heard footsteps outside in the corridor, his heart turned to cold lead and sank like an anchor into the depths of his gut. Fear paralyzed him.

Every time, he expected a heavy boot to kick in the door, shattering the fragile lock.

Every time, he expected to find small, brutish eyes staring at him, a guttural voice shouting demands before hard blows fell.

The kick never came. The door remained shut. The night deepened.

He wished he had a baseball bat.

The train's gentle, rhythmic rocking was soothing, and Will was soon snoring gently.

An hour or so later, the train came to a stop. Gaspar wished he'd brought a map; the town's name was unfamiliar. He pressed his face to the glass, fogging it with his breath. A few people boarded. Only a single woman got off, dragging a heavy, wheeled suitcase behind her.

Another stop, another.

At the third stop, Gaspar saw two men leave the train wearing the familiar coats and hats. He wiped away the fog and pressed his face closer to the glass.

The plan worked—moments later, he saw the two men who had been following them racing after the decoys. They caught them near the station building at the far end of the platform.

The train was still stopped in the station.

"C'mon," Gaspar urged the train. "Come *on!*" It did not move.

One of the men grabbed at the passenger wearing Will's coat. He pulled the Red Sox cap off the man's head and threw it to the ground. Gaspar could see them arguing.

The train didn't move.

Suddenly, the men seemed to realize their mistake. They turned and shouted frantically, pointing at the train. They ran.

Closer, closer.

The train started moving.

The men ran faster.

The train gained speed.

The men sprinted, waving and calling. This time, Gaspar realized, they had no hope of catching up. He let out the breath he'd been holding.

The men were still standing on the platform, staring, arms at their sides, when the station disappeared from view.

Count Bethlen Tamás waited in his study, using one of the rapiers from the wall to spar with an imaginary opponent. The blade was one of his favorites; the balance was perfect. He dropped the rapier on his sofa when the phone rang and raced to answer it.

"Yes?" he said in Hungarian.

After a moment, he said, "Damn! Which train?"

Finally, he said, "No, no. It doesn't matter. I know where he's going. Find a train to Rome. I don't think I can get men to the station before he arrives, so call me when you get there. I'll have instructions for you. More men will be on their way to join you."

In their tiny crew compartment, Gaspar watched the shadowed European countryside go by. He thought about trying to get some sleep; they'd be in Rome soon enough, but he was wired.

Will looked up from his book. "Mind if I ask a question?"

Gaspar shrugged.

"You gave up baseball."

Gaspar nodded. "Retired. That's not a question."

"A switch-hitting first baseman with power . . . mostly from the right. . . ."

Gaspar glared. "Still not a question."

"Mind if I ask why?"

Gaspar sat up, blinking. "What the hell do you mean? My wife died!"

"I know why you stepped away. I guess I don't really understand why you stepped away . . . I mean, like . . . forever. I mean, maybe it'll pass, right? The grief."

"No," said Gaspar. "See, that's the difference between sorrow and grief. Sorrow heals. It passes. Sorrow is a season. Grief is forever. Grief defines you."

"So you just . . . what? Give up? Like, everything?"

For a long moment, Gaspar didn't speak, and neither did Will. And then, almost before he realized it, Gaspar took his mask off and started speaking again, if only to keep the silence from becoming too dark, too oppressive. "Baseball . . . it's like anything. If you're gonna do it, really do it, it takes love. When Beth died . . . ." Gaspar had to struggle to find the words. "All my love for the game . . . it was just . . . you know. Gone. Everything. It all died with Beth."

"Man. I don't know what to say."

Gaspar shrugged. "But then I look at you and Ana . . . and I remember. What it felt like to be that in love, that alive."

"She's amazing, isn't she?" Gaspar rolled his eyes. After a moment, Will added, "I hope we can find what you and Beth had. Of course, I can already hear my friends back home. They'll tell me to slow the hell down."

"Yeah," said Gaspar. "They will. Tell 'em to piss off."

Will raised his eyebrows.

"Life is short," said Gaspar. "Believe me. That's the one thing I'm smart enough to know for sure. Make the most of every precious, fleeting, goddamn moment." He nodded to Will's book. "No offense, but look at you. All those books. I mean, Beth was a reader, too. But dude, she *lived*. And you . . . you never even took time to see the world."

Will looked back at the window. "I guess I was waiting for the right moment."

"The right moment . . . dude, it never comes. You have to make it. That's what Beth used to say. I mean . . . what if Beth had waited for the right moment? Huh? Think about that next time you're thinking of playing it cool with Ana."

Will smiled. "So I should have told her."

"It doesn't count if you don't."

Will nodded. "Tell me something. Why do you want the gem so bad?"

Gaspar looked at him, wondering what the hell he meant.

"It's not like you need the money," said Will. "Is it just to keep that count from getting it?"

"I told you already. If I've told you once, I've told you fifteen times. Beth wanted me to have it."

"You said that, yeah. But that was before we had guys who are very probably trained killers on our butts. The stakes are a little higher, now."

"Beth wanted me to have it. That's enough." Gaspar found, suddenly, that he had to fight to keep from choking up. Dammit, he was not going to cry in front of this guy. "I just want some . . . piece of her. Something that means she's not gone." He took a deep breath to compose himself. "Like I told you. I want something to hold on to. And by God, I'm going to get it. And I'm going to hold onto it with both hands."

Will was quiet for a long time before he spoke again. "Would you do it again? Knowing how it was going to . . . you know."

"End?"

Will nodded.

"Yeah," said Gaspar. "Yeah, I totally would. Even knowing all the agony that comes after, I'd do it all again. In a heartbeat. Between the grief and . . . and no Beth at all, I'd take the grief every time. And I'd thank God for it."

"It doesn't have to, you know," Will said after a long moment. "Define you, I mean. Grief."

Gaspar didn't answer, but he thought about those words for a long time, and he was still thinking about them long after Will fell asleep.

An hour or two later, Will was again snoring gently. Smiling, Gaspar turned his attention to the financials from Will's shop. The smile faded. The numbers in their columns were precise and clear. There was little room in the tidy rows for hope to hide. Spreadsheets are the antithesis of faith.

Gaspar reminded himself to ask Will about his idea later. Whatever it was, it had better be a doozy.

12

As the Romans Do

unrise turned the ancient city of Rome to gold. Will gaped at Gothic buildings already decorated tastefully for the holiday as the cab spun them through the narrow street like a bullet fired from a gun. Gaspar barely noticed. His attention was focused on the Maps app and the latest coordinates he'd been able to decipher with the book Beth had left for him in Budapest.

Gaspar pointed at a street just ahead. "There! Turn there. Left."

Will flipped frantically through his Italian phrase book. "Uh . . . *sinistra! Sinistra!*"

Tires squealed as the cab made the turn.

"Well," said Will, "on the outside chance anyone was following us, we've almost certainly lost them. Also, my breakfast."

"Shouldn't be much farther," said Gaspar. "Just ahead. I think."

"Look," said Will. "A bank. That's gotta be the place, right?" Gaspar only nodded. "Uh, you okay?"

"This is close to where the cops found Beth. After . . . you know. This . . . this is probably the last place she ever visited."

"C'mon," said Will, putting a hand on Gaspar's shoulder. "Let's see what she left you."

Moments later, having confirmed Gaspar's identity, a bank manager led them across the lobby and to a vault filled with safe deposit boxes. One of them was Beth's. Gaspar's, now. He checked his notes and entered the combination. When it opened, he nodded to the manager.

"Grazie," said Will.

The manager returned the nod and left as Gaspar put down his overnight bag and the briefcase with the two books. Then he peered into the box. Inside, he found a thin envelope. His fingers trembled a bit as he reached out to touch it. Beth had put this here. It was one of the very last things she'd touched in this world. Crap, if he wasn't careful, this guy really was going to see him cry.

"Huh," said Will. "No book. So I guess we're still missing one volume."

"So far," Gaspar agreed.

They took the envelope to a small table just outside the vault. Gaspar opened it carefully, finding two more parchments in a clear plastic folder and a large, antique key on a silver chain. The first parchment showed a map of what Gaspar guessed was a much older Rome. He passed the map to Will.

"Think that map is . . . of, uh, here? Rome, I mean?"

"Yeah," said Will. "Good thing Rome doesn't change much. Look, I think we're supposed to follow it to this place." He pointed. "See? Holy crap." Will looked at his phrase book. "If I'm reading this right, it's a monastery, but it's called the Graveyard of Secrets!"

"Yeah, nothing creepy about that at all. Any idea where it is?"

Will nodded. "Yeah; it's close. I think we can walk. Which is good, because I don't think I can stomach another Italian cab ride."

Gaspar chuckled. "I hear you. What about the other page? It's another map, I think. But look . . . is that . . . inside somewhere?" He passed the parchment to Will.

"Jeez," said Will. "It looks like a labyrinth! Huh. Yeah, I see why we'll need a map."

"If there was ever a place called the frickin' Grave-yard of Secrets," said Gaspar, "I guess it would be like that." He took the map back from Will and examined

179

it more closely. When he turned it over, he found a yellow sticky note that Beth attached. She'd written a few lines in the neat hand he knew so well. Unconsciously, gently, his fingers traced the last two words. He handed the note to Will.

These items, along with the engraving of the gem, were with your father when they found his body.

Finish what he started, my love.

Will's eyes were wide. "Gaspar, she didn't know about that count. Did she?"

Gaspar shook his head. "Dad . . . We always thought it was just a . . . a random mugging or something. Oh my God. You don't think. . . ?"

"I don't know what to think," said Will. "Except that we'd better freakin' hurry."

"Yeah. I think you're right. Help me grab our stuff, will you?"

Will and Gaspar passed the old, stone monastery's entrance twice before they finally found it. Will shook his head and looked at his phone again. "Gaspar, this place is huge. But I swear, it's not even on any of my maps."

"Just the one Dad had," said Gaspar. "And Beth."

"She really got around, didn't she?"

Gaspar shrugged. "Apparently. And I didn't even know. I thought she was just ... visiting family and stuff."

"I guess she kept the books, huh?"

"That she did."

"And she found this place! Which is pretty close to amazing because it's like someone here doesn't want to be found. Not exactly welcoming, is it?"

"What d'you expect from a place called the Graveyard of Secrets? A neon sign? A red carpet?"

"I see your point," Will acknowledged.

"C'mon. Let's go in."

They found themselves in a long entrance foyer with walls of cold stone. The air smelled dank and stale. At the far side of the room, a stocky monk sat behind a desk of ornately carved wood. Gaspar and Will approached the man slowly. He looked up from his book and spoke rapidly in Italian. Will fumbled for his phrase book. Seeing Will flipping through the pages, the monk said, *"Americano?"*

Will nodded.

The monk spoke again, this time in English. "This place is not open to the public."

"Just a sec," said Gaspar. He reached into his coat pocket for Beth's envelope.

"Uh, un secondo. . . ." Will managed.

Gaspar opened the envelope, revealing the key on its silver chain. "Uh, I think this belongs here." The stocky monk's eyes widened when he saw the key. "I'm, uh, looking for something called the Graveyard of Secrets," said Gaspar.

"Your name?" the monk asked.

"Gaspar Bethlen. This is my assistant, Will Klaus."

"Detective," said Will.

The monk picked up an antique rotary phone that, Gaspar couldn't help thinking, was probably the most modern thing in the building and dialed. After a moment, he spoke softly, making it difficult for Gaspar to hear him. "Someone has come. A Gaspar Bethlen. American. He has a key."

After a moment, the stocky monk hung up the phone. "The Keepers will see you, my child. It seems they have been expecting you."

"Thank you," said Gaspar. "Will, here, take my bag, okay? And gimme that other map."

Outside, two men in expensive Italian suits and sunglasses watched the monastery entrance. One of the men tapped a mobile phone and held it to his ear.

"Bethlen is inside," the man said.

—❧❦❧—

"This place really is a maze," Will said as they turned down another narrow passage.

"Good thing we got a map."

"We've got to be, like, miles underground now."

"You're exaggerating," Gaspar muttered, hoping it was true.

"Maybe," Will acknowledged, "but where even are we?"

"Where Beth was," said Gaspar. "That said, look." He pointed first at the map and then ahead. "I think that just might be our destination, just ahead, yeah?"

Gaspar pushed a door open, and the two men stepped, blinking, into a vast chamber lit by dozens of lamps, many of which hung from the tiles of a great domed ceiling. A winding staircase climbed up to balconies that circled the room, and corridors led off in a dozen or more different directions. Bookcases lined the walls, all the way to the lip of the dome far above.

"My God," said Will. "Look at these books! I bet . . . jeez, I bet most of them don't exist anywhere else in the world. I think I could die very happily in here."

Gaspar smiled. "Could you even read 'em?"

"I can learn. Knack for languages, remember?"

"What about Amazing Ana?"

"Yeah, I'd have to go get her first. Of course, I'd probably have to figure out how to smuggle her past the monks. . . ."

"Later," said Gaspar. "I think we have company." Three monks were approaching them, while nine more held back. "Think they're . . . uh, friendly?"

"Well," Will said, "they're monks, so I think the odds are with us. Also, Beth sent us here."

"Point."

One of the monks, a plump man with white hair cut very short, approached them and extended his hand in a gesture, Gaspar couldn't help thinking, of both welcome and blessing. He found himself relaxing. The monk spoke in English with an almost musical Italian accent. "Welcome, Gaspar Bethlen."

Gaspar wasn't sure what the expected response was, so he bowed his head in what he hoped was an appropriately respectful manner. "Uh, yeah. Hi."

Will was still looking around, gaping. "My God. What is this place?"

A second monk spoke. This man had a ring of thinning red hair surrounding a bald pate and spoke with a Scottish accent. "We are humble servants of the church, my son."

"But for nine centuries and more," the plump monk added, "we have guarded the secrets of the great families of Europe."

"Whoa," said Will. "Wicked!"

The Scottish monk chuckled. "Quite the contrary, my child."

A third monk, younger and thinner than the others, spoke next. He, too, had an Italian accent. "How may we help you, Mr. Bethlen?"

"To be honest, I'm not sure," said Gaspar. "My wife wanted me to come here. Unless I'm, like, way off base here, I think you might have a book for me."

The Scottish monk nodded. "The first volume of *The Roots of the Bethlens*. Your wife has already established your claim quite satisfactorily."

Gaspar smiled. "Of course she did."

"Assuming, of course," the plump monk added, "that you are, in fact, Gaspar Bethlen."

"I have my passport," said Gaspar. "Oh, and my birth certificate. Some, uh, other documents. They're right here in my bag." Gaspar unzipped his overnight bag.

The plump monk smiled. "Your wife was very thorough, I see. Yes. That will suffice."

Gaspar handed him the documents. The monk took the passport to a computer on a desk behind him and scanned it under an illuminated reader like the ones at the airport.

"Uh, how long will that take?" Will asked. "We're kinda in a hurry here...."

At that moment, the computer beeped loudly. The monk turned back to Will and smiled. "Not long." Then, to Gaspar, he said, "Mr. Bethlen, your identity is confirmed." Seeing Gaspar's obvious surprise, the monk added, "We are quite well funded and most decidedly a part of the twenty-first century."

The Scottish monk turned back to his brothers. "Do the Keepers agree?"

One by one, the twelve Keepers nodded solemnly.

The plump monk nodded again. "Your vault is number 379943. You'll find that the book is there, along with something else."

"A gem?" Gaspar guessed.

The plump monk shook his head. "No. A package. Your wife left it with us. For you. Come, I'll show you."

The thin monk raised his hand, another gesture of blessing. "Blessings, Mr. Bethlen. May God's grace give you peace and lead to you what you seek."

Gaspar crossed himself, feeling like a child and hoping the gesture was appropriate. The monks seemed pleased. One by one, most of them left the great chamber, leaving Gaspar and Will alone with the plump monk.

"Gentlemen, this way, if you please?" the plump monk said. "You may leave your bags here, if you like."

Gaspar set his overnight bag down next to Will's, but he kept the briefcase.

In the stone-walled entrance foyer far above, the stocky monk at the ornate desk looked up from his dusty book as four more men in Italian suits pushed their way through the heavy entrance door, moving purposefully toward the entrance to the Graveyard of Secrets.

The stocky monk rose to his feet, but the men did not slow or speak. One of the men started to force the second door open.

"Arresto—!" the stocky monk began.

Before he could finish, one of the men raised a high-caliber Magnum Research Desert Eagle pistol with a suppressor. The monk gasped and raised his hands.

The plump monk led Gaspar and Will into a narrow chamber lined with ancient vaults like the drawers in a mausoleum. The place was labyrinthine and vast, with corridors and stairs leading off in a bewildering number of directions. As near as Gaspar could tell, all seemed to be lined with more of the crypt-like vaults. *Yeah, that's not creepy at all*, he thought.

"No wonder they call this place a graveyard," said Will.

"No kidding," said Gaspar. "God only knows what's buried down here."

"And He alone," the monk agreed.

"Here we are," the plump monk said. He pointed at a brass plaque engraved with the number 379943. "Your key will work here, and nowhere else. Hear this. Do not try any of the others; they are protected by mechanisms both subtle and dangerous."

"Seriously?" said Gaspar.

The monk nodded. "We protect great secrets here, Mr. Bethlen. We take that responsibility very seriously. This place is dangerous to those who do not belong. You, however, belong, but only here, at this one vault. Please, proceed."

Gaspar nodded. He inserted his key carefully, and, with effort, gave it a twist. The mechanism groaned, and Gaspar heard the deep and echoing moan of stone grinding against stone.

Will looked at the monk with his eyebrows raised. "Counterweights?"

The monk smiled coyly. "This place is called the Graveyard of Secrets. We protect them, my son."

The vault slid open. Gaspar looked at Will and took a deep breath. He had to wipe his suddenly damp palms on his pants. "Okay. Yeah. Here goes." Will smiled and nodded to him.

Gaspar peered into the vault drawer. Inside, he found another leather-bound book. It matched the other volumes of *The Roots of the Bethlens*.

"Well," said Gaspar. "It seems I have a complete set."

"Wicked," said Will.

"Damn straight," Gaspar agreed. "Uh, sorry, Father."

"Brother," the plump monk corrected him. He smiled.

Gaspar also found a brown paper-wrapped package in the vault. It was addressed in Beth's hand to:

My Beloved

Gaspar smiled as he slipped the book and the package into his now-full briefcase. Then he turned to the monk. "Thank you," he said, his voice heavy with a brewing cauldron of emotions he couldn't begin to count or name. "Thank you for this."

The monk nodded and smiled. "We honor our ancient oaths, Mr. Bethlen. Now come, let us—"

Before he could finish, three men in suits appeared from the corridor, walking with focused haste and grim determination. None of them wore masks. The first man was carrying a pistol with a long suppressor screwed into the end of the barrel.

The plump monk stepped forward. "What—!"

The men ignored him.

The closest man had his narrowed gaze locked on Gaspar. He, too, spoke English with an Italian accent. "Before I shoot you, I would like to know if you have retrieved all three of the books."

Gaspar took a deep breath, and another. *Okay, keep calm, keep calm....* He held out his now heavier briefcase. "They're all right here."

"Gaspar—" Will began.

The man with the pistol stepped closer, and closer again. "Show me."

Gaspar moved toward the man slowly, with the briefcase extended in his left hand.

"Open it," the man in the suit said. He did not lower the gun.

Gaspar obeyed. The man stepped closer still and bent to peer into the case.

"Give it to me," the man said.

At that moment, Gaspar kicked, hard, catching the man between the legs. The man howled and doubled over in pain.

"No," said Gaspar. He snapped the briefcase shut again.

Gaspar threw a punch with his free hand, catching the man under the chin and knocking him down. The gun slid down the corridor.

Gaspar was aware of Will moving, trying to pull the monk after him. "Father, run!"

"Brother," the monk corrected him.

"RUN!"

The other men seemed to be recovering from their surprise and were reaching for weapons. *Uh oh,* Gaspar thought. That's when an idea struck him. It was desperate, probably stupid, and had he had time to think, he almost certainly wouldn't have tried it. He didn't, and he did.

Gaspar seized the key on its chain from his pocket and dove for another of the vaults—one that wasn't his.

From behind, he heard the monk cry out in alarm. "Bethlen, *no!*"

Gaspar jammed his key into the vault and grunted as he turned it.

At once, he heard again the sound of heavy counterweights shifting as the ancient mechanism worked. Great slabs of stone, each weighing tons, crashed down from the ceiling on both sides of the corridor, sealing the vaults. The air was thick with dust then, and Gaspar coughed violently.

Another crash boomed behind them. Then, at the far end of the corridor, another stone slab slammed down, raising another great cloud of dust.

"Holy crap, Gaspar!" said Will.

Gaspar shook his head. "Okay. That's not what I thought that was gonna do."

They heard another echoing crash, louder than thunder, and then another, several meters closer. They heard another, and another after that.

Gaspar looked back. The corridor was being sealed, section by section. They would be trapped in moments.

Gaspar pushed the surprised monk ahead of him, while Will pulled.

"Run!" Will shouted.

They bolted, as the stone slabs fell, one by one, almost like they were chasing them, falling closer, closer. . . .

The men in suits recovered and followed, running for their lives.

Gaspar, Will, and the monk turned a corner, sprinting. The men in suits were right behind them, barely making the turn as a stone slab fell, rumbling the very walls and sealing the corridor behind them.

At the far end of the corridor, Gaspar heard another groan as counterweights shifted again, straining to push the final slab before the main vault entrance—*up from the floor.*

"Run!" Will cried out again.

Gaspar heard another sound, stone grinding on stone, from above. He craned his head and saw stone seals about the size of his outstretched hand slide away from openings in the ceiling.

Uh oh.

Seconds later, jets of water that Gaspar guessed must be flowing from the canals above streamed down, flooding the corridor. Soon the water was ankle—and then knee—deep. Running was getting harder with every step. Gaspar bowed, protecting his briefcase with his body. The water was rising fast.

"It's flooding," said Will. "Right. Of course it's flooding."

The slabs fell faster. Gaspar looked back over his shoulder. Behind them, one of the men in suits stumbled, but the others didn't slow. Before the fallen man could regain his feet in the rising torrent, another stone slab slammed down, crushing him.

"Holy—"

"Keep running!" Will shouted.

The falling slabs were closer—they were barely ahead of the crashing weights. The exit was just ahead, but Gaspar was beginning to think they weren't going to make it. The slab coming up from the floor ahead of them was chest high and rising.

Gaspar saw Will leap, climb, and make it over the rising slab. Gaspar shoved the monk, sending him sprawling over, too. He pushed himself harder, harder. Then he leapt, throwing his briefcase. His fingers grasped the top of the slab. He heaved himself up. Grunting, he reached the top of the slab, but it was rising with him, fast, pushing him close to the stone ceiling.

Oh shit oh shit oh—

He was going to be crushed, just like the man behind him.

At the last instant, he slid over the top of the slab, feeling his back scraping against the rough ceiling, and dropped hard to the floor of the domed chamber.

The slab boomed against the ceiling above, sealing the passage and showering them with a cloud of dust.

The men behind him weren't so lucky. They were trapped in the corridor. The stone was nearly thick enough to muffle their screams. Nearly.

The monk raced to a set of waist-high levers set into the floor and, using all of his body weight in the effort, moved one. Gaspar heard more counterweights and the distant sound of water draining from the still-sealed corridor.

The monk made the sign of the cross and mouthed a silent prayer.

"Amen," Gaspar muttered.

Will was panting and his eyes were wide. "Those men—"

"Will be dealt with," the monk said.

Will turned his gaze to Gaspar. "There's gonna be more outside."

Gaspar nodded and turned to the monk. "Is there, like, another way out?

The monk shifted uncomfortably and did not meet Gaspar's gaze. "We are the Keepers. Our oaths do not permit us to interfere in the matters of the families whose secrets we guard."

Just then, from above, they heard the distant sound of church bells echoing. The monk smiled and gestured to the stairs behind him. "But of course," he said, "all are welcome to join us in holy prayer, my child."

An hour or so later, Gaspar and Will followed a procession of monks as they left the gates of the chapel and walked through an open Roman plaza. As they entered the bustling square, Gaspar looked around. "I think we're safe."

"Yeah," Will agreed. "For now."

Gaspar and Will pulled off the hooded robes they'd borrowed and handed them back to the plump monk. Another monk returned their bags.

"*Grazie*, Brother Keepers," said Gaspar.

The plump monk held a finger to his lips and then made the sign of the cross in benediction. Gaspar slung his bag over his shoulder, carrying the briefcase in his other hand, and slipped into the crowd, with Will following close behind.

Count Bethlen Tamás missed the days of the landline sorely because no matter how hard he jammed the End Call icon with his thumb, it was nowhere near as satisfying as slamming an old-fashioned receiver down on its cradle, and his fury needed an outlet. He considered, briefly, hurling the handset against the far wall, but he had to remind himself that he was on a budget. Hired muscle was expensive, and it seemed he would need more before this matter was concluded at last. Then, he would be able to hurl as many handsets as he wished.

Abban stood by the doorway, waiting, arms folded across his ape-like chest, one eyebrow raised, an impertinent gesture that the Count had always found particularly irritating. The man was forgetting himself. Did no one respect the old ways any longer? The will of the nobility was to be enforced, not questioned.

"The men you hired for me in Rome have failed," the Count told Abban. "The Americans have eluded them, and they still have my books."

Abban shrugged. "I can hire more. They must still be in Rome, yes? We can find them—"

"No," the Count said. "They won't be there long. Don't worry. I know where they'll be going next."

Abban couldn't—or didn't bother to—hide his surprise. "How—?"

"Because it's where *I* went," the Count snapped. "But I didn't have the bloody books, so it did me no good! I want you to go yourself. Take Jael. I will hire more Italians to support you. And wear a damned suit! I want to you both to look like gentlemen."

"I don't think it's gentlemen you want for this kind of work," Abban said.

"Remember who you represent," the Count said, and there was ice in his voice. "You leave within the hour. I'll have a jet ready."

13

The Star in the East

ill and Gaspar moved fast, weaving through side streets and alleys, looking over their shoulders constantly for signs of pursuit. "Look," Will said when they paused to catch their breath. "The Metro. It's their subway."

"Dude, I know what a Metro is," said Gaspar. "Any idea where it goes?"

"Somewhere that's not here," Will pointed out. "Right now, that's good enough for me. Rome's a big city. Let's make it harder for the Count's men to find us. Yes?"

"That's actually not a bad idea," Gaspar acknowledged. "C'mon."

They used Gaspar's credit card at a ticket machine and chose a direction at random. When they reached the Termini Station, which seemed to be a central hub, as near as they could tell from the map, they changed lines and, again, chose a direction at random. After passing a few stops, they exited. They found a shop and purchased new coats and hats, hoping that would make them at least somewhat harder to spot. Will bought an Italian phrase book. "My phone's getting low on batteries," he explained.

Then, suddenly, Gaspar realized he had absolutely no idea what to do next. Nothing in his life had prepared him for running through Europe from hired killers. He opened his mouth to speak, but no words came out. He hadn't even thought to look to see where they'd gotten off the frickin' train. He literally had no idea where they were, beyond somewhere in the greater Rome metropolitan area.

"We need food," Will suggested. "And caffeine. Definitely caffeine. And we need to plan our next move."

"I'm for all of those," Gaspar agreed. "Yeah."

Then, because Will had read more than his fair share of thrillers and detective novels, they found a crowded café with good views in all directions—and multiple exits should they have to bolt.

Once they'd ordered, with the help of Will's phrase book, Gaspar pulled the brown paper-wrapped package from the briefcase. "Ready for another clue, detective?"

"Always," said Will.

Gaspar fumbled with the paper and then opened the box. Inside, he found a folded note along with a business card clipped to an index card and a CD. On the index card, Beth had neatly transcribed a URL.

Gaspar opened the note first and read aloud:

Here is your next clue, my love. To claim your legacy, you will need the answer to four questions.

Who is the founder of your line? To where did he travel? What led him there? What did he find there?

Learn his name first. Then you can begin to answer the others.

Text your answers to the same number, 47613!

Will's brow furrowed. "What in the world is all that?"

Gaspar offered Will his best *Seriously?* glare. "You tell me. Detective."

"I'm, uh, working on it. Let's start with the clues, shall we?"

At that moment, the waiter brought their plates of steaming pasta carbonara and crusty bread with olive oil, along with bottles of sparkling water and two espressos.

Gaspar scowled as the waiter departed. "Why can't you get a decent-sized cup of coffee and a plain old regular glass of stupid water on this continent?"

"Why can't you get pasta and cheese like this back in the States?" Will countered. "What's the business card?"

"A university professor. Richard Summers. Astronomy. Here in Rome."

"That's convenient," said Will. "Any idea what that has to do with your family?"

Gaspar pursed his lips as he thought. "My dad was a professor."

"But religion, not astronomy. He specialized in the Nativity."

Gaspar nodded as he dipped a piece of the bread in the olive oil. "Beth was one of his students. Did you know that?"

"No," said Will.

"That's how I met her."

Will twirled some pasta around his fork. "Wow, but this is good. How about the index card? That's a URL?"

"YouTube," Gaspar acknowledged with another nod.

"Shall we give it a try?"

Gaspar fumbled with the phone. He made a fat-fingered typo, so he had to reenter the URL. When he did, a video of a familiar old children's song began to play.

John Jacob Jingleheimer Schmidt,
His name is my name too.
Whenever we go out
The people always shout,
There goes John Jacob Jingleheimer Schmidt!
Tra la, la, la, la, la
John Jacob Jingleheimer Schmidt,
His name is my name too—

"Okay," said Will, "I think that's enough."

Gaspar nodded and stopped the music. "His name is my name, too."

"That's not much help either," said Will. "Not yet. What's the CD?

"The Greatest Hits of Bill Haley and the Comets," said Gaspar.

Will grinned. "Oh! The 'Rock Around the Clock' guys. No kidding. I guess they had other hits. Who knew?"

Gaspar returned the grin. "I thought you'd be too young to remember them. Because I sure as hell am."

"They did the theme on the first seasons of *Happy Days,*" Will explained. "I'm part of the TV sitcom rerun generation, don'tcha know."

"Any idea what it means?"

"Maybe there's a clue in the lyrics?"

Gaspar shook his head. "I don't think Beth would've expected me to be carrying a CD player along."

201

"Good point. She probably would have sent another YouTube link if we were supposed to listen to a specific song." Will shook his head. "So unless your ancestor is the Fonz, this detective is stumped. Pass me the pepper, will you?"

Gaspar sighed and opened the final volume of *The Roots of the Bethlens,* the one the monks had been keeping. "We need to know what's in this book. Maybe we need this to unlock the clues."

"That makes sense. At least we have all three now. Hey, let me have it. I have an idea."

Gaspar slid the book across the table to Will. Will pushed his plate aside, opened the book, and began photographing the pages with his phone. "I can text them to Ana," he explained.

"Do it fast," said Gaspar. "We don't know where those guys are."

"They don't know where we are either," said Will. "At least we'll be fed and caffeinated. Want another coffee?"

—◦❦◦—

They'd just finished their third espressos when Will's phone buzzed.

"Hello?" Will said. "Ana, hey! Yeah, yeah, we're okay. Just a sec. I'm gonna put you on speaker."

Will tapped the icon and put the phone on the table.

"Hi, Ana," said Gaspar.

"Hi, Gaspar!" Ana said. "Will, I just got the pages you sent."

Will grinned. "Excellent. Can you read them?"

They heard Ana take a deep breath. "It's difficult. The writing is . . . archaic. More so than the other volumes. This is an ancient record. But I think I've got most of it. It's fascinating! It was begun by a man named Bethlen. That was his only name, not just the surname. He left the monastery of his father with his two sons."

"The two branches of the Bethlens," said Gaspar.

"Yes," said Ana. "To his older son, Bethlen bequeathed his lands and earthly wealth. To the other, the legacy."

"The gem," said Will.

"Maybe," said Ana. "The secret, anyway. So it could be either, both, or neither. The book doesn't say. When war raged across Europe, one of your ancestors took the legacy back to the monastery, so the holy men there could protect it until his progeny could someday return and claim it."

Will looked up at Gaspar. "Dude, what is it with your family and monasteries?"

Gaspar shrugged.

"But I bet that monastery is our last stop," said Will. "The other one, I mean. Where the first Bethlen was."

"But here's the interesting part," said Ana. "Guess what Bethlen's father's name was?"

Gaspar saw Will's eyes pop open wide as a realization struck him. "It was Gaspar, wasn't it?"

Ana laughed. "It was! How did you know?"

Will whistled the second line of "John Jacob Jingleheimer Schmidt."

"Oh," said Gaspar, realizing. "His name is my name too. Good job, detective. You got that clue before me."

"Apparently," said Ana. "I missed some adventures."

"That you did," said Gaspar.

"I'll fill you in later," Will promised.

"Anyway," said Ana, "Gaspar seems to be a family name. Dating back to the founder of the Bethlen line. How about that?"

"Yeah, nobody hangs a name like Gaspar on a kid without a damn good reason." Gaspar saw Will grinning and scowled. "Uh, no offense," Will added.

Gaspar rolled his eyes. "If I had a dollar for every time some playground punk called me Gaspar the Friendly Ghost. . . ."

"I confess I might have used a nickname," said Will. "If I. . . ."

"I had one in college," said Gaspar. "But I made damn sure it didn't stick."

Ana laughed. "I have to know. What was it?"

"Rock," said Gaspar.

"Rock?" said Will. "That doesn't sound so bad. Better than ghost, anyway."

"It was short for 'Rock the Gas-par.'" He sung the last words to "Rock the Casbah," the tune made famous by The Clash. "Also? If I hear a peep of that again, so help me, I will punch you, Klaus. No matter who I hear it from. Ana, if you ever want Will here punched. . . ."

Ana laughed. "I will call you Rock."

Will suppressed his laugh if not his grin. "We better get back to business," he suggested. "What else is there, Ana?"

"Just what we already know," said Ana.

"Any idea who this first Gaspar might have been?" Gaspar asked.

"I'll do a Web search on Gaspar," said Ana. They heard her tapping on a keyboard. After a moment, she said, "*Hmmm.* Not much help. There are more than ten thousand hits. A lot of them are about the famous American baseball player."

"I think we can rule him out," said Will. "His only gem was a baseball diamond."

"Seriously?" said Gaspar.

"Sorry," said Will.

"Let's see," said Ana. "There's a Portuguese sausage company, an eighteenth-century pirate—"

"Pirate would be cool," said Will.

Gaspar shrugged and chuckled softly. "Might explain the gem."

205

"There's also a city in Brazil," Ana continued, "one of the Magi, a Flemish artist, an actor in Argentina—"

"Wait," said Gaspar. "Did you say Magi?"

"I did," said Ana.

"Did I miss something?" said Will.

"The Magi," said Ana. "The wise men who visited the Christ child in Bethlehem!"

"Ha!" said Gaspar. "Here I'm ahead of you. Detective. Gaspar was supposedly one of the three wise men. Although it helps to have grown up with a dad who's a Nativity scholar. Since it was Dad's area of study, maybe there's a connection?"

Ana's voice was quiet. "Maybe ... oh my God! Maybe that's the secret!"

"Wow," said Will. "That would be ... quite a lineage."

"I was joking," said Gaspar.

"Still, it's certainly an interesting idea," said Ana.

Gaspar shook his head. "No. Uh uh. That's impossible."

"Gaspar, it adds up!" said Will. "Your Dad's research! His whole life's work!"

"I'm starting to believe the pirate theory," said Gaspar.

"I think this is ... interesting," said Ana. "Don't dismiss it so quickly."

"C'mon," said Gaspar. "We're talking about the literal frickin' Magi. Gold, myrrh, frankincense! That just can't be right."

Will frowned. "Why not?"

"What do you mean why not?" Gaspar shook his head again and wished he had another coffee. "I mean, come the hell on! There's no proof Jesus even existed."

"Actually, that's not true," said Will. "There's—"

"Really?" said Gaspar. "Really? A lecture? That's what you think I'm looking for here?"

"Well," said Will. "There's one way to find out. Text the answer."

"Whatever," said Gaspar. He nodded and entered GASPAR THE MAGI and hit send. After a second, a reply came. Gaspar gaped, shook his head, and then read it aloud, "That's right, my love! Now the next one!"

"If it's true, we should know the answers to the remaining questions!" said Will. "Who is the father of your line? Gaspar the Magi. Where did his journey take him?"

"To Bethlehem, the city of David," said Ana. She sounded excited.

Gaspar shook his head but entered the word BETHLEHEM and hit send again.

Seconds later, he read the next reply aloud: "Yes! And what led him there?"

"I don't believe it," Gaspar muttered.

"What led him?" Will asked. "We know that, too, right? The star in the east. The star of Bethlehem!"

"Try it," said Ana.

Gaspar entered THE STAR IN THE EAST and hit send.

A few seconds later, he received a reply: MORE SPECIFIC?

Will read it aloud and then mused, "I guess the star in the east is a little too obvious. Try the star of Bethlehem?"

Gaspar did so, and after a moment received the same reply. "No dice."

"Huh," said Will. "More specific. A mystery that scholars have been trying to solve for two thousand years. Well. I guess we'll just have to solve it. How hard can that be?"

Gaspar chuckled. "Yeah. Good thing I got a detective."

"The answer will be something precise," said Ana. "Don't you think? Maybe I can do another Web search. Aren't there a lot of theories about what the Star of Bethlehem was? A, uh, stellar conjunction or something?"

Hearing how Ana's quick mind worked, Gaspar had to suppress another grin. It really was like having a second Will on the phone. "If there's a lot, that's not going to help us," he said. "I mean, unless we try them all one by one?"

"You make an excellent point," said Ana. "I suppose the mystery would not have remained unsolved if one could simply Google the answer."

"I think there's an easier way," said Will. He held up the business card, grinning. "I think this is something an astronomer can help with."

"I guess it's time to go pay this professor a visit," said Gaspar.

"Be careful," said Ana. "Both of you."

"Ana," Will began. "I . . . I. . . ." He didn't finish. He fumbled with his face mask.

Gaspar rolled his eyes. "Oh, for God's sake, you wuss. Tell her."

After a too-long, awkward moment, Ana was the one who broke the silence. "Would it help if I said I love you too, first?"

Will beamed. "It might. I love you, Ana."

Gaspar could almost hear Ana smiling through the phone. "Come back soon."

In her flat, Ana smiled as she tapped the icon to end the call. She floated around her living room and realized she'd been humming an old Hungarian folk song, one her parents used to dance to in long-ago, half-remembered happy times. She wondered what it would be like to dance with Will in a club with real music, perhaps from the current century. *Awkward, most likely*, she admitted to herself. But she could work with him.

Just then, Ana heard a sudden sound at her front door. She stopped and spun, startled. Her eyes went wide and her heart pounded.

She heard another crash, at the door again, louder this time. Her hands covered her mouth as she gasped.

A short and surprisingly not-terrifying cab ride took Gaspar and Will through the southeastern suburbs of Rome to Tor Vergata University. The campus was sprawling and, to Gaspar's eye, unexpectedly modern. He'd been expecting less concrete and more, well, Gothic.

It didn't take them long to find the office building they were looking for, but Gaspar kept looking over his shoulder as they walked, watching the other pedestrians intently. None of the students looked especially like thugs, but Gaspar eyed them suspiciously all the same.

"Maybe they gave up?" Will suggested, and Gaspar heard hope in his voice. Gaspar didn't share that optimism.

"Is that what you think?"

Will didn't bother to answer.

They found the office they were looking for on the third floor. Gaspar gave Will a glance, shrugged, and knocked.

After a moment, a thin, balding man in his fifties opened the door. He was dressed in jeans with a business shirt and tie under a tweed jacket. "*Sì?*"

"Professor Summers?" Gaspar said, hoping the man spoke English.

"That's me," the man said, pushing his wire-rimmed glasses back into place. He had a friendly smile and a British accent.

"I'm sorry to disturb you, sir. My name is Gaspar Bethlen. I think you might have known my wife, Beth—"

"Why yes!" the professor said. "She said you'd be by some day. I'm just finishing a call. Rather important, really. Why don't you wait in the library? It's just downstairs and right across the way there. I'm afraid my office is rather, uh, close, as you Americans might say."

Gaspar and Will found a table in the comfy, book-lined room. The volumes there weren't much help; Will's Italian wasn't great, even with his new phrase book to help. Instead, he researched on his phone. "There's not much about the Magi in the Bible," he said. "They only appear in one Gospel."

"Does it say where they came from?" Gaspar asked.

"No," Will admitted.

"So we're still at square one."

"It doesn't give their names, either," Will added. "In fact, it doesn't even say how many there were."

Gaspar shook his head. "No. Three. Three kings. You know." He sang a line from the old carol: *We three kings of Orient are . . . Blah, blah, blah, but see it says three!*

Will chuckled. "Uh uh. Three *gifts* are mentioned, and the fact that there was more than one. The truth is, a lot of the stuff most of us lay folk think is in the Bible . . . just really isn't."

Gaspar raised his eyebrows. "And how do you happen to know that, detective?"

Will grinned. "I read one of your dad's books. Remember?"

"Touché."

"Look, I have a cousin. His name's Jason Cook—he's American but he's living in London so the time zone's not going to get us, or not much. Anyway, he just finished his doctorate in comparative mythology and folklore. Not exactly your dad, but maybe he'll know something. Or know someone who does."

"Can we call him?"

"He's on WhatsApp. I'll get him now." When Jason answered, Will put his phone on speaker. Will outlined the situation quickly.

"Ouch," said Jason. "I'm afraid that's a little out of my area of expertise. I don't know much more than what they taught us in Sunday school. And not as much of that as my mom is probably hoping."

"I see," said Will, disappointed.

"But listen," said Jason, "I have a friend who might know more. Do you remember my pal Jessie Malone?"

"I do," said Will. "One of your grad school friends, right? Another American in London?"

"That's her," said Jason. "Anyway, she knows a bit more about biblical history than I do. And trust me, she's kind of an expert on Christmas miracles, too. Give me ten or fifteen minutes, and I'll have her WhatsApp you."

True to Jason's word, Jessie Malone called a few minutes later. After introductions and small talk, Jessie began to tell them what she knew of the wise men.

"There's not much at all about the Magi in the modern Bible," Jessie explained. She had a nice voice; Gaspar found himself liking her.

"Will was just telling me that," said Gaspar. "And that we don't know where they came from."

"True enough," Jessie said. "The Bible only says that wise men came from somewhere to the east. Although the phrase 'from their own country' implies somewhere other than Judea or Palestine. In fact, the Matthew Gospel's not even clear on *when* they arrive. Most assume it's at the Nativity—I should mention that Matthew's Gospel makes no mention of shepherds or the stable and manger—but some scholars argue that the text actually has the Magi arriving when Jesus is a toddler, or even a young child. For one thing, Matthew uses the word for *child* rather than *infant.*"

"Wait," said Gaspar. "I'm sure I remember the shepherds in the Bible. Angel of the Lord, sore afraid, and all that. Right?"

"Those are in *Luke,*" said Jessie. "In fact, only Luke covers the birth at all; Matthew is more concerned with matters that occurred before and after the Nativity. The Magi seem to fall into that latter category. Luke, on the other hand, doesn't mention the Magi *or* the star, or the flight into Egypt."

"So where does all the three wise men stuff come from?" asked Gaspar.

"Oh," said Jessie, "there is a wealth of folklore about the Magi. Some of it comes from the so-called apocryphal Gospels, books that didn't make the cut when the modern Bible was finally assembled. Others seem to be just legends."

"So they're just nonsense," said Gaspar. "Fiction."

"Oh, I certainly didn't say *that*," said Jessie. "First, many modern scholars argue that some of the lost Gospels, like Thomas, for example, perhaps *should* have been included. Which, let me tell you, shocked my poor undergrad self to the soul. Although I'm afraid the Infancy Gospels don't usually make even the most radical cuts. They seem to be at best simple accumulations of folklore, albeit fascinating ones. One of my colleagues who actually focuses on this stuff calls them Jesus fanfic. But as I of all people can attest, folklore usually has an original source. Sometimes, tracing that source can lead to some surprising truths."

"So what *do* we know about these Magi?" asked Gaspar. "Anything?"

"Well," Jessie began, "This really isn't my area, and I haven't done any serious study since I was an undergrad. But I did three semesters, so I'll tell you what I remember. The word *Magi* is the Latin form of a Greek word, *magos*, which is a derivative from Old Persian *Magupati*, the priestly caste of a branch of Zoroastrianism. As part of their religion, these priests paid particular attention to the stars. In fact, they gained an international reputation for astrology—an impressive feat for the times."

"You mean like . . . horoscopes?" said Gaspar.

"You have to remember, at that time, astrology was a highly regarded science," said Jessie, "later giving rise to aspects of mathematics and even astronomy, as well as the modern practice of fortune-telling going by the same name. A clearer indication of their astrological credentials is in the phrase which the King James Version of the Bible translates as *enquired of them diligently*. That's actually a Greek technical word referring directly to astrology, with no direct translation into English. Their religious practices and use of astrology caused derivatives of the term *Magi* to be applied to the occult in general and led to the English term *magic.*"

"So if these priests *had* seen something unusual in the stars, some sign or augur—"

"There is every reason to think they would have followed it," said Jessie. "Even to the ends of the Earth. That's something else I can relate to. Although to be honest, even given the conditions of the day, it's not as far as you might think from Iran to Palestine."

"Funny, isn't it?" said Will. "The long-awaited Messiah is born, and God doesn't send out invitations to the rabbis and Jewish elite. He tells lowly shepherds and astrologer priests of an entirely different religion."

"Jessie, do you think it's possible that there was a *literal* Star of Bethlehem?" Gaspar asked.

"Why not?" Jessie countered. "Surely, more miraculous things have happened. I'd say life itself, or even the totally impossible existence of the universe, is a greater wonder by far. Compared to that, a star in the east is nothing."

"Then you don't think the author of Matthew might have, like, just . . . invented the Star of Bethlehem?" Will probed. "Maybe to help link the birth with the Old Testament prophecies or something?" He looked back at Gaspar and winked. "I also got that from your dad's book."

"Scholars have certainly made that argument," Jessie conceded. "But frankly, I don't think it holds water.

While it's true that the author of Matthew obviously couldn't have been an eyewitness, he seems certainly to have been, at the very least, working from a well-established oral tradition—although linking the events directly to the Old Testament prophecies may have been the Matthew author's own addition. But had Matthew been just, like, concocting events to match the old prophecies, it seems to me he could have picked some more obviously appropriate ones and, frankly, made a better job of it. In any case, the idea that Matthew would have just made up the star out of the blue seems a little far-fetched. He relied on an established oral tradition, I think."

"We need to know about that star," said Gaspar. "Anything you can tell us."

"I'm afraid you might need an astronomer for that," Jessie admitted.

Will grinned. "We just happen to have one. Here comes Professor Summers now!"

"Hey," said Jessie, "call me back, okay? I'd love to hear what he has to say."

"You bet," Will promised her.

Will ended the call just as Professor Summers joined them. "Sorry for the delay, gents," he said as he pulled over a chair and sat.

"Not at all," said Will. "Thank you for sparing a few minutes for us."

Professor Summers nodded. "How can I help?"

"Professor," said Gaspar, "do you think it's possible that there was a . . . a literal Star of Bethlehem?"

The professor chuckled. "That's what your wife wanted to know. Astronomers like me have wondered about that for two thousand years. I've heard theories. Fireball meteors. A supernova. But none of those really fits the bill, eh?"

Will shook his head. "I don't think so."

The professor smiled. "I'll tell you what. Let's go to the planetarium and take a look, shall we? That's what I did with Mrs. Bethlen. I think something I showed her there gave her an idea, but to be honest, I'm not sure what!"

The university's planetarium wasn't at all like the one Gaspar and Beth had visited at the Museum of Science back in Boston. That one had featured high-tech projectors and 4K screens. This one was an old place, small, with layers of stars and planets driven across the dome by elegant gears and brass clockwork. It was a delicate and beautiful instrument that made Gaspar think of some fantastic, steampunkish orrery imagined by Leonardo da Vinci or Jules Verne.

While Professor Summers worked the antiquated levers that moved the mechanical stars in the dome of the sky, Will got Jessie on the phone again and introductions were exchanged.

"Now then," said Professor Summers. "We're going to attempt to solve the age-old mystery of the Star of Bethlehem. Before dinner would be nice. Where are we so far?"

"This is what we know," said Jessie. "First, the star seems to have appeared at least twice—once as a sign to the Magi in their own country, and then as a, uh, directional sign over Bethlehem. Sort of like old-world GPS. Next, the star must have had a specific astrological significance to them."

"Some special meaning," said Will.

"Exactly," said Jessie. "Second, according to the biblical account, the star moved—it went before them. Finally, it stood over Bethlehem to pinpoint the location of the baby Jesus."

"Handy," said Gaspar.

"Indeed," Professor Summers agreed.

"Third, the star was seen in the east," said Jessie. "There may be even more to that. The Greek phrase used in Matthew, *ex en Anatole*, is considered by many scholars to be a technical term for an acronychal rising."

"Say what?" said Gaspar.

"An appearance of a star in the east just as the sun sets in the west," Professor Summers explained.

"Oh," said Gaspar. "So what we need to do is look for is an object that can meet all that criteria."

"Let me show you some of the ideas I showed Mrs. Bethlen," said Professor Summers. "First, way back in the year 1603, the famous astronomer Johannes Kepler suggested a planetary conjunction. His calculation showed that a conjunction of Jupiter and Saturn occurred in the year 7 BCE. The two bright objects seemed to combine to make one new one."

"I've heard that theory," said Jessie.

The professor adjusted his controls, and the great clockwork spun and whirred as the stars shifted their positions in the dome above. "There. You see?"

The two lights came near to each other, like a pair of ballroom dancers bowing, but did not touch.

Gaspar shook his head. "They're close. But they don't really look like one star, do they?"

"And the Magi were experienced and knowledgeable stargazers," said Will. "No way this would have fooled them. No way. And it doesn't move, appear twice, or hang over one place."

"You're right," said Jessie. "I think so, anyway. Plus, conjunctions don't move, so it wouldn't fit the criteria in the Gospel. In any case, it would have been brief. Those Magi would have had to race like crazy to follow it. Not to mention the fact that they knew the night skies; they would have known what a conjunction was. Finally, the astrologers of the day kept fantastic records, and the conjunction doesn't seem to have caused much of a fuss."

"Did any events cause that kind of, um, fuss?" asked Gaspar.

"I'd be interested to know that myself," said Professor Summers. "In any case, the only object I can think of that would fit all of that criteria is a comet."

"I should have thought of that!" Will exclaimed.

"Yes," Jessie agreed. "Me, too. In fact, the Jewish historian Josephus, nearly a contemporary of Christ's, mentions a sword-comet that 'stood' over Jerusalem in the year 66 CE as a harbinger of doom. The Persian astronomers made similar notes. In fact, the word Josephus uses for 'stood' is the same one that Matthew uses when describing the star in his Gospel."

"Yes," said Professor Summers. "I'm aware of the notes the Persian astronomers made. I made the same suggestion to your wife. Here, I'll show you." The professor moved the levers again, and the stars shifted. A great comet shaped from illuminated brass appeared on the eastern horizon. "This is the sky in the year 66."

"A comet. . . ." Will mused. Gaspar could see a change come over his face as an idea struck him. "Gaspar, let me see your CD."

Gaspar reached into his jacket and pulled out the CD Beth had given him. Bill Haley and the Comets. He handed it to Will.

"Could this year 66 comet have been Halley's comet?" Will pronounced Halley the same way that Bill Haley had: *Hailey*.

221

The professor cleared his throat. "Halley." He pronounced it like Halle Berry's first name. "To answer your question, almost certainly. Most of the world made note of it, including the Persian priests."

Gaspar shook his head. "That can't be it. The year 66 is, like, way too late for the birth of Christ."

"But the comet returns," said Will. "Right?"

Professor Summers nodded. "Every seventy-six years."

"Wait," said Gaspar. I know the traditional date for the birth of Christ—December twenty-fifth in the year one—is obviously a mistake, if only because shepherds would have known better than to be outside with flocks in the middle of winter. I learned that much from reading Dad's stuff, anyway. So, uh, when *was* Christ born?"

"The usual 'cut off' for the earliest possible date is considered to be around 8 BCE," said Jessie. "I also read some of your father's work, Mr. Bethlen. In school."

Gaspar smiled.

"Halley would have come around in about 12 BCE," Will calculated. "Is that right?"

Professor Summers nodded. He adjusted his levers, turning the sky back. The comet rose again. "I showed this to your wife as well, sir."

"But that's four years too early," said Gaspar.

"At least," Will acknowledged.

"Is it?" asked Jessie.

"Uh, what do you mean?" asked Gaspar.

"Well," said Jessie, "a detailed study of both the Roman historical records and the New Testament accounts suggests that the crucifixion happened around the year 36 CE, rather than the more traditionally accepted 33 CE. I'm just rechecking my notes, but yes. The year 36 is widely accepted by just about all New Testament scholars today. Let's take that as a starting point for dating the birth."

"That sounds reasonable," said Gaspar. "So it's simple. Subtract thirty-three. That gives us the year 3 CE, correct?"

"Not so fast," said Jessie. "Why thirty-three?"

"That's what the Bible gives as Christ's age when he was crucified," Gaspar said. "Uh, isn't that right?"

"No," said Jessie, "the New Testament never gives an age. More, the generally accepted, traditional thirty-three just doesn't ring true, not if you read the text carefully. Which, I must say, also shocked my undergrad self. First, Jesus is referred to as rabbi."

"Doesn't that just mean teacher?" said Will.

"Mostly," said Jessie. "But there's more to it. To be called a rabbi in Jewish society way back then, one would have had to be close to fifty, at the very least. Also, Bishop Irenaeus wrote as early as the second century CE that Jesus was fifty when he taught. Irenaeus was a student of Polycarp, who knew people who had actually *seen* the living Jesus. More, the Gospel of John refers to Jesus as 'not yet fifty,' seeming to imply that he is at least close to that age. John also relates that Jesus compares his life to the temple in Jerusalem; he calls it 'forty and six years in the building.' The temple didn't take that long to build. So what did he mean?"

"Christ is saying that he is the same age as the temple," said Will. "Right?"

"That puts Christ at forty-eight when he was crucified, agreeing with all sorts of other hints and clues that he was nearly fifty," said Jessie.

"If I'm doing the math correctly," said Professor Summers, "Jesus would have been born in the year 12 BCE." He started adjusting his levers again.

"The exact year the temple that stood in Jerusalem in Jesus's day was built," said Jessie.

"And a year that Halley's comet appeared in the east!" Will exclaimed.

Gaspar's heart was thumping. This was what Beth has discovered; this was the solution to her riddle.

This, this was the answer.

It had to be. It just had to be. He could feel it. He could almost feel Beth there with him. He could almost feel her smiling.

"Just so," said Professor Summers. "And unlike the conjunctions, Halley *was* noted with awe in the Mediterranean and Middle East regions."

"In 12 BCE," Jessie added, "the chroniclers noted that the comet was considered an omen of great import, a harbinger of the dawn of a golden age."

"And it fits our other criteria, doesn't it?" said Professor Summers. "It would have appeared twice, once heading toward the sun, once passing back on its orbit back into deep space. It would have appeared to hang . . . or to stay over one point."

"Oh my God," said Will. "Oh my God."

Gaspar winked at Will. "You *are* a detective."

"I get the job done," Will said. "With a lot of serious help from my friends. Thank you, Jessie. I owe you big time."

"Pay me back by telling me how all this ends, okay?" said Jessie.

"I promise," said Will. He ended the call and looked over at Gaspar and grinned. "Go ahead. Try it."

Gaspar nodded and opened the text app on the phone. As Will watched, Gaspar typed HALLEY'S COMET and hit send.

"Here goes nothing," said Gaspar.

"Or everything," said Will.

The second that passed seemed to take an eternity, but the answer came: RIGHT! TELL PROFESSOR SUMMERS HE CAN GIVE YOU YOUR NEXT CLUE.

The professor laughed. "Bravo, gents. And yes, it seems I do have a package for you, don't I? I promised her I wouldn't tell you until she gave the okay. Let's run by my office, shall we?"

—◦❦◦—

After thanking the professor and saying their good-byes, Gaspar and Will found a bench in the courtyard. The sun was already setting, and most of the students were gone. "So what do we have?" Will asked, nodding to the package.

"One way to find out," said Gaspar. He tore away the brown paper and opened the box. Inside, he found a new golf shirt still with its tags, a paperback book, another card with a YouTube URL, and a sealed letter. Gaspar recognized the ivory linen stationary that Beth always used. *Had* always used. He closed his eyes for a moment and then opened them again. On the envelope, she had written:

My Beloved

"Golf shirt," said Will. "Sweet. What's the book?"

Gaspar held it up. The cover photo shows kids playing in a swimming pool. "*Pool Games for Children.*"

"Huh. No obvious help there."

"I guess not," said Gaspar. He put the book on the bench and unfolded the golf shirt it, running his hands along the fabric. Beth had touched that shirt, his Beth.

"What's the URL?" Will asked.

Gaspar shrugged. "Try it for me, will you?"

"Sure." Will entered the URL into the browser on his phone. "It's called 'The Call and the Answer' by a group named De Dannan. Ring any bells?"

"De Dannan is a traditional Celtic group from Ireland," said Gaspar. "Let me tell you. Beth dearly loved the old music, as she called it."

"Was she Irish?"

Gaspar smiled fondly. "So she claimed. The AncestryDNA test disagreed, but that didn't sway her."

The singer, an Irish woman, sang, and the voice and words were so lovely that Gaspar felt his heart break anew with every chorus:

> *You are the call, I am the answer,*
> *You are the wish and I am the way,*
> *You're the music, I the dancer,*
> *You are the night and I am the day,*
> *You are the night and I am the day. . . .*

"That song," said Will. "Nothing against the cool shirt and the phone and all, but so far, I think that's the best gift yet. What a lovely, lovely message to send. Wow. You wanted something to hold onto, man. That just might be it."

"You may be right," said Gaspar. He shook his head; he had to get himself under control. He was not, *not*, going to cry in front of this nerd. He swallowed and

227

managed a nod. "You may be right. But knowing my Beth, it's a clue as well as a love note. That's so totally like her. . . ."

"I wish I'd known her better," said Will. And then, suddenly, he laughed. "Oh. I see it now. Of course it's a clue. Of course it is."

"Oh?" said Gaspar. "Figured something out, have you? Detective?"

"Gaspar, your nice new shirt. It's not a golf shirt! I mean, it is, but they also call them polo shirts! See? Look at the logo."

Gaspar looked. Embroidered on the left breast was a tiny figure mounted on a horse and wielding a polo mallet.

"See?" Will continued. "Even the brand is Polo." He flipped through the pages of the pool games book.

Gaspar frowned. "So?"

"And the song! 'The Call and the Answer.' That's also the name of a kind of children's game. The kind where the *it* player calls, and the other players must respond. Games like Blind Man's Bluff or. . . ."

Will held up the book, which he had opened to a chapter on a familiar water game. They finished the sentence together: ". . . Marco Polo!"

"Not bad, detective," said Gaspar. "Not bad at all."

"I'm checking the Marco Polo page on Wikipedia," said Will. "Oh. Hey. You're not going to believe this."

"What?"

"Marco Polo claimed to have visited the tombs of three men called Melchior, Balthasar ... and Gaspar."

"The Magi. Huh. So what do we do with that?"

"Try the letter?" Will suggested.

Gaspar took a deep breath. He wasn't ready for that. He wasn't ready at all.

Maybe he could put it off. They could find a place to spend the night. They could think, make a plan. . . .

And he'd still be no more ready then than he was now. Besides, the Count's men were still out there, somewhere.

Gaspar took another breath. With trembling fingers, he opened the envelope. Carefully, he unfolded pages that still carried the faint ghost scent of Beth's perfume. And ah, Christ, he was starting to cry after all, and right in front of Will.

His eyes were wet with tears, so it took him a long time to read the words that she had written:

My Love, my heart, my dearest darling,

It is so hard to write these words, my dear, sweet man, because there is so much, so very much I wish I could say to you. I have tried to say it all, every day during our precious, golden time together, but as I near the end of this journey at last, I know that all the days in all the years in all the great and endless eons of the universe are not enough, not nearly, to say all the things there are to say to the one you love. Forever is not nearly long enough, a thousand times forever is not, and our time is so short, so fleeting. It makes me sad to think how much time we wasted on the inconsequential things, the things that never matter, not in the long run. But then, maybe they do matter. Maybe everything matters, even the smallest things, because they are all a part of our love, our life, and everything that we do for love is what matters most of all in the world, isn't it? Our lives are like the wink of a firefly, flashing with glorious light, and then gone. But for that moment, oh, how we shine!

My heart is so full, so full of love for you, and so full of joy when I think of the life we've shared, and all the happiness we've known. You have been my sun and my stars, the bright light of my life, the center of all joy. How can I stand to leave you? Oh Gaspar, my Gaspar, my love. I miss you already, and I haven't even left you yet!

Ah, but this is not the time for goodbyes, my heart. This is a time for the giving of a gift! This is my last gift to you, my love, one last Christmas memory, to celebrate all the Christmas mystery puzzles that have come before. I had planned simply to give you some great and elaborate family tree, perhaps with some small artifacts from all the places your family touched as they traveled through all the long years. For what better to give a man made an orphan than the great gift of roots?

But, oh! I found so much, so much more than I expected! Can you imagine what it was like, my heart, to slowly discover the great mystery of your past? To slowly uncover the great and marvelous legacy that you alone can claim as heir? I hope, my love, that by following the clues I've left for you, you can share in some of the excitement. How I wish, how I wish I could be with you at the end!

By now, you must know that my gift to you is a touchstone, a connection to your past. I have given you <u>family</u>, Gaspar, the way you gave one to me. You know that, don't you? You were my family, dear Gaspar, and no woman ever loved her family more.

And by now you know that you are the heir to a legacy, something wonderful. I imagine you're thinking there will be a clue in this letter telling you what it is. Alas, my poor dear, there is not. I don't know what it is. I don't know what secret your blood entitles you to know. Oh, how I ache to! How I wish I could be there, with you, to solve it at last! I don't know the answer, although of course I have a guess, just as you must yourself. Ah! But I know what you must do to find out!

The clues I have given you, in this package and in the others, will lead you to the tomb of the man who founded your family line. There you will find another monastery, this one of a very different sort. This is the place of the Magi, my heart. For 2000 years now, the brothers have guarded the tomb of your ancestor. When some war or another flared up around them, your grandfathers took the secret, your legacy, to the brothers there, and charged them to guard it. Then your family came to America, and the hope of a new life. They never returned to claim it, and now you are the last of your line, the last man who can.

Go to them, my love. You must show them your books and your documents. Prove you are the heir. And then you must answer their questions. That is important, a password of sorts, I suppose. Answer, and they will give you your inheritance, the proud legacy of your family, my love.

Ah, but where do you go? Where do you answer these questions? Oh my love, I can almost hear you asking that! It makes me laugh, and I find I have to wipe away a tear. I will tell you only this. I don't know. But you have an advantage I did not when I began my research.

You have my gifts, dear heart. You have all the clues you need. You can solve the last one.

If you have solved the clues in this package, you will know a name. He found the tomb. He visited it. Now, my heart, you must begin where he began. That's where his record is kept.

Oh, good luck!

And now, I am going to close by giving you a command, my heart, and you must obey, because the last wish of a dying woman is sacred. I won't ask for your promise, because I know you would never refuse me. This is it, then. My command: I want you to _live_, Gaspar. Live your days, all of them, and make them all count. Every last, precious one of them. Every minute, every second. Be a part of the world. Experience. Create. Love. _Matter_. That's the real reason I gave you these gifts, you know, and this adventure. I know you will want to throw your life away because you'll think you don't want it anymore. You would have made of our home a *coffin, but you are still alive. Don't you dare, don't you <u>dare</u> shut yourself off and throw away the precious gift time has given you.*

I think perhaps that only when we begin to near the end do we realize how very much every moment is worth. Life is so short, and we are so fragile. But every second is a miracle; every heartbeat is more precious than all the wealth in all the universe. Find joy again, my dear, because you are living for both of us now, and I shall expect great stories from you when we are together again at last.

Because my love, we <u>will</u> be together again. That is the miracle of Christmas, the gift. In the past, I have always been with you as you solved your mystery each year. This year, I am not. But I know that somewhere, somehow, I will be watching over you, my dear. How do I know this? Your ancestor found the answer to that question. Now you must, too.

There is a bridge between this world and the eternal, the divine. Anything that loves never dies, and that which is loved lasts forever. This is the great truth I have learned in all my days with you. And know, I know, my dear, that someday we will be together again. On that day, we will be together forever, and maybe then, I'll finally have the time to find all the words that I need to tell you how very much I love you, and will always love you, and how grateful I am for all the joy you have given me. You've been my life, Gaspar, and I am so, so very grateful.

So for now, go and live, my heart. That is my last command. Live!

Oh my love, my love. I love you, Gaspar. I love you so very much. It is unfair to expect so much of this poor paper and wretched ink, for letters and words were never meant to contain the depth and might of the love I have for you. It is like trying to fit an ocean in a teacup.

I have to leave you for a while, and I am at peace with that. It doesn't frighten me because I know that love endures. I love you always and forever, with all that I am and all that I ever hoped to be. When the last night falls, I will be waiting for you. I will be your star to guide you. Know this, my heart, and remember it.

Oh, Darling!

Your Beth

Gaspar read the letter three times. He tried to read it aloud to Will, but his voice broke. The sobs came then, and right in front of Will, after all his promises to himself, and in that moment, he found that he just plain didn't care. Weeping, he handed the tear-stained page to Will, and the young man read the words to himself.

"Oh my God, Gaspar. What a wonderful, amazing woman."

Gaspar's voice failed him again, so he merely nodded.

"We need to figure out what to do now," Will said hesitantly.

Gaspar forced another nod.

"But . . . the Count's men can't know to look for us way out here, huh? Let's take a walk. Get a bite or something. That'll . . . you know. Give you a minute and all."

"Thanks," Gaspar managed. As they stood, Gaspar added, "Will, if you don't mind, walk a little ahead of me, okay? I just . . . I kinda need a little time to myself, and this is probably the best I can do. Just find us a place, okay? Anywhere's fine, as long as we have to walk a little while to get there. Okay?"

"Sure," said Will. "Whatever you say."

And Will?"

"Yeah?"

"Why don't you take a moment to call Ana?"

Will smiled and nodded.

Will led them on a long, circuitous route, heading more or less back in the direction of the old city. Gaspar never thanked him for that simple kindness because he could never find the words to measure the depth of his gratitude.

They dined on pasta with olive oil, herbs, and fish still fresh with the brine of the sea, accompanied by hot bread and wine, spicy and sweet, that sang on the tongue. In the evening, it was too cold to sit outside, but the café windows gave them a good view of the city in its twilight hues, where Christmas lights and gas lamps made it sparkle. When the waiter cleared away their dishes, Gaspar ordered a bottle of port for dessert. Will was looking at his phone.

"Whatcha reading there, dude?"

Will turned the phone around to show the screen. *"The Travels of Marco Polo.* I downloaded the e-book."

"I guess it's time to start thinking about a plan," Gaspar said.

"You sure you're okay?"

"I'm . . . yeah. I'm okay. Just tell me what you found."

Will nodded. "Okay." He looked back down at his phone. "Marco Polo claims to have visited the tomb of the three wise men. The Magi. So there's our connection. Problem is, he doesn't say where it is."

Gaspar rolled his eyes. "Frickin' of course not. Didn't Marco Polo go, like, all the way to China?"

"He made some stops along the way."

"Too much to hope he left a map, huh?"

"Nothing . . . published."

"Right," said Gaspar. "Right back where we started, then."

Will shook his head. "Maybe not. According to legend, there's supposed to be a drawing. In his original manuscript."

"Can we get a copy?"

Will shook his head. "It was never published. For some reason. But the original, yeah . . . that's in the Libreria Vecchia—the Old Library in Venice. Which, by the way, is the answer to Beth's last clue. Marco Polo began his journey in Venice!" Will looked back at his phone, but then he sighed. Gaspar couldn't help thinking he looked defeated. "But it's almost never displayed. And never to the public. I don't know how we can get them to show us."

Gaspar grinned.

Will raised his eyebrows. "I take it you have an idea?"

"I need a rare book."

"I'm totally your guy. Which one?"

Gaspar's grin widened. "One any museum or library would sell their nuts for."

Will shook his head. "Huh?"

"Or at least trade a quick peek at an old manuscript for."

"Oh!" Will said, catching on at last. "So not something we're gonna find at a . . . legitimate dealer. But yeah, maybe. I'll make some calls."

Gaspar sighed. "I'm gonna need an ATM."

"You're gonna need a whole bank," Will told him.

"Find me a book," said Gaspar. "I'll get us train tickets to Venice."

The antiquarian bookshop in the heart of Rome was closed and locked for the night. One light glowed softly in the back room. The back room, too, was locked.

The proprietor, a man who preferred not to offer his name, came wearing white gloves and holding an ancient, leather-bound volume. *"The Prayer Book of Charles the Bold,"* the man said. "A masterpiece of the art of the illuminated manuscript."

"A librarian would want that?" Gaspar asked.

The proprietor looked shocked by the question. "Any good librarian would sell their mother to the gypsies for just a look at this!"

"Perfect," said Gaspar. "Now what?"

"Now," said Will, "we haggle."

The proprietor's eyes popped open even wider. "Haggle? *Mio Dio!* This book is priceless!"

Gaspar sighed and reached for his wallet. "Mastercard?"

14

The Secret Map

he change in the train's gentle motion as it neared Venice was enough to wake Gaspar from sleep. Will was already awake, and he was smiling.

"Is there coffee?" Gaspar asked. "Please tell me there's coffee."

"Yeah," said Will. "I asked the porter to bring us some here. The carafe's over there. Some pastries, too."

"Thank God."

"Thank the porter."

Gaspar rubbed his eyes and poured himself a steaming mug. It was hot, slightly bitter, and delicious. "So what's got you grinning like a jackass this early?"

"An email from Ana," said Will. "I missed it before."

"Ah. Yeah, I can see how that would do it."

Will laughed. "Well, yeah. That alone. But she had some good news. Well, maybe. Remember the idea I had? For the toy shop?"

"You never actually told me what it was," Gaspar reminded him.

"Right. Sorry. I guess we've been a little busy, huh?"

"A little."

"Anyway, remember the movie crew we saw setting up to shoot back in Budapest?"

"Yeah. Did you ever find out what that was?"

"Some high-tech thriller thing," said Will. "It's called *Challengers*. It actually sounds pretty awesome. Unfortunately for the crew, they had to shut down because their props and stuff never showed up thanks to all the supply chain hassles."

"What kind of props?"

"High tech computer gizmos, weapons, stuff like that. It's got a spy, a shaman, an assassin, a daredevil pilot, an inventor, a magician . . . and they all use special gadgets. Which they don't have. Anyway, I think the folks at the toy shop can make all that, and right there in Budapest."

"Sweet! Is there money in that?"

"Not much," said Will. "I offered to do it for free."

"Free! Dude, I know you're not much of a businessman, but I don't think that's gonna help much."

Will laughed. "I offered to make the props free. It's a pretty low-cost investment. But in return, we get the rights to make toys and high-end replicas for the collector's market. They get 10 percent of net, but the rest is ours."

"Sweet," said Gaspar. "That actually sounds like a pretty good idea."

"I hope so," said Will. "Let's just hope it's not too little too late. Ana's talking to the bank. Fingers crossed, eh?"

Gaspar was not surprised to learn that Will had never seen Venice, at least not outside of a book. Gaspar knew from experience that the pictures didn't begin do it justice. They had arrived late at night, when the city was shrouded by darkness. Even then, it had taken his breath away. The city lights had been reflected in the shadowed waters and Will had experienced the dreamy sensation of floating through stars.

On their way to the hotel, Gaspar kept looking over his shoulder.

"See anyone?" Will asked him.

"No one that looks like a hired thug, or who looks like they're following us," said Gaspar. "Of course, that might just mean they're better thugs."

"Good point," said Will. "And jeez, thanks for putting that idea in my head."

"I guess it's too much to hope we lost 'em, eh?"

Will took a deep breath. "We know the Count's been working on this problem for a very long time. If he'd managed to get the books, he probably would have already solved this whole thing. I think we have to assume he knows as much as Beth knew. Maybe more. So he'd probably guess we came here. You?"

"I was thinking pretty much the same thing," said Gaspar. "Let's . . . just be damn careful, huh?"

"No argument from me."

Morning came. They hadn't seen any signs of pursuit, but Gaspar wasn't ready to relax his guard. Gaspar and Will had to take a boat through the famous canals to reach their destination. One of the public transportation motorboats would have been more efficient; but the first viewing in the crisp light of morning should be presented with suitable flair, Gaspar decided, so he decided to spit at the danger and hired a gondola. If they did have a tail they hadn't spotted, a gondola should be hard enough to follow, he supposed, and they might be more likely to blend in with the tourists.

Gaspar watched Will regard the sun-drenched columns and balconies, the arcing bridges and dark tunnels, and the tall domes and palaces of timeless, crumbling

Venice with stunned awe. The air was ripe with the mingling, pungent scents of canal water, cheese, spices, smoke, and fish. Even in winter, the city was busy; plazas and cafés bustled with people and the magnificent, broken statues of saints and angels. Here and there, they caught hints and echoes of faint music, wafting like breezes, sudden, teasing, and vanished. Gaspar smiled to see Will, overcome with an overload of beauty, wiping tears away from his cheeks.

"I wish," said Gaspar, "I had the time to show you Venice as she deserves to be seen, dude. I'm telling you—she would break your heart into a thousand million pieces."

"I think she already has," Will said softly.

"Maybe we'll come back someday," Gaspar said. And for the first time since Beth's death, he realized, suddenly, that he *did* want to travel again. He wanted to see things. He wanted . . . he wanted to live.

"I'd like that," said Will. He smiled. "Maybe we can bring Ana, too."

Gaspar chuckled. "Maybe so, maybe so."

The boat pulled up to a dock, and Gaspar helped Will climb out. To reach the Old Library, they had to cross a wide stone-paved plaza, where flocks of birds scolded couples holding hands on benches, children throwing coins into a fountain, and old men eating pastry with their espresso. Most of the tourists wore masks, but Gaspar could see the smiles in their eyes.

Will, Gaspar couldn't help noticing, was grinning like an idiot. "The Libreria Vecchia. Sixteenth century. It's the masterpiece of designer—"

Gaspar raised his eyebrows and tried not to smirk. He didn't imagine he was doing too good a job.

Will mimed the steel trap again, complete with the *tw-WAP!* noise. "I'm telling you. A fact's gotta chew off its own leg to get out of this brain."

Gaspar shook his head and rolled his eyes. "The poster on your bedroom wall. Was it *Star Wars* or *Tron?*"

"Uh, *The Phantom Menace,*" Will admitted.

"The Phantom . . . ! Dude. Even among nerds you're lame."

"And the Red Sox."

"Okay, touché," Gaspar conceded.

The banter helped calm his nerves to a degree, but all the same, Gaspar found himself looking around suspiciously. "See anybody . . . you know. Hired thuggish?"

Will shook his head. "No. Not yet. But if they're here, or close, they won't stop us going in. Getting out's going to be the hard part."

"Right," Gaspar said. "Especially since we don't have an exit strategy."

"We don't even have an entrance strategy," Will pointed out.

"I was planning to just knock and ask for help."

"Good thinking," said Will. "'Cause that's been working out great for us."

"Which is why we need a getaway plan."

"Right," said Will. "We need a car."

"No cars in Venice." Gaspar grinned at Will's embarrassment. "That fact must'a chewed its own leg off, huh?"

"You got me." Will chuckled and checked his phone. "Here we go. Just outside the city. There's a parking garage called Tronchetto. We can rent a car there."

Gaspar nodded once. "Okay. Go get a car. Take our stuff, will ya? Be ready to move."

"Gaspar—"

"I can do this, Will. Beth knew I could do this. And don't worry; I'll be careful. Just make sure we can get the hell out of here, okay? Fast if we have to."

"Okay," Will agreed.

Abban and Jael wore suits with black shirts and ties. Abban thought the ensemble was . . . *inappropriate* given the work they'd come to do, and the way the clothes made them stand out among the tourists with their blue jeans and hoodies. But Count Bethlen had his standards, and he wrote the checks. Jael kept running his fingers under his collar—the man had a neck like a tree stump—and Abban had to put his hand on his arm to remind him to stop.

245

At that moment, Jael pointed. Abban looked, and saw one of the Americans, the taller one, entering the Old Library, just as the Count had predicted.

"Where is the other one?" Jael asked.

"It doesn't matter," said Abban. "We will find him later."

Abban tapped his mobile phone and notified their backup. Then, the two men moved quickly and with ruthless precision.

Gaspar entered the Old Library and gawked, despite himself, at the magnificent, cavernous room. He wished he had time to just stand and look. Beth would have wanted him to stand and look. He didn't though. He did, however, take a moment to simply breathe. He'd spent a lifetime visiting libraries and bookstores, first with his dad and then with Beth. It was the scent of his past, of his life, one he knew as well as he knew the smell of newly mown grass and roasting hot dogs in a ballpark. He breathed and let the scent of dust and musty paper fill and comfort him. He made a mental note to bring Will back someday. Will and his Ana.

Then he moved. A help desk waited just ahead. Gaspar needed to focus. He needed to find a head librarian, or whoever the hell was in charge around here.

—❦—

Less than twenty minutes later, Gaspar found himself sitting in an office across a dusty, antique desk from an older Italian librarian in a dapper but somewhat dated suit. Gaspar placed his neatly wrapped bundle on the desk and forced a smile that he hoped would come across as charming. "I'm told you're the gentleman I can talk to about a . . . little donation."

"I'm sure that's very generous, Mr. Bethlen. But the Old Library isn't . . ." The librarian smirked. ". . . a used bookshop."

Gaspar opened his bundle and watched the librarian's eyes pop open, wide as dinner plates. The man gasped out loud. "Dear God. Is that . . . a *Charles the Bold*?"

Gaspar nodded. "One of the proofs."

The librarian gasped again, and Gaspar had to force himself not to laugh. The man even gasped with an Italian accent. "That can't be! None exist!"

"One does," said Gaspar. "The last copy in existence, or so I'm told. But to be honest, the guy might have just been trying to drive up the price. Oh, and, yeah, it's the original binding. Uh, that's important, right?"

The librarian gaped. "This book is priceless. Priceless!"

"Oh, believe me, it had a price. But I think it needs a new home. Maybe we can make a little . . . uh, deal. What do you say?"

The librarian sighed and shook his head. "Our budget is limited, as you can imagine. We couldn't begin to offer a fraction of what this is worth."

Gaspar leaned back in his chair and smiled. "Well, how 'bout a little . . . trade then? See, there's something here I'd like to take a look at. Just a look. And then this is yours. Think we can make a deal?"

The librarian looked up and offered Gaspar a nervous smile.

"Oh, and I'm gonna need a receipt. Tax write-off and all. I sure as hell hope so, anyway."

The librarian took Gaspar to a vault in a subbasement, a place where manuscripts were stored, far from public view, and where skilled artisans worked to restore ancient volumes. A few loose pages and cracked bindings lay spread on a massive wooden table, along with glue, twine, scraps of leather, and other supplies. At present, the place was deserted, although Gaspar guessed that someone had been working there recently; a pot of glue sat on a metal rack warming over a burner that reminded Gaspar of high school chemistry class. On the walls, locked glass cabinets held books that, Gaspar was willing to bet good money, not even Will or Ana knew existed.

Gaspar followed the librarian to the table and placed his volume on a chair. The librarian watched it with greedy eyes. The man forced a smile through thin lips. "So as you can see, Mr. Bethlen, your book will be cared for, protected, and treasured. Forever."

Gaspar offered the man his hand to shake. "Then we have a deal?"

The librarian hesitated. "Just . . . look, right? You won't touch?"

Gaspar nodded.

The librarian pointed to a gilded volume in a glass case that stood on a pedestal on the far side of the work-table. "This is the book, written in the hand of Rustichello da Pisa, who recorded the words of Marco Polo himself when they were imprisoned together in Genoa. Marco Polo described his journeys in the years 1271 through 1295, and Rustichello recorded every word. It is said he had it bound himself. Every other edition in the world comes from this one. This is the first of four books, the one that describes his journeys in the Middle East. I believe that is the one that interests you, yes?"

Gaspar nodded as he bent to examine the book. It was smaller than he'd imagined, and beautiful. The leather was stained and worn, and the edges of the pages were gilded.

"Marco Polo was the greatest traveler of his day," the librarian continued. "He journeyed from Italy through the Middle East, all the way to Asia. He claimed to have met Kublai Khan himself! Those volumes are here, too, if you'd like to see them also."

"Maybe, but I think this is what I need." Gaspar looked back at the man. "You really think that's true? About, uh, Kublai Khan? And all the other stuff?"

The man shrugged. "Who can say, eh? But then, how else would he have known of Kublai Khan's existence?" He hesitated for a moment. "I myself have held this treasure twice. Quite a privilege, yes? But I must tell you, Mr. Bethlen. I have never seen a map."

"Open it," Gaspar said, nodding to the case.

The librarian produced a tiny brass key and twisted the lock. The case opened, but the man hesitated. "Mr. Bethlen, please. The Marco Polo manuscript is never displayed. Scholars wait years, decades, for a glimpse. It—"

Before he could finish, they heard a sudden crash behind them. Gaspar spun.

Two men in suits had kicked the door in, splintering the wood. They weren't wearing masks, so Gaspar could see their faces. He knew the men. He had seen them before, in the Count's manor back in Hungary.

The librarian gasped but recovered quickly and shouted in Italian. *"Qual'è il significato di questo!"*

The two men moved closer, pulling handguns from beneath their jackets.

Gaspar didn't hesitate. He grabbed the jar of hot glue and threw it at the thugs, splashing the thick liquid in their faces.

The men cried out in pain. The nearer man fired wildly, shattering the glass in front of the Polo manuscript. They staggered forward, guns in hand, trying to wipe the goo from their faces. They stumbled closer, and closer still. They reached the worktable and leaned against it, wiping frantically at their faces.

With a great heave, Gaspar pushed the table over, trapping the struggling thugs beneath its great weight. He knew that wouldn't slow them for long.

The librarian let out a cry—part gasp, part girlish scream. He scrambled after the books and loose pages, ignoring Gaspar and the trapped men.

Gaspar knew that the smart thing to do now was to run, but he also knew he'd never have another chance. He had to find the map.

Seeing that the glass cabinet was open, the glass shattered, Gaspar grabbed the Polo manuscript and opened it, turning through the handwritten pages. Then he started over, going through the pages again, more slowly this time.

There's no map.

He turned back to the scrambling librarian. "There's no map!"

The librarian ignored him as he frantically gathered the fallen papers. The two thugs struggled wildly, screaming, still trying to wipe the hot glue from their eyes while simultaneously trying to free themselves from the weight of the table.

Gaspar started to go through the book again, but as he did, he happened to bend the lower gilded edge of the side opposite the spine just so, so that only the smallest bit of every page was visible. Gaspar gaped. There was a hidden picture there. When the book was closed, only gilding showed—but when the spine was bent at a slight angle, fanning the ends of the pages just enough, an image appeared on the fore edge.

"Whoa!"

It was a map.

No wonder they never published the map. It was hidden!

Gaspar snapped a photo of the map with his phone. The he turned back to the librarian. "Uh . . . thanks. You can keep the book."

Gaspar saw that the two men had managed to cooperate enough to begin lifting the heavy table. They were nearly free. He placed the Polo manuscript back in its place carefully and ran.

Moments later, he exited the Old Library and found himself back on the plaza, blinking in the sun. Not far away, he saw three more men in suits. None of them were wearing masks. *Of course hired killers don't wear masks. Why would a hired killer give a rat's ass about protecting other people?* One of the men was pointing at him and shouting in what he guessed was excited Italian.

Gaspar turned and ran, racing through crowded streets, dodging street vendors, performers, and pedestrians. He didn't have to look back to know that the three men were after him.

Gaspar turned and raced along the Grand Canal, which was crowded with boats. *They may not have cars here,* he thought, *but they still have frickin' traffic jams.*

Suddenly, Gaspar skidded to a stop. Two more men in front of him were moving to cut him off. One good thing about the suits and the lack of masks—at least they made the thugs easier to spot. Gaspar spun, but the men behind him were gaining. One way to go—he cut left, racing along a canal that was narrower than the Grand Canal, if not by much. It, too, was crowded with boats. *So, what? Is there, like, a multi-boat pileup somewhere?*

Just then, he saw more men in suits, coming from the direction he'd been running. Their hands were in their jackets, probably reaching for weapons, Gaspar had to assume. Which meant that only the bustling crowd on the sidewalk was keeping them from firing. That wouldn't stop them for long.

Gaspar couldn't go back, and he couldn't go forward.

He was trapped.

He looked around frantically. There were buildings to his right and suited, maskless men behind and ahead. There was only one way to go.

Gaspar sprinted toward the crowded canal and leapt to a boat, landing on its middle bench. The boat lurched, but he didn't slow, not to regain his balance, not even to think. If he did, even for a single split second, he knew it would all be over. If he somehow managed not to split his head open, he'd be in the water. If he didn't drown, he would be easy pickings for the men in suits.

He took another step and jumped again. He leapt to the next boat and then to another—never relaxing his momentum as he sprung across the canal, boat to boat, like a skipping stone.

With one final leap and stretch, he made it to the far side. Looking back, he watched two of the men behind him tumble into the water. He grinned, but it faded in a wink. At least two more men were on this side of the canal, and they were closing.

Gaspar ran. He turned a corner, still sprinting, but slid to a fast stop—another, narrower canal blocked his way. He turned, but the men behind him were gaining. He spun back to the canal and spotted an empty gondola.

Without hesitating, he grabbed the steering pole just as the men reached him. Swinging the pole like a quarterstaff, he caught one man in the jaw, knocking him down. Before the other man could react, Gaspar swung the pole low, sweeping the man's feet out from under him, landing him hard on his seat. Gaspar moved behind the man and kicked, sending him spilling into the canal.

Gaspar turned to run back the way he came, back in the direction of the Grand Canal, but he stopped. Two more men were racing toward him, weapons drawn.

Again, only the crowd kept them from firing. He was cut off. Men and women pointed and screamed, and ran in all directions. Gaspar turned again, still gripping the pole, and ran. Now, he was heading straight back to the narrower canal, with nowhere else to turn. He could see only one chance. It was crazy, but the alternative was men with guns.

He closed his eyes and mouthed a quick prayer. He'd hated his track days back in school. He'd taken up the sport only to improve his skills as a ballplayer. Now—again—that discipline was the only thing that might save his life.

It's just like track back in school, he told himself. *It's just like track back in school—*

Gaspar picked up speed. He prayed that his guess about the depth of canal was right—the pole had to reach the bottom to steer the gondolas, right? He reached the edge of the narrow canal, jabbed the long pole into the water, and vaulted across. He let go of the pole, landed on the tips of his toes on the far side, now facing back the way he'd come, flailed his arms wildly, and leaned backward. Somehow, he managed not to tumble back into the water. He turned and ran wildly, with no thought given to direction. He kept moving forward, sprinting, gaining speed, until he lost himself in the crowd.

He ran a few more meters until he reached another canal. For a change, luck was with him. A motorboat taxi was there, empty and waiting. And—*thank God!*—there was only one. Gaspar leapt aboard.

The pilot looked back at him expectantly.

Dammit, where the hell was he supposed to meet Will again? That's right....

"Tronchetto! Uh ... Parking Garage ... uh. ..."

He scrambled for the phrase book, patting his pocket. No luck. Will had it.

He tried faking Italian and speaking with an Italian accent. That usually worked in the North End back in Boston. "di, uh *parkingo garagio*. ..."

The pilot rolled his eyes and shook his head as he pulled out into the canal.

Looking back, Gaspar saw at least two more men in suits arriving at the spot where he had jumped into the water taxi. The pilot sped up. Gaspar saw the angry, frustrated men shouting. There wasn't another boat or taxi waiting; they had no way to follow. For the moment at least, he'd lost them.

Gaspar closed his eyes and let out a breath.

The sun was almost directly overhead when Gaspar sprinted toward the garage, looking for a sign for the rental car area. Before he reached it, a tiny Smart Car pulled up to him and beeped the horn. Will was driving.

Gaspar jogged to the car and opened the passenger door, wondering how the hell he was supposed to fold himself up and fit inside.

"This is supposed to be a car?" he shouted.

"It's the best I could do," said Will. "Will you just get in?"

"This is worse than Ana's car!"

At that moment, Gaspar heard a sound. He turned his head and saw two men on motorcycles riding at speed. One of them had a gun. He fired. The bullet hit the garage's concrete wall just to the right of Gaspar's head.

"Get in!" Will shouted.

Gaspar folded himself and slammed the door. "Go! *Go!*"

The coming motorcycles had the drive blocked. Before Gaspar could close his door, Will shoved the car into reverse and sped backwards, weaving around the approaching traffic. The motorcycles roared after them.

"Where are we going?" Will asked.

"Out of here!"

Will looked over his shoulder, dodging around angry Italian drivers. He didn't get far. "Crap," said Will.

Gaspar looked up and saw another armed man on a motorcycle closing from behind. They were trapped again.

There was only one way to go. Will shifted back to drive and turned back into the massive parking garage.

"Will, for God's sake, *this isn't away from here!*"

"I'm open to suggestions."

With the cycles in hot pursuit, Will raced through the deck, dodging traffic and angry pedestrians. A car was backing out, but Will didn't slow.

"Will," Gaspar shouted, pointing, "you're not gonna make it!"

The tiny car's wheels squealed as Will spun around the backing car and then swerved again to avoid more pedestrians. Gaspar couldn't understand any of the words they were shouting, but the hand gestures were certainly clear enough.

Gaspar looked back over this shoulder. The cycles were gaining. Will accelerated and Gaspar's stomach lurched. As he turned a tight corner, he clipped the passenger mirror on a concrete pillar, knocking it loose.

"Will!"

"Don't worry," Will said. "I got the extra insurance."

"Good thinking," Gaspar growled. "Yeah. 'Cause that's totally what I was worried about. Whoa, careful!"

Will raced around the tight corners of the deck. His tires squealed again as he avoided pedestrians and cars without slowing. Gaspar could smell the stench of burning rubber.

"Whoa!" Gaspar said again. "People! Don't . . . hit . . . the . . . *people!*"

Will kept weaving to avoid cars backing out at the same time from opposite sides of the aisle. He didn't slow. "You'd make one hell of an Italian cab driver," Gaspar said.

"We need to find the down ramp!" said Will.

"This *is* the frickin' down ramp," said Gaspar. "There's only one frickin' ramp! We're just going the wrong way!"

Gaspar looked back again. The cycles were right behind them. They weren't going that way, even if Will could somehow find a way to turn around.

Near the top of the deck, close to the adjacent office building, they seemed to be cut off again. They'd reached the end of the ramp. Unless they could turn around, there was nowhere else to go. Gaspar looked around frantically. They could not turn around.

Will jerked the wheel, turning the only way he could —right into an open freight elevator. He slammed on the brakes.

"Elevator," Gaspar said, glaring at Will. "Good thinking."

"Hit the button!" Will yelled.

Gaspar leapt out and pushed the DOWN button. Then, frantically, he mashed the CLOSE DOORS button again and again. The three motorcycles roared closer. One of the men raised his weapon, but the heavy doors slammed down just in time. Gaspar raced back to the car. He slammed the passenger door just as the elevator started moving.

"Okay, that was too close," said Gaspar.

"We're not out of here yet," Will reminded him.

Seconds later, the elevator doors opened—not the ones they'd entered, the ones behind them, but the doors in front of them—the doors that opened inside the office building.

"Okay," said Gaspar, "that's not good. *Hey!*"

Will punched the gas. Surprised and screaming workers dove out of the way, yelling angrily as they passed. Gaspar was glad he didn't speak Italian.

"What the hell are you *doing?*" Gaspar demanded.

"Getting away!" said Will.

"This isn't away! We're inside the frickin' building!"

"Still open to suggestions."

Gaspar looked back over his shoulder again to see second elevator door open. The three men on motorcycles came roaring out. The terrified office workers dove for cover again. Will floored the Smart Car and its engine whined as it raced through crowded hallways, making a circuit around the building. Gaspar closed his eyes and flinched, but the car was just small enough—barely—to make the tight turns. Will didn't slow.

Gaspar looked back again. The cycles, faster and more maneuverable in the tight corridors, were gaining. Screaming office workers dove out of the way.

Will turned a corner. Just ahead of them, a crowd had gathered, talking in the halls. Will beeped the horn. The men and women scattered, screaming and shouting, and making more of these hand gestures. The cycles were right behind them. One of them knocked over a plant.

Gaspar looked forward again just as Will turned to avoid a janitor mopping the floor and then again to spin past four workers carrying a heavy metal desk. The janitor spilled his soapy water and, as the Smart Car passed, the startled men dropped the desk.

The lead cyclist slipped in the spilled water and, swerving to avoid the desk, wiped out, skidding into the wall. The other two tried to avoid him—unsuccessfully. The corridor was too narrow. It was a pileup.

"What happened?" said Will.

"Just go!" said Gaspar. "Go!"

Will went, turning another corner and sending more workers scrambling. Just ahead they spotted an opening, the main entrance. Will punched the gas again and crashed through the glass doors, barreled down a small flight of concrete stairs and across the sidewalk, and sped out into the main road.

Lost in traffic, he zipped away.

About a half an hour or so later, Will found a place to stop. "Any idea where we are?" asked Gaspar.

Will shook his head. "I can narrow it down to away from Venice, but beyond that, I was pretty much just thinking to go far and fast."

"That was a good plan. Now, though, I think we need a better one."

"Did you find Marco Polo's map?"

"I did," said Gaspar. "It was totally hidden. He showed Will the photo he'd snapped with his phone.

"Whoa, wicked!"

Gaspar grinned. "See? Now *this* is some cool detective work."

"How in the world did you figure that out?"

"Just genius deduction," said Gaspar, grinning. Will raised his eyebrows. "Okay, it was luck. Here, let me see your phone. I need the Maps app."

"Anything?"

"Yeah," said Gaspar. "Persia."

"Persia. . . ." Will began. "Wait, *Iran?*"

"Yeah." Gaspar nodded and held up both phones. Gaspar's still displayed the photo; Will's showed a map of Iran. "The maps match. Kinda. If you squint."

Gaspar zoomed the GPS display. "Marco Polo found the tombs near a place called Saveh. Just south of what's now Tehran."

"Okay," said Will. He took his phone back from Gaspar. "I guess we know what's next."

"What's that?" said Gaspar.

"Well, we find a city with an airport."

Gaspar nodded. "Yeah. Ideally, in a city that's not Venice, since that's where the Count's men are looking for us."

"Here, looks like we can make Pisa in about four hours, or Rome in six. I'll see where I can get us a flight. Tonight if possible, but I guess tomorrow morning is more likely, since we'll need to apply for a travel authorization from the Iranian Ministry of Foreign Affairs. Huh. I wonder if Beth already took care of that?"

"She didn't know the final destination," Gaspar reminded him.

"Not the exact location, no. But if she read Marco Polo, she would have narrowed it down to Iran. I'll call your travel agent. Mind driving for a while?"

Gaspar shrugged. "I guess not. If I can manage to get behind that wheel."

"Good. I'll plan. And call Ana. Oh, and I need to get in touch with the toy shop."

15

Red Sox Nation, Iran Chapter

ill found Gaspar and handed him a boarding pass. "Here you go. We fly to Istanbul and then change planes for Tehran."

Gaspar shouldered his carry-on bag and the case with the books, and they started walking to the gate. Gaspar frowned. "Do they, uh, like Americans there?"

"We can tell 'em we're Hungarian if it'll make you feel better," Will suggested.

"I don't speak Hungarian," Gaspar reminded him.

"Neither do they. Relax. Westerners travel there. It should be fine, especially if you know someone."

"Uh, do we know anyone?"

Will grinned. "Would you believe there's a chapter of Red Sox Nation in Iran? American baseball is actually popular there." Will showed Gaspar his phone, which displayed a Web page with Gaspar's picture in his Red

Sox uniform. The writing was in what Gaspar had to assume was Farsi. "Turns out you've got a fan club there."

"Huh," said Gaspar. "Who knew?"

"I confess it was a surprise to me, too," Will admitted.

"Hey, did you get ahold of Ana?"

"No," said Will, frowning. "And she didn't answer my texts."

"She must be busy at the bank." Gaspar tried to smile and hoped it didn't look forced. "Probably working on your toy shop."

"Maybe," said Will. Gaspar didn't think Will sounded convinced.

In Istanbul, they changed planes for the flight to Tehran. As the plane left the Istanbul airport, Gaspar said, "Here we are. The last leg."

"Then all we have to do is find this monastery," said Will.

"That's about the size of it," said Gaspar. "That might not be as hard as it sounds. On the map at least, Saveh doesn't look all that big. If there's a monastery anywhere close to there, or ruins, or old tombs, someone will know. I mean, like, how many can there be? And if not, well, we do have a map. It's a little out of date, but I'm guessing it's better than nothing."

"Sounds good to me," said Will. He opened his phone and started reading.

"*The Travels of Marco Polo* again?" asked Gaspar.

Will nodded. "I'll let you know when I get to the part about the Magi tombs."

"Cool."

Will shifted in his seat and adjusted his safety belt. "So tell me, Gaspar. Do you really think we solved the mystery? Do you really think Halley's comet was the Star of Bethlehem?"

"Well, I mean, why not?"

"Well . . . I don't know. It just seems kind of . . . *ordinary.*"

"It is to us now, I guess, but I bet it wasn't to the ancient people. Like the professor said back in Rome. It was a thing of awe and wonder. We've forgotten that to our loss, I think. Maybe miracles have become too common."

"You might be right."

"In any case, why *shouldn't* God use a ball of snow and rock to lead the Magi to the place where His son was born? Huh? Hadn't He used the base stuff of creation to accomplish His divine will before? Aren't we humans supposed to be, like, shaped right out of the dust of the earth? Right? Didn't the miracle with the wine start with water? Feeding the multitudes with a couple of loaves and a fish or two? Wasn't the womb of an ordinary, mortal dust-to-dust woman supposed to be the gateway by which He entered creation, the Word made flesh and all that? Yeah? Isn't that how the story goes? Jeez, listen to me. I sound like my dad. Besides, we know Beth thought so. That's good enough for me. More than."

"I suppose."

"But don't forget, even if we *have* guessed the right answer, if the Bethlen family riddle really gives us the ultimate clue—in the end, it doesn't really matter, does it?"

"I'm not sure what you mean," said Will. "Sounds like a pretty darn important answer to me."

Gaspar smiled. "Dude, you're totally like a kid who gets so enamored with all the paper and ribbons that he forgets to open the gift. Comet, supernova, planetary conjunction, or just big, brilliant old star that appears right out of nowhere. Whatever it really was, in the end, that's just the package. I mean, right? It's fascinating trivia, but in the end, it's just that—trivia. It doesn't matter. The deeper truth, the true gift, that's what's inside."

"What is it?" Will asked, his voice barely a whisper.

"Don't you know?" Gaspar smiled again. "Dude, it's a miracle, of course. It's a frickin' miracle."

The airport in Tehran was shiny and modern. Despite the fact that the signs were in Farsi, it could have been pretty much any airport in any city in the world, a fact that Gaspar found oddly comforting. Once they made it through customs and to baggage claim, they found eight smiling Iranian men, all in their mid to late twenties, waiting. One of them was holding a cardboard sign bearing the name Gaspar Bethlen handwritten in Magic Marker. All of the men wore Red Sox caps; most of them wore coordinating jackets or shirts. Three of them were waving Red Sox pennants. Gaspar eyed them carefully and smiled. They had the look of athletes, amateur ballplayers, maybe. They reminded him of the guys he'd played with in high school and college. He found himself liking them.

The man holding the cardboard sign grinned and waved. "Mr. Gaspar! Mr. Will! Welcome, welcome! I am Masood Mortazavi. Welcome!"

Masood's van carried them down a dusty road south of Tehran. Gaspar and Will sat on the bench seat behind Masood. Another of the Iranian men in a Red Sox ball cap sat next to Masood. The rest of the men had crowded into the two benches behind them. Gaspar was busy signing baseballs and bats.

Not long after, Gaspar and Will had their first good look at the Iranian city of Saveh. Like most of the places they'd visited, Saveh was a place of contrasts, Gaspar couldn't help noticing. Time and geography were jumbled, as though acres and eons had been shuffled like cards and dealt at random on a table of desert sand. The grounds surrounding a modern industrial complex gave way, suddenly, to reveal a breathtaking mosque with its onion-domed minarets. On one street, they found a cluster of homes that could have been built at any time in the past few decades, while on the next street, they saw houses that must have been built centuries before. They passed a thriving market bazaar that, modern clothing and the occasional automobile aside, would not have felt out of place in the time of Christ. A lush and thriving green park, a cultivated and manicured oasis—Gaspar had no idea how it was irrigated—ended, suddenly, in a vast desert, where the buildings had been shaped from stone and sand. The winter sun was pale and harsh, and the cold air tasted of dust.

The road through the desert took them south of Saveh. Will, who had been reading, sat up. "Interesting," he said. "I found Marco Polo's account of finding the tomb of the Magi."

"What does he say?" asked Gaspar.

"Well, he says he found a great castle in the desert," said Will. "Masood, do you know of any ruins in the area? A fortress, maybe. Or old tombs?"

"You mean Kala Atashparastan," said Masood. "It is a castle, yes."

"That seems kinda unlikely," said Gaspar.

"Just wait till tomorrow," said Masood. Gaspar saw the man's reflection in the rearview mirror. A smile curled the corner of his lip.

"Anyway," said Will, "Marco Polo claimed to have gone there. He said he found the Magi, buried in three sepulchers of great size and beauty. Listen to this . . . this is how he described them: 'Above each sepulcher is a square building with a domed roof of very fine workmanship. The one is just beside the other. Their bodies are still whole, and they have hair and beards. One was named Balthasar, the second Gaspar, and the third Melchior.'"

"Huh," said Gaspar. "Fascinating!"

"I think there's more," said Will. "Let me read a little farther."

"How much longer?" Gaspar asked Masood.

"Not very," Masood told him. "There's only one good hotel. Very famous. I know the owner. I made a reservation for you. You got the information I sent you?

"I did," Will said without looking up from his phone.

"Masood," said Gaspar, "thanks. All of you."

Masood grinned. "Anything for Gaspar Bethlen of the Red Sox of Boston!"

Will leaned forward in his seat. "What can you guys tell us about this Kala Atashparastan place?"

"The castle you mentioned!" the man sitting next to Masood said. He was the man the others called Mo, which Gaspar was pretty sure was short for Mohamed. "Of course! Several miles into the desert. A holy place, or so they say, old as dirt. Sufi, I think."

"No," the man sitting behind Gaspar corrected. Gaspar couldn't remember his name to save his life. "It is Zoroastrian."

"I am pretty sure it is Sufi," said Mo.

"No," said Masood. "It is Zoroastrian, not Islamic. That's why nobody goes there much. I mean, except for the people who live there."

"It's not a ruin, then?" Gaspar asked.

"It's a community," said Mo. "But they keep to themselves. Very secret."

"But it's really, like, a castle?" Will looked back down at the book on his phone. "Marco Polo said he found a great castle in the desert where the people worshipped fire."

"Fire?" said Gaspar. "That doesn't sound too likely, either. Uh, does it?"

"Who knows what Sufis do?" said Mo.

"Zoroastrians," said Masood.

"I don't know what they do, either," said Mo.

"Me neither," said Gaspar.

"No one really knows about that place," Masood admitted. "It is a mystery. It is a place of legends. A place of secrets."

"But . . . fire?" said Gaspar.

"Fire," Will confirmed. "There's a whole story here about the Magi, the child Jesus, rocks, and . . . yeah, fire."

"Huh," said Gaspar.

"Is it really a castle?" Will asked.

"Just wait," said Masood. "I can take you there in the morning if you like."

"That'd be great," Gaspar said. He wrote his name on another baseball and tossed it over his shoulder. He turned to reach for another. With huge smiles that Gaspar could see even with their masks on, all six of the men on the back benches reached forward eagerly with balls, bats, and baseball cards. Gaspar grinned. "I may have to sign some of these tonight and give 'em back to you tomorrow. That okay?"

"Mr. Bethlen, please," one of the men said. Gaspar couldn't remember his name, either. "Can you please explain the infield fly rule, yes?"

The front desk clerk at the hotel had a lovely smile, Gaspar couldn't help noticing, and spoke excellent English with an accent that he could only describe as musical. As she handed them their keys—real, honest-to-God keys, not cards, Gaspar noticed with satisfaction—she said, "Mr. Klaus, your package arrived and was delivered to your room. Mr. Bethlen, your guest has arrived before you. He is waiting for you in your room."

Gaspar's body felt numb as his blood turned to ice. He realized he was gaping and forced himself to close his mouth. "Uh . . . guest?"

The clerk nodded. "Yes sir. Your relative. A Hungarian gentleman. You were expecting him, yes?"

"Yeah," said Gaspar. "I suppose I was at that. Is he alone?"

The clerk nodded again. "He is. Is there a problem, Mr. Bethlen?"

"Not yet," he said, hefting one of the baseball bats he'd brought in to sign.

Gaspar's room was on the second floor. He and Will took the stairs and crept quietly down the hallway.

The door to Gaspar's room was ajar. Gaspar looked at Will. Will nodded. They were as ready as they would ever be. Hoisting the bat again, Gaspar kicked the door open.

They found Count Bethlen Tamás seated at a table in the small sitting room outside the suite's bedroom. He did not stand before speaking. "Pray, lower your club. I am alone and unarmed. Alas, getting a revolver onto a commercial airliner takes more skill and resources than I can muster, I fear. Getting one into this barbarian country? *Bah.* It is more than I can manage. Come. Let us talk like gentlemen . . . if you can manage it."

Gaspar did not lower the bat. "What do you want, Tamás?"

The Count peered into Gaspar's eyes. Gaspar met his gaze without flinching, and the Count was the one who looked away first, turning his head down as if to study the tile in the floor.

The Count spoke hesitantly. "As I recall, you came to my house looking for help. You found me . . . a desperate man. A broken man. Perhaps you can understand that, yes? You know what it is, I think, for a man to lose his entire world."

Gaspar closed his eyes and sighed. When he opened them again, he said, "I asked you a question. What do you want?"

The Count opened his mouth, but he did not speak. After a moment, he closed it again. He bowed his head and his shoulders drooped. His body seemed to collapse, like a hot air balloon when its fire is quenched. He took a deep breath before answering. "I've come to ask for your help."

"You've gotta be kidding," said Will.

The Count ignored him. "I don't know how much you know about my house—"

"That manor," said Gaspar.

The Count nodded. "It is a proud part of my family's—" He swallowed. Gaspar could tell the words were hard for the man. He didn't care. "—of *our* family's past, of our heritage. It is a proud part of Hungary's culture. I call it my house, but it was never that. I only hold it in trust. I hold it for our family, sir. I hold it for our people. It is a part of our very soul, both as a family and as a nation. It is far more than a house. Those books you have taken belong there."

For a brief moment, the Count met Gaspar's eyes. But despite the passion in Bethlen's voice, Gaspar didn't see fire. He saw cold calculation. The count looked away again. "It is a trust," said the Count, "that I fear I have failed."

Gaspar closed his eyes and sighed. "I suppose there's a point to this?"

"You'll find this difficult to understand, American," said the Count. "Your branch of the family abandoned Hungary when the storm clouds gathered. What do you know of our land, and what it has suffered? What do you know of your *people?* You left your heritage behind. *Bah.* You're not a Bethlen. The great families leave their spirits behind when they flee. You are a man with his soul cut out. I do not say that to accuse, merely to point out the facts of the matter. The treasure that belongs to the Bethlens, and the Bethlens alone—your line left it in the hands of Arab strangers. You ask my point? It is simply this. The legacy you've come to claim means nothing to you. Nothing. Else, why would you have left it behind for so long?"

"You presume a great deal," Gaspar said. He didn't bother to cool the rage that he felt coming to a boil in his gut; he let it heat his words. "You have no idea what this means to me."

The Count shrugged. "Perhaps. I have no doubt you will get a very good price when you sell it." Gaspar felt his eyes narrow. "But let me ask you this. Do you really need the money? While you are only modestly wealthy by the highest of American standards, perhaps, you are more than comfortable. You will live the last of your days without want. You can buy nice things; you can travel. What more do you need?"

"I'm not sure I understand you," said Gaspar.

"Are you in danger of losing your home, sir?" said the count. "Of losing your very heritage? The last remaining vestige of your family's sacred honor? Of losing a bit of your nation's very soul? I think not, sir."

"Ah," said Gaspar. "I see now. You think this is about *money*. Don't you?"

"You think my friend will give you his inheritance, so that you can pay your debts and save your castle," said Will. "Is that what this is about?"

The Count shrugged.

"If you think this is about money for Gaspar Bethlen, you really *don't* know what you're talking about," said Will.

"Is that seriously it?" said Gaspar. "So . . . what? Have you been trying to eliminate the last heir, so you can claim the legacy for yourself? And now you're hoping to force or cajole me into giving it to you? Is that what you want, Tamás? Is that it?"

"I want what should be *mine*," the Count snapped. He spat the words as though the very act of speaking them was distasteful. "I do, in fact, know about you." The Count pointed with a bony finger as he met Gaspar's eyes again. "And you, you plainly have no interest in the proud legacy that comes with the Bethlen name!" Gaspar could see spite rising in the old man like bile, and his eyes grew large in their sockets as he spewed his sentences. "*Bah.* You're not a Bethlen at all. Your fathers fled to the plastic, greedy world of America. How dare you, how *dare* you return now and try to claim kinship? How dare you claim the legacy that belongs to the Bethlen name, and to Hungary?"

Gaspar shook his head and sighed again. "If you've come to ask me for something, you have a strange way of going about it."

The Count took another breath and then nodded before he continued, softly. "You are correct, sir. This is . . . difficult for me. I shall speak frankly. I have not come to ask, American. I have come to beg. If I am not good at it, forgive me. I am a proud man from a proud line. I have had little practice. Nonetheless, I beg you. Give it to me. The gem. Give it to me, Gaspar. Please. Save my home. Save my family's honor. Save *our* family's honor. If you care anything, anything at all for blood, or for the past, save this last shadow of glory." He swallowed again. "Please, sir. I beg you. Please."

Gaspar frowned and shook his head. "Please, spare me the *noblesse oblige*, shining symbol to the suffering, disenfranchised people of Hungary bullshit. You've lived in a frickin' castle, while thousands of your countrymen are homeless. Do you think they sleep more warmly at night knowing that one of the old families endures in its seat of power? You've been a man of means, but you've squandered your resources in the name of pride and pretension. You've done no good with the gifts you were given. No, Count. I find I can't muster one frickin' speck of sympathy for you or your plight. There is no nobility in you. You are a small, selfish, and petty man. Get out of here. Now."

"I beg you," the Count said again. "Please.

"I might have been more inclined to help you if you hadn't attacked my friend and me." Gaspar was silent for a moment before he spoke the next words, the guess he hadn't really articulated before, not even to himself. "And if you hadn't killed my father. You did, didn't you? And you let us think it was a simple mugging."

The Count dropped his humble mask and sneered. "I did no such thing. I hired men to retrieve that which was rightfully mine. Italians can be . . . enthusiastic. Your father paid a thief's price."

Gaspar saw Will's eyes go wide. "Gaspar, if he killed your dad. . . ."

Gaspar felt his body go numb again as he realized. When he spoke again, his voice was barely a whisper. "Beth."

The Count scowled. "I see that coming to you cap in hand and expecting you to be reasonable was a waste of time. You, sir, are not a gentleman. Therefore, I shall not act as one, either." He looked again and turned his cold gaze to Will. "Young man, pray, step to the window."

The Count gestured behind him. Gaspar watched as Will stepped past the Count and pushed the curtain aside. Without letting go of the bat, Gaspar followed and peered down at the street one floor below.

There, in the circle of pale light from a streetlamp, Gaspar could see two of the Count's men—the ones they'd seen first in the Count's manor, and then in Venice—holding a struggling Ana. Each of them had a firm grip on one of her arms. Her hands were bound in front of her with thick rope, and she was gagged.

"Ana!" Will cried. He pounded his fists on the heavy glass.

"I believe you remember my associates, Masters Jael and Abban?" said the Count.

"Ana!" Will called again. "*Ana!*"

"Do not underestimate me," the Count said. I will do what I must to protect that which is mine by right. Do not make the mistake of thinking I won't kill again."

Certain they had been seen, the men forced Ana into a waiting car. Seconds later, they sped away into the night.

Will turned back to the Count, and Gaspar saw that his eyes were wild with fury. "You son of a bitch. Your own granddaughter!"

"I did what I had to," the Count said, and Gaspar heard a sneer in his voice.

Will leapt for Tamás's throat, forcing him back. He held him against the wall. The Count grabbed Will's arm, but rage gave the younger man wild strength.

"Where is she?" Will demanded. *"Where?"*

Gaspar pulled the struggling Will back. "Easy."

The Count slumped, gasping. "She is a traitor to her name and to her heritage. She is of no bloody use to me. You want her? Claim the gem. Give it to me. The gem and the books. And then the bitch is yours. Now then. Do we have an understanding?"

Gaspar took a deep breath, his fists clenched, and nodded.

"Excellent," said the Count. Do you see how much simpler matters are when we bargain like gentlemen? Where is the gem?"

"Tell him, Will," said Gaspar.

"A place called Kala Atashparastan," said Will. "In the desert."

The count nodded. "I'll be there at sunrise, waiting with my men. Claim the gem and give it to me, and the girl is yours. But mark me. If I catch even the faintest whiff of treachery, she is dead. Do we have an understanding?"

Defeated, Gaspar could only nod again.

16

Kala Atashparastan

he morning sky was turning pink as an older white pickup truck left the suburban area and turned into the lonely desert. A loose tarp covered the cargo bed. In the cabin, Masood drove. Gaspar and Will sat next to him. Neither of them had slept much. Neither of them spoke.

For the first several miles, Gaspar found the desert fascinating, and even beautiful in a stark and harsh sort of way. After an hour, however, he began to find the landscape, with mile after mile of gently sloping dunes of khaki sand, monotonous.

The exhaustion of a sleepless night overtook them. Gaspar had begun to doze a bit when suddenly, as they crested the slope of a hill, he felt Will reach over to put a hand on his shoulder.

"Oh my God!" Will said, his voice barely a whisper.

Gaspar looked and gaped.

The monastery was nearly the size of a small mountain rising from the desert. Indeed, its terraced walls, levels, narrow windows, arches, and square towers seemed to have been hewn directly from the living rock of the desert itself. It was the red tan of the desert, save where light glinted like stars when it caught bits of glass or mosaic, and three great domes capped with blue tile that shimmered like still lakes. It was a mighty place, a place of peace, and it had stood for countless ages against the relentless pounding of time and the ravaging storms of desert sand. Smoke rose from a few of the chimneys, and Gaspar saw lights in some of the windows. Even in the distance, they could hear the sound of bells, low and solemn, discordant, but strangely merry at the same time. Gaspar's cheeks were damp, again, with tears, despite the danger, and as he wiped them, he felt his heart lift, arise, borne aloft as though on wings of song and prayer.

The outer areas, surrounded by two concentric walls, seemed to be deserted. The outer wall looked to be at least thirty feet tall, Gaspar guessed, and the inner wall was probably five feet or so taller. As near as he could judge, some forty feet separated the outer wall from the inner, and the inner wall from the castle inside. Narrow ladders led to the top of each of the two concentric walls on the outside.

"No wonder Marco Polo called the place a castle," said Gaspar.

"Told you," Masood said, grinning.

Will didn't say anything. Gaspar looked over at him and forced a smile. "We'll get her back, Will."

Will didn't look at him. "Tamás isn't planning on letting her go, you know."

"I know," said Gaspar. "Maybe—"

Will pointed ahead. "Uh oh."

Two SUVs were parked to block the road just outside the walls. The gate was closed. Masood brought the pickup truck to a stop.

"Looks like the Count got here early," said Gaspar.

The doors of the SUVs opened, and ten men climbed out. Gaspar recognized some of them from Hungary, including the two they'd encountered at the manor, and later in Venice, the men the Count had called Jael and Abban.

Abban held the struggling Ana. Her hands were tied, again or still, and she was gagged. Abban held a knife to her throat. The Count was the last to climb out. He stood close to Ana.

Gaspar and Will climbed out of the pickup. Gaspar reached for his metal briefcase, the one that held the books.

"That's close enough, American," the Count said. "The books. Give them to me."

"Let Ana go first," Will demanded.

"You are in no position to bargain," the Count said. "Cooperate, or I'll kill her right here and then my men will take the books."

"I thought you wanted the gem—" Gaspar said, stalling.

"With the books, I shall not need you, American. I can claim it myself. Now then. My men may not have been able to bring guns with them, but the barbarian Arab markets have nonetheless provided." The men reached into their jackets for long hunting knives. "But there is no need to be unpleasant. I shall try again to be a gentleman. Pray, do likewise. Throw the books to me. Gently."

Gaspar closed his eyes, sighed, and nodded.

"Gaspar—" Will began, but Gaspar ignored him and tossed the briefcase to the Count. It landed in the dust at his feet, spreading sand over his shoes. Tamás bent down, opened the case, checked the books, and snapped it back shut, satisfied. Then he turned back to his men. "Kill them all. Kill the Americans first."

Ana struggled mightily, and Gaspar could hear her screaming behind her gag, but the brute Abban did not relax his iron grip.

Gaspar watched as the Count's men stepped forward slowly, coordinated professionals, moving to surround them.

"You should have kept your bargain, Tamás," Gaspar said.

"You think to threaten me?" the Count said. "I believe you have not counted our numbers."

"You've got hired goons——" Gaspar looked at the Count's men and smiled. "——no offence——" He turned his attention back to the Count. "——but I brought Red Sox Nation."

At that moment, Masood climbed out of the cab, carrying three baseball bats. At the same time, the blue tarp flew away from the bed of the truck and seven more men, the Iranian baseball fans that had met Gaspar and Will at the airport, leapt out from under it.

The man called Abban looked over at Jael and spoke in Hungarian. "*What* nation?"

Jael shrugged. "Maybe a terrorist cell?"

Gaspar reached into his pocket and pulled out a baseball. He looked at Will and smiled again. "You know, I *have* missed this."

With a sudden motion, he threw the ball with all the strength in his arm and hit Abban, the man holding Ana, smack in the forehead. He dropped like a stone, moaning. Ana, free, tried to run, but Jael grabbed her. As she struggled and tried to kick, the remaining men charged at Will and Gaspar.

Masood gave Gaspar and Will baseball bats, keeping one for himself.

Gaspar tensed and readied himself. Their attackers were obviously professionals, but the Iranians were athletes, ballplayers, and the bats gave them reach. Gaspar smiled. He liked their chances.

The first man reached Gaspar. Gaspar swung the bat like he was driving for the Green Monster at Fenway, but the man danced back. Gaspar was vaguely aware of the men around him doing pretty much the same thing. Will and the Iranians swung their bats while the Count's men tried to close. For the moment at least, they were putting up a good fight.

Gaspar took his eyes off his attacker long enough to see the Count grab the briefcase with the books and flee toward the ladder leading to the top of the first wall, the outer one. He called to Jael as he ran. *"Velem! Hozd a lányt!"*

Jael dragged the still-struggling Ana as he turned to follow the count.

"Ana!" Will shouted.

Gaspar saw Will trying to get to her, but the Count's men were there. He fought, blocking a knife blow with his bat.

To his right, Gaspar saw one of the Iranian men fall, bleeding from a stab wound in the side. Gaspar rushed to his side, taking down the attacker with a blow to the shoulder before he could stab again. The man grunted and dropped his knife. The man who had been attempting to reach Gaspar lunged, but Gaspar turned and caught the man with a hard swing to the gut and then to the side of the head. The man crumpled, moaning in pain.

Gaspar looked up. The Count, Jael, and another man had reached the ladder at the outer wall. Gaspar saw Jael slash Ana's bonds and, still using the hunting knife, forced her up ahead of him. They started the climb. They were getting away.

Another of the Iranian ballplayers—the man they'd called Mo—fell, badly hurt. Gaspar hadn't seen what had happened, but he moved in to protect the man, swinging his bat wildly. Gaspar saw blood on the sand.

Gaspar and Will fought harder, swinging their bats like the blades of a pair of windmills, growing desperate. The men with the knives dodged nimbly but did not retreat. Gaspar swung hard and caught a man in the jaw. He heard the sickening sounds of bones snapping before the man fell. Another man jabbed with his hunting knife, but Gaspar blocked the blow with his bat. His counter missed badly.

The Count's men were still closing in, tightening their noose around Gaspar, Will, and the Iranians.

The Count and the men with Ana were still climbing the treacherous, narrow ladder. They were nearly to the top. "*Dammit,*" Gaspar muttered.

As Gaspar watched, Will blocked a knife swing, but the swipe lopped the top off of his bat. Will, desperate, lunged forward and caught the attacker under the chin with the freshly-hewn end. The man stumbled back, and

Will clubbed him on the top of his head. He dropped and was still.

Another man was about to stab Will from behind, a Gaspar tackled him. The man struggled like a wildcat, and Gaspar held him. "Go get her!" he yelled to Will. "Go!"

Will didn't hesitate. He sprinted across the sand to the ladder and started climbing, following after Ana.

The man Gaspar was holding struggled and fought. Gaspar dropped his bat and slugged the man with his fist, again, and again after that. The man slumped. Gaspar punched him twice more, ignoring the pain in his hands, and then the man was still. Grabbing the bat again, Gaspar climbed back to his feet and looked around, trying to take the scene in quickly. He thought that he and the Iranians were starting to get the edge on the Count's men, but the fight was still brutal and intense. He looked to his left just in time to see another Iranian fall, hurt. Gaspar couldn't tell how badly.

Gaspar was afraid. Every instinct told him to run, but he didn't. Gripping his bat, he waded back into the fight. He couldn't stop. If he stopped, he was dead.

Another man attacked with his long knife, but Gaspar got him in the wrist with a sharp blow from his bat. He dropped the knife and fell back, but another man was there to take his place. Gaspar took the man down, swinging his bat with his left hand. Then he tossed the

bat to his right hand and swung again, taking down another man.

He saw Masood grinning. "Switch hitter," Masood
said. "With power from both sides."

Gaspar grinned back at him. "Tell that to Will,
okay?"

Gaspar looked quickly to check on Will. He was
about halfway up the outer wall ladder and climbing
fast. *Way to go, dude.*

Meanwhile, the Count, Ana, Jael, and Abban had
reached the top of the wall and were now descending
what Gaspar guessed must be a stairway on the other
side of the outer wall. They'd moved fast, and Gaspar
thought of all the fencing trophies they'd seen back in
the Count's sitting room. The Count was an athlete and
apparently a good one.

Gaspar turned his attention back to the fight. Only
a few of the Count's men were standing, and Red Sox
Nation fought like demons. A man charged Masood
from behind, but Gaspar was there, swinging his bat like
a scythe.

Will reached the top of the outer wall. The wall was
about five or six feet wide and paved with pale blue tiles.
He crossed and looked down. The thugs called Jael and

Abban were dragging Ana across the courtyard and to the far wall. There, another ladder led up to the inner, taller wall. The Count was right behind them, moving fast.

Colorful banners hung from the inner wall, each adorned with symbols that Will did not recognize. He wished he had time to study them, because they struck him as both beautiful and holy.

Will looked down. Narrow, uneven stairs carved into the stone on the inside of the wall led down. There was no handrail, so Will had to move carefully. Carefully, but fast. Those men had Ana.

Across the courtyard, Abban was already forcing Ana to start climbing the second ladder, the one that climbed the inner wall. She was moving slowly. They'd hurt her.

Will moved faster, as fast as he dared. If he fell, he wouldn't be able to help anyone.

Below, another Iranian man fell, bleeding from his arm, but Masood caught him. Gaspar slugged the man who'd attacked him. The man didn't get up again. Gaspar spun, holding the bat ready, and looked around. Only two of the Count's men were standing. Seeing their chance, they both ran, racing toward the ladder at the outer wall. The direction Will had gone.

Masood looked at Gaspar. "Farid is hurt. So is Mo. These men need a doctor."

Gaspar nodded. "I understand. Go. Take them."

Masood hesitated. "Mr. Bethlen—"

Gaspar put his hand on the man's shoulder. "Go, pal. And thanks. I owe you. All of you."

Masood nodded. "Go Red Sox! Defeat the Yankees of New York." He grinned. "And these bastards."

Gaspar grinned back at him, winked, then turned and ran toward the ladder. He reached it and looked up.

It was a long way. And the ladder did not look sturdy. In fact, it looked downright precarious.

Will climbed this thing, Gaspar told himself. *If that nerd can do it, I can sure as hell do it.*

His heart pounded and his palms were starting to sweat. He had to wipe them on his pants. He closed his eyes.

Behind him, he heard Masood's truck roar away. He had to start up. He had to climb. He had to.

I can do this. I can do this. I can frickin' do this.

It took all the effort he could muster, but Gaspar put his foot on the bottom rung and then the rung after that.

⊰⊱

Will sprinted to the inner wall and started up the second ladder. He was gaining. The Count and his entourage had not reached the top yet. Ana, bless her, was slowing them. As he watched, he saw one of the men backhand her with a closed fist.

Faster, he admonished himself. *Dammit, Klaus, faster!*

- ❧ -

The first of the two men who had fled the fight reached the top of the outer wall. The second man was right behind him. Before the second man could step off the ladder, Gaspar grabbed him by the leg and heaved. The man fell backwards, screaming.

The other man turned and kicked, but Gaspar avoided the blow and, while the man was off balance, made it to the top of the outer wall. By then, the man had set himself again. He was ready. The man swung his knife and Gaspar ducked—and nearly tumbled off the wall.

"Heights—" he muttered aloud.

Gaspar punched, but the man stepped back, avoiding the blow. The man swiped again with the knife, but Gaspar ducked under it and lunged forward, catching the man in the gut with his shoulder. The man grunted and dropped the knife. Gaspar kicked it off the wall. They were both unarmed.

The man swung at Gaspar with his fist. Gaspar stepped back to avoid the blow—and nearly tumbled backwards and off the wall. Gaspar glared at the man. "Dammit, I . . . frickin' . . . *hate* . . . heights!

Will reached the top of the ladder on the taller inner wall and tried to move carefully and quietly. The Count and the others were just starting down the stairs on the far side. Ana, still gagged, had managed to slow them down, at least somewhat. Will could see that she was bleeding.

Just as Will stepped off the ladder, Ana met his eyes and tried to scream behind her gag. Will held his finger to his lips, but it was too late. The man called Jael spun. His eyes widened for a single heartbeat and then he raced at Will, going for the body slam. Will was ready. At the last second, he ducked, dropping to one knee, and used Jael's own momentum to flip him over his shoulder and off the wall.

Will turned and saw that Jael had managed to grab the ladder as he fell, one rung and then another, grasping at each just enough to slow his fall. Nonetheless, he landed hard in the sand some thirty feet below, missing the jagged rocks by less than a yard. He grunted, barely moving.

Will turned in time to see Ana kick Abban hard in the leg. It hurt him enough to make him mad. He turned, his hand raised to slap, but Ana kicked again, this time in a spot that made Will cringe in reluctant sympathy. Abban crumbled, releasing Ana. She managed to spit out the gag. "Will!"

The Count backed away, closer to the stairs that led down on the far side, watching. He clutched the briefcase with the books to his chest.

"*Állítsd meg!*" the Count cried in Hungarian.

Stop him, Will translated in his head. *Great.*

Abban was still hurting, but he lumbered toward Will. The man looked like a mountain in a suit. Will ducked under Abban's first punch and landed a blow of his own. It didn't seem to hurt Abban much, but he dropped his knife. It slid to the edge of the wall.

Will looked up and met Abban's gaze. He truly hadn't hurt the man; he'd only made him madder.

"*Will!*" Ana screamed.

Will reached under his jacket, but, belying his size and mass, Abban's hand moved like a crack of thunder, grabbing Will's arm just below the wrist. He squeezed, and Will's eyes nearly popped out of their sockets.

Uh oh.

—❦—

At the top of the outer wall, the lower one, Gaspar stepped back to avoid another blow from the man he fought. His heart pounded. He was close to the edge; if he had to back up again, he knew he'd fall.

Dammit, I hate frickin' heights!

Gaspar knew he needed to end this, and fast. The man was a killer, but Gaspar was a trained athlete. The man swung again, aiming for Gaspar's eyes. Gaspar ducked under the punch and, still hunched, charged forward like a linebacker, using the same move again, but harder, and drove his shoulder into the man's gut. The man tumbled down the narrow stairs and then off, landing in the soft sand.

Gaspar looked across the courtyard, to the higher, inner wall. Will was struggling with one of the Count's men, the one called Abban. It didn't look good.

Will needed help. He needed it right now.

Count Tamás Bethlen watched as Abban struggled with the smaller American. Abban had the man at the edge of the wall; in a matter of seconds, he would push the little man off and it would be over. At that moment, Ana raced forward, clubbing Abban on the back of his thick neck with both of her hands. The blow didn't seem to faze Abban, but it distracted him long enough for the small American to regain his footing and land a desperate punch. The surprised Abban stumbled back. Abban wasn't used to victims who fought back.

The Count scowled. His traitorous granddaughter had interfered in his business one time too many. It was time for the bitch to learn her place. Holding the heavy briefcase against his body like a battering ram, he sprinted directly at Ana. She heard him coming and turned, but too late. His charge caught her full on, knocking her off the wall. He had to skid to a stop to avoid following her.

The Count looked down. Somehow, she'd managed to catch hold of the very edge of the wall.

Gaspar saw that Ana was in trouble. She was holding on to the edge of the inner wall by the tips of her fingers. Her grip was worse than precarious. He frowned. He wasn't going to get there fast enough to help her.

Unless. . . .

Seeing one chance, Gaspar turned and pulled the narrow ladder up to the top of the outer wall. It was heavy and swaying in his grasp. Gaspar held it steady; there was a pretty damn good chance that if it fell, it would take him with it. Gaspar walked the ladder to the far edge of the wall with careful, teetering baby steps.

He paused for second, trying to judge the distance to the inner wall.

It's long enough. It's long enough. . . .

His arms strained as he tried to lower the ladder gently.

Please, God, let it be long enough.

He let the ladder fall across the gap between the walls. It caught, making a precarious, rickety bridge. He closed his eyes for a second, gathering courage.

It's not that high. It's not that high. . . .

Without looking down, he started across, running rung to rung. The ladder bent under his weight. Gaspar looked across and tried to tell himself that the far end of the ladder was not starting to slip.

It's not that high. . . .

Gaspar dared to look down and saw the jagged rocks far below.

"It's totally that high!" he shouted out loud.

Abban was still off balance from Will's punch. Taking advantage, Will managed to push the big man away with a body slam and race to Ana. Will bent down and grabbed her arms, just below her wrists. Grunting, he tried to pull her up. Just then, he heard a noise behind him. Abban had recovered and charged, slamming into

Will from behind. Somehow, Will managed to keep himself from tumbling off the wall, but he lost his grip on Ana's arms.

Ana screamed as she fell again, but when Will looked, he saw that she had managed to catch the top of one of the great banners that hung from the top of the wall.

Will turned, but something else had caught Abban's attention. Gaspar was coming, using the ladder from the outer wall as a bridge. That gave Will a chance. Holding on to the edge of the wall, he lowered himself down. "Ana! Grab my legs!"

———※———

Gaspar saw Abban step out onto the ladder bridge, coming to meet him. "Aw, c'mon! Can't we just try to beat the crap out of each other on the other side?"

Abban didn't slow. He raised a hand behind his head. Gaspar knew he was trying to end the fight with a single punch. Gaspar managed to avoid it, leaning back, and somehow managed not to lose his shaky footing. A wave of vertigo surged through him, and Gaspar had to fight not to vomit—or pass out.

Gaspar tried to land a return punch, but in doing so he nearly lost his footing. Abban, a professional killer, dodged it easily. He smiled.

In the distance, from somewhere within the walls of Kala Atashparastan, the Castle of the Magi, bells tolled.

———❦———

Brother Reza had served as the bell ringer at the Kala Atashparastan Monastery for more than forty years. In that time, he had only missed his duties twice. It was a simple job, but it was his, and he considered it a great honor. To him, the sounds of the bells were music, and everyone knows that music pleases the Holy Maker. The wind billowed his white robes as he pulled the ropes.

As the bells rang their songs, Brother Reza looked out over the monastery's courtyards and out at the stark beauty of the sun-bathed sands below. Then he gasped. Down below, people were fighting. Fighting! And on the holy ground!

Brother Reza turned and ran back down the stairs. Moments later, he charged into a room where more of his brothers had gathered. Brother Reza yelled at them in Farsi, telling them what he'd seen.

One of the brothers hurried to a vintage wall phone and dialed. Brother Reza closed his eyes and prayed that the police would arrive swiftly.

Will allowed himself a quick sigh of relief as Ana managed to grab his leg, first with one hand and then the other, and hold tight. He struggled to pull them back to the ledge, but the weight of two bodies was too much for him. He grunted and tried again, but it was no good. It was all he could do to hold on.

C'mon, Gaspar. . . .

And then he had a new problem.

The Count saw Will and Ana's predicament and leapt forward, stomping hard on Will's hands. He cried out in pain. Somehow, he held onto the ledge.

"*Will!*" Ana screamed.

The Count raised his booted foot again.

Terror rose in Gaspar's belly like the tide. Abban's fists were like a storm, like a force of nature. Worse, it was getting harder with every pounding heartbeat to keep his footing. He was sure that the stupid ladder was slipping.

He was going to fall. He knew it. *Oh, God, oh, God,* he was going to fall.

301

He aimed a clumsy jab toward Abban's face, but the big man slapped it effortlessly aside. Abban leered at Gaspar. "I watched your wife die, American. Now I'm going to kill you."

And then Gaspar felt something change within him. Hot terror cooled to cold fury. The world seemed to slow. Every heartbeat was an eternity.

"Like hell," Gaspar said.

Abban swung, but Gaspar knocked the punch aside with his left arm and punched with his right. Gaspar felt cartilage break. He punched again and again after that.

Abban stumbled back and Gaspar nearly fell, but the ice of his rage helped him regain his footing. He raised his fist again.

"This is for Beth, you son of a bitch."

Gaspar put all the power he could muster into one last blow, this one with his left fist. He felt the strike connect, and Abban reeled.

In the next heartbeat, Abban stumbled back.

In the next, he lost his footing.

In the heartbeat after that, Gaspar realized something. This wasn't for Beth. Beth had loved life, every heartbeat. Beth wouldn't want a man to die, not even a brute like Abban.

In the next heartbeat, Gaspar dived, landing belly first on the rapidly shifting ladder. He reached out, stretching as only a Gold Glove first baseman could, and for a second, he caught a handful of Abban's shirt.

Only for a second.

Abban's shirt tore, and then the big man fell to the jagged rocks, where his final scream was abruptly silenced with the sickening, chopped melon sound of a body breaking.

Gaspar looked down. Below, he saw the man called Jael and the man he'd fought on the far side of the wall. Both men had made it back to their feet. The man called Jael pointed to the fight on the inner wall. The men started moving toward the second ladder.

In front of him, Will hung from the edge of the inner wall. Ana clung desperately to his legs. Gaspar slid on his belly along the ladder, knowing he would never make it to the inner wall in time to help.

As Gaspar watched, the Count stomped at Will's hands. Will cried out in pain, but he held on. The count raised his foot again, higher.

In that moment, Will's hand darted like a striking Cobra. A knife had fallen by the edge of the wall. He lunged and grabbed it.

"Ana," Will shouted, "hold on!"

Gaspar thought Will was going to slash at the Count's foot, but he had other ideas.

Will let go of the ledge with one hand and, in the same motion, slashed the nearest tie holding the banner. Gaspar could only gape as, with all the grace and panache of Errol Flynn in the old pirate movies he used to watch with his dad, Will swung down on the heavy fabric. Ana held on for dear life.

Gaspar leapt and reached the edge of the inner wall just as the ladder tumbled down and smashed on the rocks. He turned his attention back to Will and gaped again.

Will and Ana fell the last few yards, landing softly in the sand.

"Wow," Gaspar said aloud. "Now that's one damn cool detective."

Ana, bleeding and hurt worse than Will had realized, collapsed. Will knelt and helped her to her feet. She was dizzy but she could stand.

The Count had been watching Will and Ana, giving Gaspar a split second to regain his footing on the top of the inner wall. Then the Count turned, waiting, his long knife ready. He slashed, and Gaspar nearly tumbled back and off the wall. Gaspar took a second to appraise the situation. The desperate Count, an accomplished fencer, was ruthless with the deadly blade, and Gaspar was unarmed. More, he couldn't step backward, not unless he wanted to join Abban on the rocks.

The fight was swift and brutal. The Count slashed again, ripping Gaspar's shirt and opening a shallow cut that bled.

The Count jabbed, but Gaspar avoided it by stepping to his right. The Count smiled. "Happy Christmas, American bastard."

The Count swiped and Gaspar ducked. With his body low, Gaspar pushed forward, the same move he used twice in the fight on the other wall, knocking the Count back. *Stay with what works.*

The blow put the Count off balance, and this time he was the one who nearly fell. Now behind the Count, Gaspar grabbed his arm and wrenched it back. Gaspar took the knife.

"Yeah," said Gaspar, "shove this up your chimney, asshole."

Ana dusted herself and looked up to see Will looking down at her with concerned eyes. Her whole body hurt, and she was bleeding, but she smiled.

"Are you okay?" Will asked her. He knelt and rubbed her wrists where the bonds had held her.

She nodded. "I will be. I think." Then she gasped and pointed. "Will!"

Will turned to see the man called Jael and another man closing, ready to attack. Ana looked around frantically. Where the hell was the damned knife? Will had dropped it when they fell. She couldn't find it.

The men came closer.

Ana clutched Will's arm. Will sighed and reached with both hands into the inside pockets on both sides of his jacket. "I didn't want to do this. I'm not a killer."

Slowly, he pulled his hands out of his jacket. Ana gasped.

Will was holding twin pistols.

Dots of red light appeared on the men's shirts. Will's guns had laser sights. Ana shook her head, too stunned to speak.

"I don't want to," said Will, "but so help me, if you take one more step, I will."

Jael and the other man froze.

Will didn't want to fight; Ana knew that. He believed in peace. Ana swallowed. Whatever Will was prepared to do, whatever he was willing to do for her, she didn't want him to do it. She remembered the fire that had been in her mother's eyes when she'd confronted her grandfather all those years ago, and she tried to kindle it in her own. She stepped in front of Will.

"You heard him," Ana said, and she was proud of the ice in her voice. "He doesn't want to kill you. I imagine you do not want to be killed. Now then. Let me ask you a question. My grandfather is bankrupt. By now you must know, he will not get the gem, even if it is truly here. I ask you. How is he paying you? Not a check, surely?"

Will chuckled softly. "Yeah, like, you guys got cash up front, right?"

The two men exchanged a glance and spoke to one another, too softly for Ana to hear the words. Then, with a shrug, they both turned and walked away.

Ana closed her eyes and let out the breath she'd been holding.

It was over.

--- ✦ ---

Gaspar followed the Count down the ladder. They reached the bottom and Gaspar pushed the Count toward Will and Ana, holding a knife at his back. Ana had just retrieved another knife from the sand. Will was holding a pair of mean-ass looking pistols. Gaspar shook his head. *Now where the hell did he get frickin'* guns?

They arrived just in time for the Count to see his men walking away, and Gaspar could see his last spark of hope fail.

"That's the trouble with hired help, Grandfather," Ana said. "You can't really depend on them, can you?"

Will smiled his lopsided grin. "Uh, technically, I'm hired help."

"Except for Will," Ana amended.

Gaspar moved the knife from the Count's back to his throat. The fury was back, colder than the sea, colder than any storm. He looked at Ana. "What should I do?"

Ana shook her head. "Gaspar, no. Don't. Please."

Gaspar looked at her, surprised. "He was going to kill you."

"This is a holy place." She closed her eyes and bowed her head. "And he is my grandfather."

Slowly, Gaspar nodded and shoved the Count away. "Get out of here. Get out of my sight, Tamás."

The Count scowled again, and Gaspar found himself wondering if the man was even capable of other expressions. "You can't be serious. My men have gone. I'll die in the desert."

"Leave, Grandfather," Ana said. She fingered the knife she'd found. "Now. Before I change my mind and kill you myself."

The Count nodded. Then, with a desperate move, he turned and kicked Gaspar's wrist. Stunned, Gaspar dropped the knife. Before Gaspar had realized what had happened, the Count lunged for it, rolled back to his feet, and slashed.

Too late.

The Count gasped. His eyes widened in shock as he died. As he fell, Ana pulled her knife free from his gut. "I warned you," she said, and Gaspar saw fire in her eyes.

Beyond the walls, Gaspar heard the sound of sirens. He forced a grin. "Oh thank God. I think that's the police. Help at last, huh?"

Just then, Gaspar heard a voice speaking behind him. "Come, come."

Gaspar turned to see a thin man with a long white beard standing before an opened door. He wore a white robe and a turban.

"Come," the man said again. "I believe you are Mr. Bethlen, yes? I am Brother Reza. We have been expecting you."

Gaspar felt his eyes pop open and his jaw drop. "You have?"

"Indeed! Please, come inside. Leave us to greet the police. We will handle this matter. Yes. It is . . . better that way, I think. We are not without influence, you know."

Gaspar bent and retrieved his briefcase from the Count's still hands.

17

The Legacy of the Magi

he walk wasn't long and, despite his fatigue and injuries, Gaspar did not find the going difficult. Will and Ana hurried close behind, following the path Brother Reza had shown them, walking slowly and gaping in unabashed wonder. Will had his arm protectively around Ana's waist.

"Dude," said Gaspar, "I have to know. Where the hell did you get *guns* for God's sake?"

Will laughed. "These?" He pulled one out of his jacket pocket and aimed skyward. When he pulled the trigger, there was no sound. Nothing happened at all. "These are some of the props the toy shop made for that movie. Remember? I had them ship them overnight to me at the hotel. I ... well, I thought I might need an ace up my sleeve. Just in case."

"But ... they have laser sights!"

"Yeah," said Will. "Cool, huh? The collectors really eat that stuff up."

For a long moment, Gaspar just stared, his mouth hanging open. And then he laughed, all of them laughed together, and Gaspar couldn't remember the last time he had laughed that long or that hard.

Another man waited for them near the gate. His skin was dark brown and weathered, and he too wore a white turban and robes, thick against the mild winter chill. Gaspar could not guess his age, but he found himself feeling suddenly young and awkward. He was not sure how to greet the man, so he folded his hands as though in prayer and bowed his head. Smiling, the man reached out and touched Gaspar gently on the forehead.

Gaspar heard Will, somewhere behind him, pulling his phone out of his pocket. "Just a sec, okay?" Will said. "I, uh, have Google Translate here. . . ."

The man smiled. "Do not worry," he said. "My English is excellent. Welcome to you all. I am Brother Babak. I speak for the brothers of the *Magupati*."

"The Magi!" said Will.

The man nodded to Will. "Yes, my friend."

"So it's *not* a Sufi monastery," said Gaspar. He grinned at Will. "We'll have to tell Masood."

"The Sufi are welcome here," said the man in the robes. "As are all men of peace and goodwill. Many of them visit us here. This is a place of understanding, of, as you would say, of common ground, of the truths that

311

should unite all men as brothers. Not of division and strife. Do you know of the Sufi?"

"Only that they are one of the world's great wisdom traditions," said Ana.

"Just so," Brother Babak said with a nod. "In any case, we've been expecting you, Mr. Bethlen."

"So I hear," Gaspar said wryly.

The man nodded, grinning. "You have, I think, documents for me? And, perhaps, three books?"

Gaspar hefted the briefcase and said, "I've got them right here."

The man nodded and accepted the case. "You'll understand that we must authenticate these, of course. Such was the promise we made, long ago. The legacy of the Bethlen family is without price."

"How long will that take?" asked Will.

"Not long," said the man. "Long enough for a cup of tea, or perhaps two if you sip quickly. And then, Mr. Bethlen, if you answer the questions, we shall lead you to what you seek."

"Thank you," said Gaspar. "But first . . . ."

"Yes?" the man prompted.

"How in the world did you know to expect me?"

The man titled his head and smiled gently. "Why, we are the Magi, of course. Stargazers. Astrologers. The secrets of the future are well known to us."

Gaspar felt his jaw drop and knew his eyes were popping again.

"Relax," Brother Babak said. "I'm joking."

"But—"

The man seemed surprised. "Seriously, you do not know? A man came before you. He said he was your relative. In fact, he tried to claim your inheritance for you. Would it surprise you to know that you are not the first to attempt to claim the Legacy of Gaspar the Magi? No, I see in your eyes that you are not surprised."

"That's the late gentleman the police are dealing with now," said Gaspar.

The man nodded, and Gaspar saw sorrow in his gaze. "Let us speak of him no more. Come, come with me. We will tend your wounds, and offer you rest. Also, our tea here is excellent, you'll find."

The tea was excellent indeed.

They rested. They were cared for. Will held Ana while she cried. She cried for a good, long time.

Later, Brother Babak, the man in the white robes, came to fetch them. "If you'll follow me?"

Ana, Will, and Gaspar stood.

"You need a doctor," Will told Ana. "That bandage is—"

"I know, and you're right." Ana smiled and touched his cheek. "But my love, I have to see this."

313

Will nodded and helped her walk.

Together, they followed the man in white. The path was paved with smooth stones; someone kept them swept clean of sand. After a time, the man stopped. "Here I leave you. Go on. Up the stairs. Then, enter the gate there and follow the corridor. My brothers are waiting for you. They will guide you."

Gaspar wasn't sure how to respond, so he went with what seemed to have worked before. He put his hands together again and bowed his head slightly. The man smiled and returned the gesture, and Gaspar's heart was light. Then, still smiling, Brother Babak turned and left them.

As they walked, Will turned to Gaspar and said, "Well, this is new. So help me, you're still smiling! You honestly look happy."

Gaspar felt the smile widen. "I can almost feel Beth here with me," he said. "I can almost see the way her eyes would light up just before she smiled. I can almost feel her breath on the back of my neck. I feel like I can wrap the very warmth of her closeness around me like a blanket, and it fills my heart with golden light."

"At the end of the last mystery," said Will.

Gaspar nodded. "The last mystery."

Will smiled again and put his hand on Gaspar's shoulder. "And soon you'll have what you came for. Beth's last gift. Something to hold onto."

Gaspar nodded.

"I'm glad I could be here," Ana said. "With both of you. I . . . I am honored."

They climbed the crooked, irregular stone stairs and came to the gate at the end of the path. This time, there was no one waiting to meet them, so Will pulled on a heavy rope that rang a great bell. After a few minutes, they heard the sound of soft footsteps and then the groan of the opening gate. A man they had not yet met was there to greet them. Other men, also dressed in turbans and white robes, stood with him.

"Welcome, my friends, welcome!" the man said. "I am Brother Solayman. Welcome!"

"Thank you," said Gaspar. He offered Brother Solayman his hand to shake. The man accepted, clasping Gaspar's hand in both of his.

"Pardon my companions," said Brother Solayman. "They do not speak your language, but they wished to come and greet you nonetheless."

Gaspar, Ana, and Will shook hands with the other men as well.

When they had finished with their greetings, Gaspar said, "I trust you found the genealogy and documents in order?"

"We did," said Brother Solayman. "And we have everything ready to return to you. Including, of course, that which you came so far to reclaim. I assume you have the answers to the questions?"

"I hope so," said Gaspar. "Would you, um, like to ask them now?"

"Not yet," said Brother Solayman. "Come, come, follow me. Here, just down the corridor." He smiled again, and light danced in his eyes. "There is something I wish to show to the heir of Gaspar the Magi."

Gaspar and Will followed the robed brothers through the gate and into a narrow corridor of sand-colored stone and clay. The corridor opened into a wide, sandy courtyard. Paths led to caves that ran deep into the vast and rocky heart of the mountain itself, and more stone steps led up to the great fortress of the monastery. The man in the white robes led them to the stair and upward. They came to another gate and followed the man through. He led them through a warren of corridors, chambers, and passageways. Some were of the same sandy stone and clay; others were covered with vast, tiled mosaics that Gaspar ached to study.

Brother Solayman kept a brisk pace, and Gaspar found that he had to hurry to keep up. As he walked, the man spoke. "You have read Marco Polo's account of his journey here all those long years ago, have you?"

"I have," said Will. "I don't know how much of it was true. I wouldn't have thought any of it was, and yet, here I am at the castle of Palasata in Kala Atashparastan."

"To believe and to question," Brother Solayman said with an approving nod. "That is the beginning of wisdom. But tell me, what did our friend Marco report?"

"He claimed to have found a town called Kala Atashparastan," said Will, "a name which he claimed meant the Town of the Fire-worshippers."

"An interesting name," said the man. "Did he say how the place came by such a title?"

"He did," said Will. "He said that the people of the town *did* worship fire."

"Fire!" said Ana. "Is that true?"

Will looked at Gaspar and raised his eyebrows. Gaspar winked.

"Uh, that's what Marco Polo claimed, anyway," said Will.

The man in white chuckled. "What else did he say?"

"Uh, about the fire worship?" Will asked.

Brother Solayman nodded as he walked. "Did he say why the men he visited worshipped fire?"

"Well, uh, yes," said Will. "It's kind of a long story."

"Go ahead and spill it all," Gaspar said. He grinned at the man in white. "My dude here is all about the research."

Ana gave his arm a squeeze. "My brilliant man."

Will blushed but continued. "In days gone by three wise men of this country went to worship a newborn king. That's how Marco Polo reported it. They took with them three offerings—gold, frankincense, and myrrh—

317

so as to discover whether this prophet was a god, or an earthly king, or a healer. They said to one another: 'If he takes gold, he is an earthly king; if frankincense, a god; if myrrh, a healer.'

"They followed a star to the place where the child was born, and when they arrived at last, the youngest of the three wise men went in all alone to see the child. To his very great surprise, he didn't find a baby at all. Instead, he found a man like himself, who seemed to be of his own age and appearance. The man accepted his gift of gold. And the youngest of the men came out, full of wonder.

"Then in went the second, who was a man of middle age. And to him also the child seemed to be of *his* own age and appearance. This man accepted the gift of frankincense. And the second of the wise men came out quite dumbfounded.

"Then in went the third, who was of riper years. It pretty much went the same as it had with the other two, and the gift of myrrh was accepted. The third wise man came out deep in thought. When the three Magi were all together again, each told the others what he had seen. They were all amazed and resolved that they would all go in together.

"So, in they went, all three at once, and came before the child and saw him in his real likeness and of his real age, for he was only a child. All three offerings were there with the babe in places of honor. Then they worshipped him. Before they left to return to their own country, by a different route, the miraculous child gave them each a closed casket.

"After the three Magi had ridden for some days, they decided to see what the child had given to them. They each opened their caskets, and each found inside a simple black stone. They each wondered what this could be. The youngest suggested that maybe the child had given it to them to signify that they should be firm as stone in faith. After all, when the three kings had seen that the child had taken all three offerings, they had concluded that he was at once God, a king, and a healer.

"But the other two older Magi, not knowing why the stones had been given to them, took them and threw them away, into a well. No sooner had the stones fallen in than there descended from heaven a burning fire, which came straight to the well and into the two stones. When the three kings saw this miracle, they wept and repented of their throwing away the stones, for in that holy moment they saw clearly that its significance of the wonder was great and good. The two kings took some of this fire and carried it to their castle and put it in one of their churches, a very fine and splendid building. I'm guessing that's close to where we are now."

The man in the turban nodded. "Just so."

"According to Marco Polo," Will finished, "they keep the fires burning perpetually and worship it as a god. Every sacrifice and offering is burned with this holy

319

fire. If it ever happens that the fire goes out, they go back to the sacred well and renew the fire again."

They had come to the end of a corridor, and the man stopped before a great wooden door, twelve feet high and easily wide enough for five people to pass through abreast. "Is that what Marco reported?" asked Brother Solayman.

Will nodded.

"And what do you believe?" asked Brother Solayman.

"I believe," Will said hesitantly, "that I am very eager to see what's on the other side of that door."

Brother Solayman smiled again, laughed, and nodded. With the help of two of the other robed men, he flung open the great doors. Gaspar entered and found himself in a vast chamber, one more magnificent by far than any cathedral he had ever entered. Will and Ana came in behind him.

Mighty pillars surrounded the hall, supporting a great domed ceiling. Tile mosaics, each nearly three stories tall, adorned the walls behind the circle of columns. The mosaics depicted the journey of the Magi with their gifts, until they came at last to the manger in the lowly stable in Bethlehem. Tile work on the inside of the grand dome recreated the night sky, with the tail a long comet pointing toward the final mosaic—the one depicting the Christ child, flanked by gently smiling Mary, so very young, and baffled, awe-struck Joseph. At the center of the chamber stood a great altar, one that, Gaspar could tell, had not been moved in but rather hewn and shaped from the stone foundation itself, from the very bones of the earth, and the chamber built around it. Upon either end of the altar burned two fires, great and golden, which gave no smoke.

"Marco Polo was not entirely correct," said the man in the robe. "We do not worship fire here. We tend it, yes, but the fire is merely a symbol of He who sent it, and He who sent divine light to guide the Magi so that they might witness a wonder. Like the star in the east, they point the way to greater truth, and greater mystery."

Great feeling fell over Gaspar, emotion he could neither name nor describe, and he fell to his knees, weeping suddenly. The fires were unlike any he had ever seen before. Their light was holy, numinous, like starlight, like the halos of saints and angels, like the first illumination at the dawn of creation, drawn forth by the voice of the Creator crying *Light!* with a sound more beautiful than all the choirs of all the angels in all the eternal heavens. Gaspar folded his hands and bowed his head, feeling as though his whole body was filled with light, pure and golden. He wanted to pray, but words failed him again. It didn't matter. The communion was deeper, purer. Tears were his prayer. He trembled, feeling cleansed and renewed, baptized with fire and tears, sobbing like a newborn gulping its first breath of precious life.

Ana smiled through her own tears. "It's a miracle, isn't it?"

No one answered her. No one had to.

When at last Gaspar found his voice again, he looked to the man in the white robe. "There are only two fires there," he said. "The third—?"

"The youngest of the Magi was wiser than the other two," said Brother Solayman. "He did not throw away the casket containing his stone."

"Which—?" The single word was all Gaspar could manage.

"You tell me," the man said, smiling. "Who was the father of your line?"

Gaspar was silent, but Ana spoke. "It's the first question. Tell him. Gaspar, tell him."

"Gaspar. Gaspar the Magi. . . ."

Brother Solayman nodded. "Just so. Where did his journey take him?"

"To Bethlehem," said Gaspar. "To the City of David."

Brother Solayman nodded again. "What led him there?"

Gaspar looked up, to the great comet worked in tile on the vast dome above him.

"The star in the east," said Gaspar. "The comet we know today as Halley."

"And what did he find?"

Gaspar knew the answer to the final question as well. On the first Christmas, the Magi had traveled from

322

their own country to witness a miracle. On that morning, a gate was opened, a gate in the form of a child shivering among the animals, between Creator and created, between Divine love and base matter, between light and dust, between that which is fleeting and that which endures, dearly, brightly, forever. Beth had understood that great truth in her final moments, and sharing it had been her final gift.

"What did Gaspar find?" the man asked again, his voice gentle and smiling.

Gaspar knew the answer the man was looking for was the obvious one, but looking into his heart, he gave another, truer one.

"Grace," he said, weeping. "Peace."

"Just so," said the man, beaming. "Just so. Come, Gaspar Bethlen. Your quest is at an end. Come with me now, please, and claim your legacy."

Gaspar, Ana, and Will followed the brothers, heirs of Magi, past the altar and into a narrow passage that ran deeper into the monastery. The path they followed led them down into the secret heart of the mountain, and Gaspar found himself muttering a prayer of gratitude that he would not be forced to find his way out alone.

At last, they came to a large room with walls covered with open square nooks. It reminded Gaspar of the inside of a honeycomb. Most of the cubical nooks were covered with curtains; but those exposed contained boxes of wood or elaborately worked metal, scrolls or books, or bits of pottery, sculpture, or jewelry.

"My God!" Ana breathed. "What *is* all this?"

"Treasures," said Brother Solayman. "Objects given to us for safekeeping, until such time as their owners return to claim them. In that way, we are not unlike our Christian brothers in Rome, isn't it so? I will tell you this: most of the items here would be the prize of any museum on earth. The secrets contained herein could shake the very foundations of what most scholars think they know about history."

"Astonishing!" said Will. "It seems a great tragedy that these items are lost to most of the world."

"Not lost," said Brother Solayman. "No, never that. Merely held in hallowed trust until the time is right. But for what it's worth, I agree with you, my young friend. I wish it could be otherwise. Nonetheless, our oaths are sacred ones. It is not our decision to make."

The man in white turned to Gaspar. "But here, one of the treasures, at least, I can show you. It is yours now, Gaspar Bethlen. Its secret is yours alone to reveal, or not."

Two of the other men brought a ladder, and one of them scampered up. Moments later, he climbed down, cradling a wooden casket in one arm. He carried it reverently to Gaspar and bowed as he presented it.

The box was smooth and dust free. Plainly, Gaspar thought, the monks here cared for the items in their custody. It was a little more than a foot long and perhaps half that wide and deep. It was very heavy and obviously very old. Gaspar held it with trembling hands, suddenly afraid that he would drop it. Sensing his uneasiness, the man in the white robe took Gaspar by the elbow.

"Come, my friend," he said. "There is a table in the next room, just through here. You can open the casket there."

The next chamber was smaller and bare save for a small table and two wooden chairs. Shards of pale, wintry sun reached through the slits of narrow windows. Gaspar placed the casket on the table. Ana and Will stood behind him. One of the monks showed him how to work the antiquated clasp.

Gaspar took a deep breath and opened the box.

The box was lined with folds of some dark, velvety cloth. Gaspar unwrapped the fabric to reveal a jewel, a jewel nearly as large as the span of his hand with the fingers outstretched. The setting was of gold, intricately worked, radiating out like rays of pure light from the brightest star in the darkest sky. The stone itself, nearly as large as his closed fist, was blue, a blue so deep that it was almost black, but as Gaspar gazed at it, he saw fire in its depths, fire like the ones burning on the altar beneath the great dome. The incandescent fire in the night-dark stone was both subtle and profound, the inner light that blazes brighter than a supernova, and suddenly Gaspar knew that the miracles he had read about, wonders like pillars of fire in the desert and even the bright star in the east, were only metaphors, candles used to describe the sun, symbols for a truth too mighty and profound for mere words and images to contain.

"I don't know what to say," Will said when he found his voice at last.

"It's like seeing a fingerprint of God Himself," said Ana.

Gaspar did not answer, but in that moment, he understood deeply in the heart why wise men would leave their hearth and home behind to follow a star into a cold world, no matter where it might lead. Gaspar felt the same urge awaken like a spark in the ashes of his soul, and he, like his ancestor long ago, felt the stir of longing, a profound yearning to travel out into the world made new, where everything lovely endures forever, and where miracles come into the lands of men through the mean doorway of a lonely stable.

"This jewel is called the Star in the East," the man told Gaspar. "When the Magi returned, only one was wise enough not to cast away his stone. We had no setting worthy for such a gift, but we did the best we could. We employed the greatest craftsmen in the world, but they had to settle for mere gold. There is no other stone like this one on Earth. It is a jewel beyond price."

Gaspar trembled, feeling renewed and reborn, baptized in the light of sacred fire. He covered the stone again with the velvet cloth, because it was already wet with his tears.

—◦◦❦◦◦—

Later, Gaspar and Will helped Ana into a small, two-seater car. "Don't worry," the turbaned man told Will. "He'll get her to a very good doctor, then he'll be right back for you."

Gaspar shook the driver's hand. "Thanks, my friend."

Will leaned in to kiss Ana. "I love you, my heart."

Ana smiled. "And I you. Come to me."

Will kissed her again. "Always."

As the car drove away, the man in the white robe approached Gaspar. "My friend," he began hesitantly, "I have an . . . awkward question that I wish to ask you. Do you mind?"

Gaspar smiled and shook his head. "I don't mind at all. Please, ask."

"It is only this," said the man. "The jewel . . . may I ask, what do you plan to do with it?"

"Do?" asked Gaspar, puzzled.

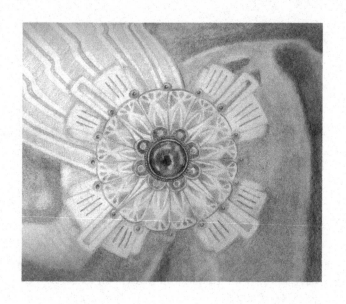

"Yes," said the man. "Will you display it in your home? Sell it?"

Gaspar shook his head. "I can't say I've made a plan yet. Now that you mention it, I guess neither of those options really seems right."

"It doesn't seem right to put it in a closet, does it?" said the man. "Or to mount it over your fireplace, eh? The Star in the East has been hidden away from men for far, far too long."

"I see your point," said Gaspar, rubbing his chin thoughtfully. "I guess."

"You must realize," said the man, "that what you have is worth *billions*. More than that. It is priceless. I say mere billions only because, if I may be frank, I can't imagine who could afford to pay even a fraction of the true worth."

"I don't really need money," Gaspar admitted. "I've made more than enough to live pretty well if I'm careful. And who knows? Maybe . . . maybe I'll make more now. I'm still a young man, after all."

"I see," said the man. "Nonetheless, I had hoped you might be willing to sell. To us, I mean. What you have— were it revealed to the world—it has the potential to do a great deal of good. Can you imagine if it were studied? Seen by pilgrims?"

"What do you mean?" asked Will.

The man took a deep breath. "For years, the heirs of the Magi have collected money from the patrons who support us, money we are forbidden to use for any other purpose than acquiring treasures like the Star in the East. If you were to sell it to us, we would display it and study it—at museums and universities all around the world. Our hope is that this relic, this mighty symbol of divine grace, might unite men and women, and perhaps begin to heal at last wounds that have endured since the dawn of civilization."

"Somehow," said Gaspar, shaking his head, "it just doesn't seem right to just, like, uh, sell something like this."

"Is it better to have the jewel lost and forgotten, stored away in some lonely place?"

"Of course not," said Gaspar.

"But what of the money? As I said, it is given for this purpose, and this purpose alone. Is it better that the money sit unused? Shall it wait, forgotten, as the Star in the East did for so long? It is the stuff of the world, not of the contemplative life of the monastery. I'm not sure we'd know how best to use it even were we so permitted."

"Isn't money supposed to be the root of all evil?" said Gaspar, smiling.

"The *love* of money is the root of evil," Brother Solayman reminded him. "It is also a tool for accomplishing great things and improving the lot of mankind. Isn't it? This sum, considerable as it is, is perhaps money that a man like you could use to do *good* in the world. It is not much, a mere fraction of what the jewel is worth—"

"Done," said Gaspar. And then he laughed. He wasn't sure who looked more surprised, Will or the man in the white robes.

"You realize," said Brother Solayman, "that while the sum we can offer is . . . large, you could do much better if you so choose."

"I'm sure," said Gaspar. "But I trust you, my friend. I know you'll do the right thing with this . . . with this magnificent and holy gift. You'll care for it and present it to the world in the way that's best. Besides, the gifts were to the *Magi*. You are their true heirs. Not me. I have seen it, and I have felt its wonder transform and comfort me. Let it pass on to others thirsty for light. As for the money, I wouldn't take it at all, but as you say, perhaps I can use it to do some good in this old world. 'Cause for the first time in a long, lonely while, I feel the need to make my days precious. I want to *live*, sir."

"I can have the money transferred to any account you choose," said the man in the robe. "Use it wisely and well, Gaspar Bethlen."

"I will," he promised. "I'll do my best."

"Gaspar, are you sure?" said Will.

Gaspar nodded. "Joy isn't in what we have—it's in what we share. Those who hoard are not happy, I think. You know, I bet that's where the term miser comes from—from miserable. What about that, huh? I don't want to be alone in a cold townhouse, not even with a fabulous jewel to gaze at through all the long hours and

331

lonely nights. That's not *life*. I used to share things with Beth, and that very act of sharing was what turned the potential into joy. Now I'll have to find some new way. To share, to matter. To be alive means to matter."

"But I thought you wanted something to hold on to," said Will. "Something to help feel close to Beth."

"Oh, I found that," said Gaspar. "I feel closer to her than I have in too long a time. I think I always will. Don't you see? Will, Beth's gift—it wasn't the jewel. It never was."

"I understand," said Will. "It was the mystery, wasn't it?"

"The mystery," said Gaspar. "Yes. That, certainly. The journey. And its answer."

"What did you find?" asked Will.

"Grace," said Gaspar. "Peace."

Two days later, Will met Gaspar in the familiar hotel restaurant in Budapest for breakfast. He smiled. This was a happy place for him. It was where he'd met Ana in person for the very first time. To his surprise, Gaspar had arrived first. He was already drinking his coffee. On the table was a package wrapped neatly in green paper. Gaspar looked up and grinned like a child.

"What's all this?" said Will.

"This," said Gaspar, lifting his mug, "is damn good coffee, water of life and all that. Not really American, no matter what they tell you, but hot, black, and wonderful all the same. This—" He pointed at a sheet of paper. "—is a wire receipt. The Magi deposited the money in my account. And this—" Gaspar pushed the package closer to Will. "—is for you."

Will sat. "Wow, that's a surprise. Jeez, man, you must have gone out at the crack of dawn."

Gaspar shrugged. "I'm still on American time. Here, I already ordered you a coffee." The waitress put a steaming cup in front of Will, and Gaspar nodded to the package. "Open it, why don't you?"

Will fumbled with his package. Meanwhile, Gaspar looked at his wire transfer receipt and shook his head. "This," he said, "is a butt load of money."

"Any idea what you're going to do with it?" Will asked as he tore free a strip of tape.

"Oh, I've got some charities in mind. Beyond that, I thought I might pay off the mortgage on a castle."

Will looked up, startled. "The Count's place?"

Gaspar laughed. "Well, he *did* have a point. It's a shame to see it torn down or slapped with some foreign corporate logo. Hungary needs its past. After all, for better or for worse, a nation's heart is in its culture."

"Uh, you're not going to, like, live there, are you?"

"Me?" said Gaspar, laughing. "Oh, no, no, not me. I plan to travel, sure, and see some of the world I'm to do all this good in, but Boston is home. No matter how much I fall in love with exotic lands and magnificent cities, sooner or later it'll always be time to go home."

"It must be nice," said Will, "to know so strongly where you belong, and what you're meant to do."

"You'll find that, too. In fact, my dude, I think you have already."

"So what *are* you going to do with the castle? If you're not going to live there? And the Count is gone?"

"I thought," said Gaspar, "that I might give it to his granddaughter."

"Ana?" Will laughed. "Awesome. She's an amazing woman."

"That she is," said Gaspar. "That she is. Can I assume you'll be staying in Hungary? With her? For a while at least?"

"I don't know," said Will. "It's awfully soon to make a decision like that. I mean. . . . Oh, jeez, who am I kidding? Of course I'll stay if I can manage it. There's no use denying it with logic and reasonable thought. I'm already crazy in love with her."

"I know."

"So what about you?" Will asked.

"What about me what?"

"What's next for Gaspar, the man who wants to start living again?"

Gaspar smiled. "I don't know. Maybe I'll try base-ball again. I hear the Sox could use a switch hitter with power."

"Yeah. Power." Will looked down, and he grinned. "From the right."

Gaspar rolled his eyes. "Those aren't the words of a man who wants me to leave him some tickets now and then. Uh, if you're in Boston, that is."

"I imagine I'm going to spend a lot of time flying back and forth. I mean, I still have the bookshop, and Dad. . . . But Ana! My God, Gaspar, I can't wait to get back to her. There's so much. . . ." Will shrugged, con-sidering.

"Speaking of that," said Gaspar, "spending time in Hungary, I mean, I have an idea for something else I might do with this money. I was thinking of setting up a foundation to invest the lion's share of it so that it can grow and do some good for a long time to come. I was thinking I might . . . oh, I don't know. Maybe invest some of it back in Hungary."

Before Gaspar could finish the thought, Will man-aged to get his box open. Inside, when he pulled aside the packing tissue paper, he found a glass figurine. It was a Victorian Santa Claus, dressed in the royal red and green robes of a king or a saint. His red velvet cap was adorned with a crown of holly. The figure was solemn and lordly but with a merry twinkle in the delicately painted blue eyes.

"Wow," said Will. "It's beautiful. What a lovely gift!"

"I imagine," said Gaspar, "that you'll find a note with it."

"You're right," said Will. He grinned. The handwriting wasn't quite as neat as Beth's, but Will recognized the familiar backwards message:

ᕼᖺᖶᒥᖶ ᑫᑌᖰᕼ

With many thanks to the coolest detective I've ever known,
— Gaspar

"Now what the heck does that mean?"

"The cool detective part?"

"Ha. I meant 'find him.'"

Gaspar laughed. "You really don't know?"

"I'm afraid I haven't solved *my* mystery yet," Will admitted.

"It's easy. Remember back in Boston when you told me about how the old families often traced their families back to one individual?"

"I do," said Will.

Gaspar asked, "You told me that your family traced its ancestry back to a Turkish Christian bishop. Am I right?"

Will nodded. "Nicholas of Myra."

"For heaven's sake," said Gaspar, "don't you know who that *is*?"

"Should I?" Will's eyes sprang wide as he looked down at the painted glass figurine. "Wait. You don't mean—?"

"Nicholas of Myra," said Gaspar, nodding. "*Saint* Nicholas." Will gaped. "What, you think you're the only one who can use Google and Bing? Huh. Maybe I'm a cool detective, too. How 'bout that?"

"You're joking."

"About being a detective? Mostly. I think."

"Whoa. Stay in your own lane there, baseball player. And I meant about Nicholas of Myra."

"*Saint* Nicholas. Who some say never really died but became a spirit, like an angel, inspiring generosity and goodwill in the hearts of humankind all across the globe. Yeah? Who's to say that this great man, made immortal, didn't wander the world, just as the legend suggests, changing his name from time to time? To Kringle, perhaps, and then to Claus. And maybe he had children—the family we know today as Klaus. Huh? Huh? Well? Why not? Is that too big a miracle for one who has followed the star in the east?"

Will laughed. "What a lovely story! Too bad it can't possibly be true."

"Now where have I heard that before? Huh?"

Will laughed again and shook his head. "Seriously. It just can't be true. It just can't!"

337

"Can't it?" Gaspar raised his eyebrows. "Well? Why the heck not? If I can be the last son of one of the three actual frickin' wise men, heir to a stone given by the Christ child Himself, why shouldn't you, too, be the son of someone every bit as famous for the giving of Christmas gifts? You're going to say it's a big coincidence that we met, that we became friends. Well, I say bull. I say it was inevitable."

"So help me," said Will, "I almost believe you. God knows I've seen enough to keep an open mind these days."

"And," said Gaspar, "since I've got all this money to invest, why shouldn't the family of the Magi and the family of jolly ol' Saint Nicholas do business together, eh? Yeah? See, I was thinking, maybe, of investing in a toy shop. Especially one with a cool new business plan."

"Gaspar, I don't even know what to say."

"We can do a lot of good together, you know. A whole lot of good. After all, dude, who better than us to remind the world what gift giving is really all about?"

"Who indeed?" Will laughed again. "I can't wait to tell Ana. Jeez. This is going to be quite a Christmas, isn't it?"

"That it is, yeah. That it is. But let's order some breakfast, huh? All these miracles and stuff make a guy hungry."

"Good plan. Then what?"

"Then," Gaspar replied, "you need to stop hanging out here with me and go spend some time with Ana."

"I like that idea. Want to come?"

"Me?" said Gaspar. "I'll be fine, and I have literally zero interest in being a third wheel today, thank you very much. In fact, I think I'll go for a walk. Take in some of this beautiful city while I'm here. Maybe do a little sightseeing." He smiled. "And spend a little time with Beth."

Afterword

Way, way back in 2001, my dear friend Carol Bales (who later became my beloved wife) and I began the tradition of creating holiday gifts of story for our friends and family. I wrote a story; she created illustrations. We bound them by hand. At the time, our plan was to do a new one every year.

Years later, I pitched the stories as a collection for traditional publishing to Lou Aronica at The Story Plant. Lou said no—these stories need to be novels. So I started rewriting and expanding them extensively. *Raven Wakes the World: A Winter Tale* and *Christmas Past: A Ghostly Winter Tale*, the first of our stories, have already been professionally published as novels and should be available now in hardcover and paperback in your favorite bookstore. *Christmas Past* is available as an audiobook.

We tried to visit a different genre every year. *Raven Wakes the World* is a sort of magic realism/mythic romance based on Inuit mythology. *Christmas Past* is our take on a different sort of myth—the ghost story and the urban legend. Our third story, *The Star in the East*, swings closer to action and adventure, with a little ancient mystery thrown in for flavor. At this point, I think next year's will be a rom-com in the tradition of the old Hollywood screwball comedies.

When we were creating the original short story version of The Star in the East, we decided to do something different. Carol did the illustrations first, and I had to come up with a story to match them. Because, you know, just getting the story done, printed, bound, and mailed before the holiday wasn't hard enough. The original illustrations included an ATM, a gem, a European manor house (Carol had just traveled to Budapest, and that influenced her choices), an immigrant family, and a toy shop. The story I came up with surprised her, I think.

If memory serves, this was the first story we created as an actual couple.

This version has been rewritten extensively. In fact, of all the stories, this one probably changed the most when it was expanded into a novel. In the original, for example, Gaspar was an old man, a retired businessman, not a rising baseball star, and the city of Rome was not visited. There was no pole vaulting, no car chase, and no battle at Kala Atashparastan. This version is longer than the original by more than three times.

341

Most of the historic details in this book are more or less correct, including Marco Polo's account of visiting the tombs of the Magi. However, I have picked the historic and biblical details and theories that best fit the needs of the story, not the ones that are most likely to be true. Hidden pictures in the gilded fore edges of books are also real things, and I highly recommend checking them with a search on Google, Bing, or YouTube. Unfortunately, Marco Polo's map is not one of them, and to the best of my knowledge, the original manuscripts are lost.

Thanks once again to our many dear friends and family members for the blessings of their love and inspiration. Many thanks to heroic beta readers Eric Bluhm, James Lock, Bill Bridges, John Bridges, Ted Anderson, Sid Taylor, Jolie Simmons, and Andrew Greenberg for helping me polish the original version of this tale, and to Mike Mikula, Nancy Fletcher, and Maryann Daves Lozano for taking a look at the first rough draft of this version. Thank you to Tomi T-Time Majoros for help with the Hungarian language (any errors are mine; he did his best) and to Steven Brust for making the introduction. Thanks to fellow authors Zachary Steele, John Topping, and Benji Carr for support and community, which helps more than you know, and to Neighborhood Church for once again giving this version of the tale a place to be born. Speaking of, thanks to pastors Anjie and Andi Woodworth for teaching me the "through me and in spite of me" prayer that I try to speak every time I sit down to write.

I am grateful to Don Dudenhoeffer, Alice Neuhauser, Bill Foley, Graham Bradstreet, John Burnet, Houston Howard, James Moore, Christopher Golden, Candice Alger, Arthur Stepanyan, and Irtaza Barlas—and the whole team at Gramarye Media—for being more than just great people and business partners, for being my second family. Finally, I am forever grateful to Charles de Lint, Paul Brandon, and the late great Ray Bradbury and Lloyd Alexander for many kind words and much encouragement. Very special thanks to the super editor/publisher Lou Aronica for pushing me to expand and elevate this story.

Thanks to Carol, love of my life.

Most of all, thank you for spending some time with this story. It means the world to Carol and me.

About the Author

After a 30-year career in new media, where his titles have included VP, Digital Media, VP, Creative, Executive Producer, and even CEO, John Adcox is now concentrating on storytelling. In addition to his writing, he is the CEO of Gramarye Media, Inc., the "next generation" book publisher, game developer, and movie studio of the future. More of his books are coming soon. You can learn more about them at http://johnadcox.com/.

About the Illustrator

Carol Bales studies, works, and teaches in a place where technology and creativity intersect. Educated in painting at the University of Tennessee and Human-Computer Interaction at Georgia Tech, she works as a User Experience Researcher for The Weather Company.

The couple lives in Atlanta, Georgia.